C000061071

CHRISTOP
THE CASE OF THE
MONDAY MURDERS

CHRISTOPHER BUSH was born Charlie Christmas Bush in Norfolk in 1885. His father was a farm labourer and his mother a milliner. In the early years of his childhood he lived with his aunt and uncle in London before returning to Norfolk aged seven, later winning a scholarship to Thetford Grammar School.

As an adult, Bush worked as a schoolmaster for 27 years, pausing only to fight in World War One, until retiring aged 46 in 1931 to be a full-time novelist. His first novel featuring the eccentric Ludovic Travers was published in 1926, and was followed by 62 additional Travers mysteries. These are all to be republished by Dean Street Press.

Christopher Bush fought again in World War Two, and was elected a member of the prestigious Detection Club. He died in 1973.

By Christopher Bush

CHRISTOPHER BUSH

THE CASE OF THE MONDAY MURDERS

With an introduction
by Curtis Evans

DEAN STREET PRESS

To

ANNA PATTERSON

With apologies for the lack of blood

INTRODUCTION

THAT ONCE vast and mighty legion of bright young (and youngish) British crime writers who began publishing their ingenious tales of mystery and imagination during what is known as the Golden Age of detective fiction (traditionally dated from 1920 to 1939) had greatly diminished by the iconoclastic decade of the Sixties, many of these writers having become casualties of time. Of the 38 authors who during the Golden Age had belonged to the Detection Club, a London-based group which included within its ranks many of the finest writers of detective fiction then plying the craft in the United Kingdom, just over a third remained among the living by the second half of the 1960s, while merely seven—Agatha Christie, Anthony Gilbert, Gladys Mitchell, Margery Allingham, John Dickson Carr, Nicholas Blake and Christopher Bush—were still penning crime fiction.

In 1966--a year that saw the sad demise, at the too young age of 62, of Margery Allingham--an executive with the English book publishing firm Macdonald reflected on the continued popularity of the author who today is the least well known among this tiny but accomplished crime writing cohort: Christopher Bush (1885-1973), whose first of his three score and three series detective novels, *The Plumley Inheritance*, had appeared fully four decades earlier, in 1926. "He has a considerable public, a 'steady Bush public,' a public that has endured through many years," the executive boasted of Bush. "He never presents any problem to his publisher, who knows exactly how many copies of a title may be safely printed for the loyal Bush fans; the number is a healthy one too." Yet in 1968, just a couple of years after the Macdonald editor's affirmation of Bush's notable popular duration as a crime writer, the author, now in his 83rd year, bade farewell to mystery fiction with a final detective novel, *The Case of the Prodigal Daughter*, in which, like in Agatha Christie's *Third Girl* (1966), copious references are made, none too favorably, to youthful sex, drugs and rock and roll. Afterwards, outside of the reprinting in the UK in the early 1970s of a scattering of classic Bush titles from the Golden Age, Bush's books, in contrast with those of Christie, Carr, Allingham and Blake, disappeared from mass circulation in both the UK and the US, becoming fervently sought (and ever more unobtainable) treasures by collectors and connoisseurs of classic crime fiction. Now, in one of the signal developments in vintage mystery publishing, Dean Street Press is reprinting all 63 of the Christopher Bush detective novels. These will be published over a period of months, beginning with the release of books 1 to 10 in the series.

Few Golden Age British mystery writers had backgrounds as humble yet simultaneously mysterious, dotted with omissions and evasions, as Christopher Bush, who was born Charlie Christmas Bush on the day of the Nativity in 1885 in the Norfolk village of Great Hockham, to Charles Walter Bush and his second wife, Eva Margaret Long. While the father of Christopher Bush's Detection Club colleague and near exact contemporary Henry Wade (the pseudonym of Henry Lancelot Aubrey-Fletcher) was a baronet who lived in an elegant Georgian mansion and claimed extensive ownership of fertile English fields, Christopher's father resided in a cramped cottage and toiled in fields as a farm laborer, a term that in the late Victorian and Edwardian era, his son lamented many years afterward, "had in it something of contempt....There was something almost of serfdom about it."

Charles Walter Bush was a canny though mercurial individual, his only learning, his son recalled, having been "acquired at the Sunday school." A man of parts, Charles was a tenant farmer of three acres, a thatcher, bricklayer and carpenter (fittingly for the father of a detective novelist, coffins were his specialty), a village radical and a most adept poacher. After a flight from Great Hockham, possibly on account of his poaching activities, Charles, a widower with a baby son whom he had left in the care of his mother, resided in London, where he worked for a firm of spice importers. At a dance in the city, Charles met Christopher's mother, Eva Long, a lovely and sweet-natured young milliner and bonnet maker, sweeping her off her feet with a combination of "good looks and a certain plausibility." After their marriage the couple left London to live in a tiny rented cottage in Great Hockham, where Eva over the next eighteen years gave birth to three sons and five daughters and perforce learned the challenging ways of rural domestic economy.

Decades later an octogenarian Christopher Bush, in his memoir *Winter Harvest: A Norfolk Boyhood* (1967), characterized Great Hockham as a rustic rural redoubt where many of the words that fell from the tongues of the native inhabitants "were those of Shakespeare, Milton and the Authorised Version....Still in general use were words that were standard in Chaucer's time, but had since lost a certain respectability." Christopher amusingly recalled as a young boy telling his mother that a respectable neighbor woman had used profanity, explaining that in his hearing she had told her husband, "George, wipe you that shit off that pig's arse, do you'll datty your trousers," to which his mother had responded that although that particular usage of a four-letter word had not really been *swearing*, he was not to give vent to such language himself.

Great Hockham, which in Christopher Bush's youth had a population of about four hundred souls, was composed of a score or so of cottages, three public houses, a post-office, five shops, a couple of forges and a pair of churches, All Saint's and the Primitive Methodist Chapel, where the Bush family rather vocally worshipped. "The village lived by farming, and most of its men were labourers," Christopher recollected. "Most of the children left school as soon as the law permitted: boys to be absorbed somehow into the land and the girls to go into domestic service." There were three large farms and four smaller ones, and, in something of an anomaly, not one but two squires--the original squire, dubbed "Finch" by Christopher, having let the shooting rights at Little Hockham Hall to one "Green," a wealthy international banker, making the latter man a squire by courtesy. Finch owned most of the local houses and farms, in traditional form receiving rents for them personally on Michaelmas; and when Christopher's father fell out with Green, "a red-faced, pompous, blustering man," over a political election, he lost all of the banker's business, much to his mother's distress. Yet against all odds and adversities, Christopher's life greatly diverged from settled norms in Great Hockham, incidentally producing one of the most distinguished detective novelists from the Golden Age of detective fiction.

Although Christopher Bush was born in Great Hockham, he spent his earliest years in London living with his mother's much older sister, Elizabeth, and her husband, a fur dealer by the name of James Streeter, the couple having no children of their own. Almost certainly of illegitimate birth, Eva had been raised by the Long family from her infancy. She once told her youngest daughter how she recalled the Longs being visited, when she was a child, by a "fine lady in a carriage," whom she believed was her birth mother. Or is it possible that the "fine lady in a carriage" was simply an imaginary figment, like the aristocratic fantasies of Philippa Palfrey in P.D. James's *Innocent Blood* (1980), and that Eva's "sister" Elizabeth was in fact her mother?

The Streeters were a comfortably circumstanced couple at the time they took custody of Christopher. Their household included two maids and a governess for the young boy, whose doting but dutiful "Aunt Lizzie" devoted much of her time to the performance of "good works among the East End poor." When Christopher was seven years old, however, drastically straightened financial circumstances compelled the Streeters to leave London for Norfolk, by the way returning the boy to his birth parents in Great Hockham.

Fortunately the cause of the education of Christopher, who was not only a capable village cricketer but a precocious reader and scholar, was taken up both by his determined and devoted mother and an idealistic local elementary school headmaster. In his teens Christopher secured a scholarship to Norfolk's Thetford Grammar School, one of England's oldest educational institutions, where Thomas Paine had studied a century-and-a-half earlier. He left Thetford in 1904 to take a position as a junior schoolmaster, missing a chance to go to Cambridge University on yet another scholarship. (Later he proclaimed himself thankful for this turn of events, sardonically speculating that had he received a Cambridge degree he "might have become an exceedingly minor don or something as staid and static and respectable as a publisher.") Christopher would teach in English schools for the next twenty-seven years, retiring at the age of 46 in 1931, after he had established a successful career as a detective novelist.

Christopher's romantic relationships proved far rockier than his career path, not to mention every bit as murky as his mother's familial antecedents. In 1911, when Christopher was teaching in Wood Green School, a co-educational institution in Oxfordshire, he wed county council schoolteacher Ella Maria Pinner, a daughter of a baker neighbor of the Bushes in Great Hockham. The two appear never actually to have lived together, however, and in 1914, when Christopher at the age of 29 headed to war in the 16th (Public Schools) Battalion of the Middlesex Regiment, he falsely claimed in his attestation papers, under penalty of two years' imprisonment with hard labor, to be unmarried.

After four years of service in the Great War, including a year-long stint in Egypt, Christopher returned in 1919 to his position at Wood Green School, where he became involved in another romantic relationship, from which he soon desired to extricate himself. (A photo of the future author, taken at this time in Egypt, shows a rather dashing, thin-mustached man in uniform and is signed "Chris," suggesting that he had dispensed with "Charlie" and taken in its place a diminutive drawn from his middle name.) The next year Winifred Chart, a mathematics teacher at Wood Green, gave birth to a son, whom she named Geoffrey Bush. Christopher was the father of Geoffrey, who later in life became a noted English composer, though for reasons best known to himself Christopher never acknowledged his son. (A letter Geoffrey once sent him was returned unopened.) Winifred claimed that she and Christopher had married but separated, but she refused to speak of her purported spouse forever after and she destroyed all of his letters and other mementos, with the exception of a book of poetry that he had written for her during what she termed their engagement.

Christopher's true mate in life, though with her he had no children, was Florence Marjorie Barclay, the daughter of a draper from Ballymena, Northern Ireland, and, like Ella Pinner and Winifred Chart, a schoolteacher. Christopher and Marjorie likely had become romantically involved by 1929, when Christopher dedicated to her his second detective novel, *The Perfect Murder Case*; and they lived together as man and wife from the 1930s until her death in 1968 (after which, probably not coincidentally, Christopher stopped publishing novels). Christopher returned with Marjorie to the vicinity of Great Hockham when his writing career took flight, purchasing two adjoining cottages and commissioning his father and a stepbrother to build an extension consisting of a kitchen, two bedrooms and a new staircase. (The now sprawling structure, which Christopher called "Home Cottage," is now a bed and breakfast grandiloquently dubbed "Home Hall.") After a falling-out with his father, presumably over the conduct of Christopher's personal life, he and Marjorie in 1932 moved to Beckley, Sussex, where they purchased Horsepen, a lovely Tudor plaster and timber-framed house. In 1953 the couple settled at their final home, The Great House, a centuries-old structure (now a boutique hotel) in Lavenham, Suffolk.

From these three houses Christopher maintained a lucrative and critically esteemed career as a novelist, publishing both detective novels as Christopher Bush and, commencing in 1933 with the acclaimed book *Return* (in the UK, *God and the Rabbit*, 1934), regional novels purposefully drawing on his own life experience, under the pen name Michael Home. (During the 1940s he also published espionage novels under the Michael Home pseudonym.) Although his first detective novel, *The Plumley Inheritance*, made a limited impact, with his second, *The Perfect Murder Case*, Christopher struck gold. The latter novel, a big seller in both the UK and the US, was published in the former country by the prestigious Heinemann, soon to become the publisher of the detective novels of Margery Allingham and Carter Dickson (John Dickson Carr), and in the latter country by the Crime Club imprint of Doubleday, Doran, one of the most important publishers of mystery fiction in the United States.

Over the decade of the 1930s Christopher Bush published, in both the UK and the US as well as other countries around the world, some of the finest detective fiction of the Golden Age, prompting the brilliant Thirties crime fiction reviewer, author and Oxford University Press editor Charles Williams to avow: "Mr. Bush writes of as thoroughly enjoyable murders as any I know." (More recently, mystery genre authority B.A. Pike dubbed these novels by Bush, whom he praised as "one of the most reliable and resourceful of true detective writers"; "Golden Age baroque, rendered remarkable by some extraordinary flights of fancy.") In 1937 Christopher Bush became, along with Nicholas Blake, E.C.R. Lorac and Newton Gayle (the writing team of Muna Lee and Maurice West Guinness), one of the final authors initiated into the Detection Club before the outbreak of the Second World War and with it the demise of the Golden Age. Afterward he continued publishing a detective novel or more a year, with his final book in 1968 reaching a total of 63, all of them detailing the investigative adventures of lanky and bespectacled gentleman amateur detective Ludovic Travers. Concurring as I do with the encomia of Charles Williams and B.A. Pike, I will end this introduction by thanking Avril MacArthur for providing invaluable biographical information on her great uncle, and simply wishing fans of classic crime fiction good times as they discover (or rediscover), with this latest splendid series of Dean Street Press classic crime fiction reissues, Christopher Bush's Ludovic Travers detective novels. May a new "Bush public" yet arise!

Curtis Evans

The Case of the Monday Murders (1936)

MURDER ON MONDAYS

WE CHALLENGE SCOTLAND YARD

T. P. LUFFHAM WAS MURDERED

ANOTHER MONDAY MURDER

HAS ENGLAND A NEW JACK THE RIPPER?

IN LONDON IN 1937 Christopher Bush was initiated, in company with colleagues Nicholas Blake (Cecil Day Lewis), E.C.R. Lorac (Edith Caroline Rivett) and Newton Gayle (Maurice West Guinness and Muna Lee, though Lee may not have been present), into the Detection Club, an organization composed of many of the finest detective fiction writers in the United Kingdom, during a cheekily sinister ceremony, devised to a great extent by Dorothy L. Sayers and involving, we may surmise, candles, guns, knives, nooses, a poison bottle or two and, as the piece de resistance, a flame-eyed skull named Eric, which ghoulishly served as the Club's mascot. Founded in 1930, the Detection Club, in addition to holding regular meetings among its membership, gave much-anticipated annual dinners--highly convivial occasions indeed, to which members could bring favored guests. It seems likely to me that Christopher Bush attended a Detection Club dinner as a guest as early as 1935, for Bush's fourteenth detective novel, *The Case of the Monday Murders* (*Murder on Mondays* in the US), which was published in 1936, is a tale in which the "Murder League," an imagined organization of British crime writers, and its fictional founder and president, Ferdinand Pole, play a major role. For fans of meta (i.e., self-referential) crime fiction, *The Case of the Monday Murders* is crime fiction at its most puckishly meta. Additionally, the novel shares affinity with two earlier Bush mysteries, *The Perfect Murder Case* (1929) and *Cut Throat* (1932), in that it concerns, respectively, serial murder and the machinations of the sensation-seeking English press. In its anatomization of naked commercial cynicism and the way writers and mass media attempt to manipulate the public for financial gain, *The Case of the Monday Murders* is one of the most fascinating and intriguingly modern of Christopher Bush's between-the-wars detective novels.

I pointed out in the introduction to *The Perfect Murder Case* that that book, Bush's breakthrough work of crime fiction, is not truly, as has been argued, a serial killer novel; yet *The Case of the Monday Murders*, which serendipitously followed into print by a mere couple of months Agatha Christie's *The ABC Murders*, the Queen of Crime's famous embroidery on the serial killer plot, unquestionably qualifies as such. (*The ABC Murders* was published in the UK in January and *The Case of the Monday Murders* in March, when the book also happens to be set.) Had serial murder been discussed at a Detection Club dinner in 1935, at a table at which both Bush and Christie were present?

Similarly, in *The Case of the Monday Murders* Bush references recently-published reminiscences by the fictional Chief-Inspector Gilliam, recalling *Cornish of Scotland Yard*, a 1935 book by ex-Superintendent George W. Cornish, formerly of the Metropolitan Police. Cornish was one of several important police officials who spoke to the Detection Club at this time, when Bush might have been present as well; and in 1936 Cornish participated with five Detection Club members (and one non-member) in *Six Against the Yard*, a collection of fictional tales about "perfect murders." Cornish's task in the book was to demonstrate how the murderers in the mystery writers' stories would have been exposed and apprehended. The same year in which *Six Against the Yard* appeared also saw the publication of *The Anatomy of Murder*, a collection of essays by Detection Club members which analyzed real life murder cases. As we will see below, the fascination of mystery writers with murder in both fancy and fact, as well as their fantasies of "getting away with murder," are explored in *The Case of the Monday Murders*.

The novel opens in March (bringing to mind the term "mad as a March hare"), at the busy offices of the *Evening Blazon*, where a missive from Ferdinand Pole, detective novelist as well as founder and president of the Murder League ("Just talk, and tea"), has set press tongues a-wagging. In his letter Pole surveys the "perfectly uncanny number of unsolved murders" that "have taken place on Mondays" since the Great War and he provocatively queries whether "by some fantastic chance most of the murders I have mentioned—or indeed all of them—have been committed by one and the same person, operating through the period of over fifteen years?" Has there really been a serial killer on the loose for over fifteen years, committing murders only on Mondays? A shocking—and to the more sensationalistic press positively salivating—notion indeed.

When it is learned that disgraced (probably pedophiliac) schoolmaster T.P. Luffham has been murdered on, yes, a Monday, it begins to appear that there might be something to Pole's wild theory—or at least that there is enough meat on its bones for the *Blazon* to feast upon for a few news cycles. Having just published his latest book, a true crime study entitled *Kensington Gore: Murder for High-brows*, upon which, you will recall, he was at work during that Chinese Gong affair (see *The Case of the Chinese Gong*), Bush's series sleuth Ludovic "Ludo" Travers, "world-famous writer and criminologist," is pursued by the press not only for his opinion about Luffham's slaying, but other unsolved murders as well (like that unsavory business at Romney Dyke). Although Travers modestly tries to stave off the newspapers, he assists, as ever before, his old Scotland Yard friends, Superintendent Wharton and Chief Inspector Norris, in their investigation of one of the strangest cases that the trio of detectives has yet encountered.

Throughout *The Case of the Monday Murders* Bush takes a dubious view of both scandal-mongering print reporters and shamelessly self-promoting mystery writers. Wealthy dilettante Travers is shocked by these people's ceaseless, cynical pursuit of their own aggrandizement, as when he discovers the lengths some go to with literary log-rolling (giving good reviews, whether merited or not, to one's colleagues in the expectation they will reciprocate). Ferdinand Pole cheerfully admits to Travers that in his guise as book reviewer "Mortimer Pugh" he indiscriminately raves about the work of his fellow Murder League members. (Members of the Detection Club who reviewed detective fiction, including that by their Club colleagues, in newspapers during the 1930s included Dorothy L. Sayers, Anthony Berkeley, E.R. Punshon, E.C. Bentley, Milward Kennedy, Nicholas Blake and Margaret Cole.) "Modern publicity requires modern methods," he explains. "Personally I'm out for any publicity which brings results. Authors have got to live, you know." As the author himself of a highly-praised true crime study, Travers worries that Pole might press him to join the Murder League, a group of men and women whom he dismisses as no better than a bunch of "performing sea-lions."

Travers also finds himself wondering just how far an egomaniacal mystery writer might be willing to go to to attain yet more publicity. Would an extreme narcissist like Pole draw a line at murder? This conversation that Ludo has with Pole prompts him to raise the question:

[Pole] cocked an important eye. "Have you read my *Three Bags Full*?"

"A very clever book," said Travers.

"Well, you'll admit that there was a murder that would have baffled any detective force in the world. That would be nothing if I were ever really on my mettle." He smiled as his mind surveyed what Travers hoped was the past. "A fine feeling of power—what?—to practically boast to the police that you've done a thing and then tell them in so many words to go to hell?"

And then he looked Travers clean in the eye with what seemed so stark a challenge that Travers was startled and his fingers went to his glasses.

"That's the sort of murder I'd commit, my dear sir. I'd remove someone who needed removing, do myself a good turn at the same time, and stick my fingers to my nose at the police."

"You terrify me," Travers told him, but with an uneasiness that was not the humorous assumption it appeared. "You almost convince me you've had the experience already."

Ferdinand Pole's self-conceit and driving need for attention is reminiscent to my mind of noted English crime writer Anthony Berkeley, an original Detection Club member whom Christopher Bush likely would have met at any Club dinner which he might have attended before writing *The Case of the Monday Murders*. Berkeley, who styled himself not only the founder of the Detection Club but the group's "First Freeman" (a made-up office that no one in the Club took seriously bar Berkeley), was a cross to bear for his colleagues, as he was painfully conscious of imagined prerogatives. "I do wish he were not so rude and silly," exclaimed Dorothy L. Sayers in a letter at one point, after Berkeley had started a dust-up with her friend, Club Treasurer E.R. Punshon, over what an exasperated Punshon termed Berkeley's "absurd claim" that as "First Freeman" Berkeley possessed absolute veto power over the admission of new members.

Berkeley additionally had a habit of writing grandiose prefaces to his mysteries announcing important breakthroughs he had made in the field—though to be fair to Berkeley he did play, particularly with his influential Francis Iles books, a great role in developing the psychological crime novel, which focuses more on suspense than detection. Like Ferdinand Pole, Berkeley also seems to have fantasized about ridding the world of undesirable people, but Berkeley, we assume, confined these fantasies strictly to paper, in such novels as *Malice Aforethought*, *Before the Fact*, *Jumping Jenny* and *Trial and Error*. (What Ferdinand Pole did or did not do in *The Case of the Monday Murders*, I leave for readers of Bush's detective novel to find for themselves.)

According to Sayers in post-WW2 correspondence concerning the Detection Club, Berkeley had difficulty getting along with the Club's non-founding members, including not only E.R. Punshon but Christianna Brand (though he partially succumbed to Brand's womanly charms) and Christopher Bush. Sayers herself defended Bush as an "extremely hard working" individual who took Club responsibilities seriously (though she allowed that "he has his faults"); and when Bush replaced the elderly and ill Punshon as Treasurer (Punshon had been recuperating at Bush's home in Sussex), Sayers relievedly observed that Bush was "now in a strong position" to withstand Berkeley's gratuitous verbal sniping. Amazingly, these events took place in 1949-50, a full dozen years after Bush had joined the Detection Club, which suggests that Berkeley could hold a grudge, whatever he imagined that grudge might be, for a long time.

Could Christopher Bush have been approached to join the Detection Club in 1935 and turned them down, only to recant and accept membership in 1937, in the meantime penning an unfavorable picture of the Club and of Berkeley in 1936? Admittedly, this is entirely speculative as far as Bush is concerned, but there is a case after the Second World War where something of the like actually happened with another mystery writer, Andrew Garve. In this case, which transpired over 1951-52, it surprisingly was Anthony Berkeley who persuaded the prospective member to change his mind about the Club, as Berkeley explained in a letter to Dorothy L. Sayers. "I met Andrew Garve at a cocktail party this week and spoke him fair," Berkeley informed Sayers in his inimitable lingo. "He seemed to have rather a wrong idea of the Detection Club, and has promised that if he is approached again he will return a different answer." Noting this development in a letter to Anthony Gilbert, a somewhat miffed Sayers declared she had informed Berkeley that it was "up to Andrew Garve to approach us, and not for us to write humbly and woo him again." (On these Detection Club controversies see my booklet *Was Corinne's Murder Clued? The Detection Club and Fair Play, 1930-1953*.) Whoever wooed whom first, however, Garve was initiated into the Detection Club in 1952. Perhaps something of the same thing had happened with Bush, though one doubts in Bush's case that Berkeley would have been the happy facilitator!

POSTSCRIPT: Two years after the appearance of *The Case of the Monday Murders*, Hutchinson in the United Kingdom published *Great Unsolved Crimes* (1938), a 351 page collection of true crime accounts authored by over forty individuals, including not only the redoubtable ex-Superintendent Cornish, but seven Detection Club members, including Anthony Berkeley, who contributed not one but two essays, one of them as Francis Iles. Christopher Bush did not participate.

CHAPTER I
THE SPLASH

THE MONTH WAS March, the day was a Monday, and it was half-past eight and a dry, bitter morning. The news room of the *Evening Blazon* had a blue haze of tobacco smoke and the sound of voices was no more than a drone. In one corner, with the Fleet Street window at his back, young Bridges, who hoped one day to be a junior reporter, was opening the letters intended by their writers for the FROM OUR READERS column and laying them out for the correspondence specialist. He was handling that job with some care. Nothing was doing in the news world and a curious paralysis lay upon the heart of things; and Ribbold, the assistant news editor, had spoken blasphemously about that pile of junk and enquired with a plaintiveness equally blasphemous when it was likely to produce something for a front page column.

Ribbold, hard-boiled as they make them, had the Sunday papers spread over his desk, and was working mechanically with blue pencil and scissors. The tape machines had ticked all night to no purpose and when he paused to light yet another cigarette from the stub of the last, he would regard with ironic amusement the slender pile of clippings that would soon be passed over to Tuke.

Marvell, the senior reporter, was with a little group at the centre table. Cane, junior crime-reporter—and holding down the crime specialist's job while Tom Stowe was on leave—was tapping a typewriter in his own corner. When he paused he would frown prodigiously, as if in his words lay the fate of empires. When Ribbold's eyes went his way, the cigarette would droop with a cynicism that had in it something different, and included the twin facts that Cane was public-school and an author of detective fiction. It was as Ribbold's eyes left Cane's direction that they fell on young Bridges, who was looking quite excited.

"This looks like something, Mr. Ribbold."

Ribbold strolled over and, while Bridges still read, took the letter from his hand. He began it with the same bored cynicism but his lips held the dead end of a cigarette by the time he had finished it.

"Good, isn't it, Mr. Ribbold! Good enough for a splash . . ."

"I'll hang on to this," Ribbold told him curtly; and went back to his desk. Marvell looked up as he passed.

"Anything good?"

"Might be," said Ribbold. Marvell followed him and was reading the letter as he went. He read it a second time as he stood by Ribbold's desk. Long and Matthews came over and read it together when Marvell put it down.

"Reads good to me," Marvell said. "Pole's the president of this Murder League, isn't he?"

"Pole's the detective-novel writer," Matthews cut in.

"Who the hell don't know that?" Ribbold told him, still turning pages and laying on the blue pencil. "And he's Mortimer Pugh who reviews thrillers for the *Colossus*."

"So I thought," Marvell said, and had another look at the letter. "What's he after? Cheap publicity for himself and the Murder League?"

"What's the real dope about the Murder League anyway?" Long asked. "Rore and Grumby publish their books, don't they?"

"Why shouldn't they?" said Ribbold, still pencilling.

"No reason at all," Marvell told him quickly. "And that's not the point. I was saying that this letter is a bid for free publicity, and I know what I'd do with it."

"How long have you been in the Salvation Army?" Ribbold cut in. "Don't you get a living out of bleeding the public the same as I do?" He called across the room. "Cane, lay off that latest masterpiece of yours and come here."

Cane flushed but came over. He was about twenty-five and looked younger, serious, shy and charmingly mannered. His left arm had a black band. Three weeks previously, it was understood, his mother had died.

"Take a dekko at that," Ribbold said. "Tell me if he's got his facts right."

Cane read the letter.

"T-t-ten minutes it'll t-t-take me to make sure, Mr. Ribbold." That was quite an engaging trick he had of sometimes stuttering slightly over his dentals when anxious or excited, though generally his speech was smooth enough, and normally even the dentals would come smoothly enough.

"Then what are you waiting for?" Ribbold asked him curtly.

"He's a damned sight smarter than he looks, that chap," Matthews said, "and he knows how to write."

"So does my fat aunt," Ribbold told him, "only she didn't go to Eton, or wherever the hell it was." Then the audience sheared off and he went on with his clippings till Cane came back well inside the ten minutes. The facts in the letter, he said, were substantially true.

"There's a fine front-page splash there, Mr. Ribbold," he said.

"Pole a pal of yours?" Ribbold asked him sneeringly.

"I've never even seen him," Cane said indignantly. "I've heard about him of course—everybody has."

"Do you tell me that!" said Ribbold, and smiled incredulously. "Perhaps you're a member of the Murder League?"

Cane flushed again. He had written a couple of detective novels and, good as they had been, had never quite lived them down.

"Anything else you'd like me to do about the letter, Mr. Ribbold?"

But Tuke, the news editor, came in then and hung up his coat and went to his desk. Tuke was lean and bony, tired, disgruntled and cantankerous; his heavy dark spectacles gave him a look that was somehow sinister. For ten years he had been news editor, but had been passed over for the managing editorship when he had come to regard it as his right. But he had always been a bit below grade, and a martinet who could never keep men's loyalties, or stand four-square to a crisis or bluff.

Ribbold gathered up his pile of clippings and came over.

"Anything broken?" Tuke said.

"Nothing much," Ribbold told him. "Everything still slack as hell. You might take a look at this letter though. Young Cane has vetted it and he says it's O.K."

Tuke fussily pressed his dark glasses tight against his eyes, ran a preliminary eye over the letter, then settled down to reading it.

Murder League,
Ragazzi's,
Pintail Street,
W.C.2.

SIR,

I wonder if it has ever occurred to the police authorities of this country, or to your readers in general, that a perfectly uncanny number of unsolved murders have taken place on Mondays.

The years since the war are the period to which I am calling particular attention for in that time there have been fifteen such mysteries. I refer to them as mysteries because they were of the public, blatant, sensational type of murder that excited general interest or indignation, and for the purpose of this brief argument the little hole-and-corner, furtive killings are not included. But would it surprise your readers to learn that of those fifteen major murders, *no fewer than thirteen took place on Mondays.*

Their popular names are: the Nottingham call-box, the Portsmouth café, the Bungay farm, the Hertford embankment, the Purley poisoning, the Romney dyke, the Vickers Street stabbing, the Birkenhead ferry, the Hyde Park strangling, and the Grimsby trawler. Of the remaining three, the Hackney shooting and the Tipton recreation-ground affairs were, I believe, solved to the satisfaction of the police, though no information has been given to the public. With regard to the famous Trunk Murder, though it is accepted for fact that it took place on a Tuesday or Wednesday, I am at this moment engaged in certain research work which convinces me that beyond question it also happened on a Monday!

In view of the facts just stated, I am sure your readers will agree that something beyond mere coincidence is in this series of happenings. What lies in the minds of these super-murderers?—for since their crimes have remained unsolved, so we ought to call them. Is there some strange benevolence that watches over the Monday Murderer? Is there among murderers some special tradition that regards Monday as a fortunate day? Or, and here I come to my vital point, could by some fantastic chance most of the murders I have mentioned—or indeed all of them—have been committed by one and the same person, operating through the period of over fifteen years?

It seems to me a matter of national importance that your readers should give their considered views.

Yours, etc.,

FERDINAND POLE.

Tuke frowned in thought.

"Pole?" he said. "Pole? I've got him. Why should we give free publicity to a noise like Pole?"

The cigarette drooped in Ribbold's mouth, and his hand went out to a reference book.

"And why shouldn't we? He gets publicity and we get front-page stuff. What's wrong with that?"

Tuke shot a look at him and said nothing. Ribbold found his page and began to recite extracts.

"Ferdinand Pole. Born 1875—which was no fault of mine. . . . Educated privately and Cranmer College, Cambridge. . . . Travelled extensively—regular little Livingstone. . . . One, two, three, four, five detective novels—last three by Rore and Grumby. . . . Founder and first president of Murder League."

He flicked the book contemptuously aside. "You know him, don't you? He's a ginger-grey, potbellied little squirt. Voice like a squeaky brake. God Almighty's vice-regent in crime. Sometime he's going to get the hell of a kick up the pants. But not from us. We're going to want him—don't you think so?"

Maylove, the managing editor, was in on time. At nine the buzzer went for conference and the usual gang trooped in. Maylove went over the heavy news and a couple of hangovers.

"Anything broken this morning?" he asked Tuke.

"Something pretty good," Tuke said, and handed him the letter.

The room watched while he read but made no stir when he finished.

"The facts are correct?"

"Absolutely," said Tuke.

Maylove lifted the receiver. "Give me Mr. Ferdinand Pole. . . . Ferdinand Pole."

He hooked the receiver back and turned to Tuke again. "Any ideas?"

Tuke pulled a wry face. "It just lags a bit short—to me. Front page, but not a splash."

"The last para wants re-writing," Marvell said. "Make it challenge the Yard and make that theory more striking about all the murders having been done by the same person."

The buzzer went. In a moment the room was hearing the voice of Ferdinand Pole like a squeak in the receiver. It was a pretentious, high-pitched voice, as if the man's pipes were choked or squeezed.

"In ten minutes then, Mr. Pole . . . Thank you. Good-by."

"Pole can talk it over here," Maylove said. "In the meanwhile, what?"

Cane cut in. "If I may say so, sir, I think it could be made a very fine splash indeed. Streamer headlines, sir—MURDER ON MONDAYS."

Maylove nodded. Ribbold broke suavely in.

"If we could splash Pole's letter for the midday, and someone bring off a nice little murder for the six-thirty—"

The buzzer went.

"Put him right through," Maylove said. "Yes, this is the *Blazon* . . . I see . . . Sergeant Harris, O-Division . . . You're plumb sure! . . . I see . . . You've passed this on to no one else? . . . Splendid! Martlet Street, between Rore and Grumby's and the print shop side door . . . Thank you. We'll be there inside five minutes. Good-by."

Back went the receiver and he whipped round on Marvell.

"Luffham's dead—the great T. P. Luffham!"

"Good God!" Marvell stared incredulously. "I thought he died years ago."

"I know," Maylove said, "I know. We all thought that. Got that address? Grab a photographer and get along down there. Long, you get the library dope."

But the door was already swinging to behind Marvell. Tuke was looking excited for the first time in months. "My God! what a splash—if it's true."

"Yes," Maylove said, "but it's got to be handled just right. Luffham was dead as mutton years ago except to us who knew him. Now we've got to bring him alive. That library dope's got dust on it. Who can we get to write him up?"

"Someone not too heavy?" Ribbold asked.

"A first-class man. A modern Luffham, so to speak," Maylove said.

"Ludovic Travers, then," Ribbold told him.

"Ludovic Travers?" Maylove thought for the merest moment, then grabbed the receiver. Ribbold reached for a reference book and began refreshing his mind on the ubiquitous Travers. Maylove was talking almost at once, for Travers was still in his flat at St. Martin's Chambers.

It was three minutes later before he hung up.

"Cane," he said, "you go to Martlet Street. Cover the story from your own angle and be of any use you can to Mr. Travers and then bring him along here. Conference adjourned for fifteen minutes!"

"Just a minute, Tuke," he said, as the managing editor was filing out with the gang. "About young Cane. Can he handle that Pole stuff if we make it front page?"

"Certainly he can," Tuke said. "He may look only a nice boy, but he knows his job. People pull his leg but he's popular. That goes a long way."

"He seems to have been a bit stolid lately."

"It's not that. He's been a bit on the quiet side since his mother died," Tuke said. "I gathered they were a very devoted couple."

"Stowe doesn't come back till Wednesday week," Maylove said reflectively. "All right then. And send Pole in here as soon as he comes. Oh, and just a minute. How's your wife getting on?"

"Slowly," Tuke said. "She'll be down there another fortnight at the least."

Tuke had married a sub-editress on the Women's Page, twenty years younger than himself. London fog troubled her and stubborn bronchitis had necessitated a holiday in a Cornish cottage.

Ludovic Travers had finished breakfast and was skimming the financial columns. That Monday morning he was on good terms with himself. Ludovic Travers the social historian, known to even the man in the street as the author of *The Economics of a Spend-thrift*, had perpetrated a volume of essays—*Kensington Gore or Murder for Lowbrows*— and had just steered it through the press. The book had arisen out of certain experiences with Superintendent Wharton and might have been described by its author as a combination of all the literary vices—the whimsical, the satirical, the flippant and the sublime. Momentarily, therefore, Travers was at a loose end and the knowledge was not unpleasing.

The telephone went. Palmer, Travers's man, was in at once.

"The editor of the *Evening Blazon*, sir," he said. "Urgent I gather, sir."

Travers's long lean fingers went instinctively to his glasses, a trick of his when travailing with an idea or at a sudden startled loss. Then he hoisted his six foot three from the chair.

"Maylove speaking, the editor of the *Evening Blazon*," the voice said. "How are you, Mr. Travers? A bit of news has just come in that might interest you—as an old Halstead man, I mean. Luffham wasn't head in your time, was he?"

"No," said Travers. "I think Luffham came about five years after my time. I knew him of course by repute—who didn't?"

"Well, he's dead," Maylove said. "We've just got the inside dope."

"Dead! Dead! I thought he died years ago."

"Oh, no. He simply dropped out. There was some scandal, you will remember. He's been living all this time in a flat in Martlet Street above that little print shop next door to Rore and Grumby."

"Good Lord!" said Travers. "I've been by there a thousand times. What did he die of?"

"Heart—plus an accident," Maylove said. And then his voice took on a definite innuendo. "You never knew, I suppose, what that scandal was?"

"No," said Travers. "I know what people said it was. I also know for certain that he tipped the bottle a bit too high."

Maylove grunted and Travers could almost see him nod.

"There's a big story in Luffham," he said. "Could you by any chance drop in and see me? Say at about ten?"

"I think so," Travers said. "But are any of your people covering that Luffham story? What I mean is, I thought of slipping round as it's not two hundred yards from here. Just ghoulishness—and general interest."

"I'll have one of our people meet you there. Ten minutes suit you?"

"Splendidly," said Travers. "Good-by. Most kind of you to ring me up."

So as he made his way downstairs, Travers was thinking about T. P. Luffham. Brilliant had hardly been the word for him, for though Halstead ranked as no more than in the first half-dozen of English public-schools, Luffham had stood head and shoulders above his contemporaries. A pungent wit and a genius for epigram had been his qualities, with the gift for rare illumination; and what had endeared him to the man in the street had been his homely deftness of phrase and his merciless onslaughts on the complacent and conventional. No symposium was complete without him and he had made more copy for Fleet Street than any man in his time. But he was no mere destructive mountebank. The lash of his tongue had brought a score of abuses to heel, and in his knowledge of economic history he had no superior.

Travers had met him once or twice at Halstead just after the war, on matters to do with the school memorial to its fallen, and two or three years later Luffham had dropped completely out. A paragraph in the press and that was all, with perhaps an appreciation or two in the staider publications, for most had imagined that a man so brilliant was merely exchanging one sphere for another, and that his pen would continue to exasperate and enliven. But Luffham dropped out altogether, and it spoke volumes for the quality and reputation of the man that his name should still have in it the germ of a big story. There had been a conspiracy of silence about the reasons for his going, with ugly rumours never officially denied, and then years later the story had got about that Luffham had died somewhere abroad.

As Travers drew near Martlet Street, which lies behind the Strand in the Covent Garden maze, he was somehow expecting to see a crowd. But the little street was its lonely, grimy self, with merely a constable on duty at the side door between the print shop and the publishing offices of Rore and Grumby. So much Travers saw from the street end and he knew that Luffham's body must have gone and the *Blazon* reporters with their stories, and then as his eyes rose from the pavement he found himself dodging a fellow pedestrian. Travers halted and the other halted too.

"Morning, Mr. T-T-Travers. My name's Cane. The editor told me you were coming and I was to see if I could be of any help."

Travers smiled, liking young Cane at first sight—his faintly ginger-brown hair, quiet, strangely blue eyes and a modesty that was unexpected from the *Blazon*.

"Most kind of you all," he said. "You're a reporter, Mr. Cane?"

"Acting crime-reporter, sir," Cane said. "Mr. Stowe, the crime-reporter, is away on leave."

Travers smiled once more. "Which explains how you knew that I was I—or shall we say, me? You've been round here before?"

"Oh, no," Cane said. "Marvell—our chief reporter—covered the story as soon as it broke. He's just gone and the body has too—in an ambulance."

Then just as it was on the tip of Travers's tongue to say that there seemed little more to do than adjourn somewhere for a coffee and talk Luffham over till ten o'clock, the side door opened and a man came out, and snapped the Yale lock behind him. Then Travers and he recognized each other and the sergeant gave a grin and held out his hand.

"If it isn't Mr. Travers! How are you, sir?"

"Pretty fit," said Travers. "This is Mr. Cane—a friend of mine. I suppose you couldn't let us have a look round inside?"

"Why not, sir?" the sergeant said. "I don't know that there's anything to see, though. Was he a friend of yours, sir, might I ask?"

The three stepped inside to the stairs, and as they mounted the first flight, Travers explained his interest in the dead man.

"Do I remember him, sir?" the sergeant said. "Do I not! One of the real sort he was, sir. Didn't give a damn for no one. And coming to his end, as you might say, sir, in a hole like this."

"I've known worse holes," smiled Travers, and cast his eye round.

The three men were on a fairly spacious landing with a tiny fanlight window at the ceiling corner, and so poor was the light that the sergeant had turned on the switch. A small table was the sole furniture of the landing and on it stood the telephone. Steep stairs, ten risers in all, and with rails both sides, even by the wall, led to a door with no intermediate landing above. The sergeant led the way there and opened the door.

The room was a kind of study, tidy and comfortable, with shelf after shelf of books. Travers opened a dozen at random and found never an owner's name.

"The woman who cleaned for him knew him as a Mr. Clough," the sergeant said, gathering what Travers was at. "We found some papers in his pocket-book saying who he really was."

To the right a door opened to a tiny bedroom that overlooked the street. A door to the left led to a still smaller kitchen-pantry, with pots and crockery and an electric cooker.

"It was the woman who found him," the sergeant said "He was lying at the foot of that landing outside What we think was that he forgot for once that there wasn't a landing outside the door, so he just stopped into space, as it were, and down he went, wallop. His heart, the doctor reckoned, did the rest."

On the table in that living-room stood a quarter bottle of whisky and a tumbler still a third full. The sergeant caught Travers's look and nodded.

"Queer sort of bird he was, sir, according to the woman. Used to sleep all day and wake up in the late evenings and go out for a meal, and then sit up all night reading. She used to get here about seven of mornings and soon as she'd tidied his bed and cooked him a spot of breakfast, he'd turn in and sleep out the day. About two in the morning the doctor said it was when he died. What I reckon is that he was having a drink and reading that book you see there, sir, and then he heard a noise downstairs—or thought he did—and went out to explore, and fell downstairs, like I said." He looked at his watch. "How long did you want to be here, sir? Why I asked was because if you weren't going at once, here's the key, seeing as you're who you are, sir. You just give it to my man outside, sir, when you come down for good."

"Thanks," said Travers. "I would like to stay for a minute or two. There's a man's whole tragedy in this room, if you know what I mean." He waved a hand at the helplessness of words. "There's an atmosphere that must grip you—if you could feel it. I'd like to, just for a moment."

He slipped him a ten-shilling note and when he had gone, stood for a time with his eyes roving quietly round, and Cane watched him, wondering what were the thoughts that made him frown or set his lips to so grave a smile. Then Travers at last nodded once or twice and seemed to come to himself.

"He was always clean-shaven," he said. "What was he like this morning? Do you happen to know?"

"He had a beard, so Marvell said," Cane told him. "A sort of bushy beard and his hair was pretty long."

"Plenty of disguise that," Travers said. "He was the dapper sort when I knew him. Maybe I've met him round in this very street of nights, or in the Strand, and never even noticed him. You never knew him when he was in his prime, I imagine?"

"No," said Cane. "I've read about him, of course."

"Amazing life he must have led," said Travers, with a ruminative nod. "There was some scandal and he dropped right out of the heart of things and hid himself here like a hermit. I suppose he had money—he must have had. A queer ironic life too, that going about at night and recognizing without being recognized."

"Pretty bad luck on me," Cane said, with a rueful grin. "A fine scoop that'd have been, Mr. T-T-Travers, if I'd been the one who got here first and made out who he was."

"Things don't happen just that way," said Travers. "But your turn's bound to come one of these days. But what's this?"

With his toe he had been idly moving the waste-paper basket and its couple of inches of oddments, and all at once something had protruded. A visiting card, it had looked, and he had leaned forward and drawn it out through the wicker.

MR. FERDINAND POLE

Marsham Mansions,
Lapford Street, W.C.2.

Travers stared and his hand rose to his glasses. Then it fell again and he passed the card across to Cane.

"There's something for you to ferret out. Do you know Ferdinand Pole?"

"Only by name—and reputation," Cane said.

"Well, he seems to have known him. Under what name, I wonder? As Clough, the hermit, or Luffham?"

As he turned to the door he was putting away that visiting card in his pocket-book, though why he made so free with the dead man's property he had no idea, unless it was from some kind of instinct. At the door he waved for Cane to pass through, but Cane drew politely back and Travers went down those steep stairs first. As he stepped to the landing, there was a clatter behind him and Cane came slithering down. He nearly brought Travers down with him and his hat shot across the landing.

"My dear fellow, you're not hurt?" Travers was all concern.

Cane got to his feet, rubbing his knee.

"I'm all right, Mr. T-T-Travers. Just slipped, t-t-that's all."

He was still rubbing his knee and Travers solicitously recovered the hat that had sailed between the side table and the far, bare wall. As he drew upright again he was holding something else between his fingers as well as the hat—what was almost certainly a six-foot length of black elastic. Cane stared as he took the hat.

"Elastic, isn't it?"

"Yes," said Travers, and frowned. His eye ran to the twin rows of rails that ran upwards with the stairs, and he frowned again. Then he examined the ends of the elastic.

"Those look to you to have been tied?"

Cane stared again, and shook his head.

"I don't follow you, Mr. T-T-Travers."

"Never mind," said Travers, and took another look at the ends. "Got a box of matches on you?"

Cane produced one and Travers began striking matches and hunting the dark corners. Then he halted and waved Cane to keep back. Another second and he was mounting the stairs again.

"Stay here a minute, will you, Cane, and don't move."

Cane stared blankly at the elongated disappearing figure. In a minute Travers was coming down the stairs again and he stopped at the foot of the landing and there hooked off his glasses and gave them a polish. He hooked them on again with a shake of the head, then once more began striking matches and searching that landing. But whatever he sought was apparently not there, for he gave yet another shake of the head as he came over to where Cane stood. He halted again and a curious smile came to his face.

"I expect I'm being several kinds of a fool but—"

And then he gave a wince of pain for something had stuck in the thinnish sole of his shoe and had gone through to the tread. He screwed round his boot and as he extracted the something, his face had an amazing beam.

"Would you believe it? Just the sort of thing I was looking for."

"Why, it's a drawing pin!" Cane said.

"Yes," said Travers and his face suddenly straightened. "I expect I'm still several kinds of a fool, but just supposing I'm not, can you keep a secret?"

"Why, yes," said Cane and gave another stare.

"Then we'll go on supposing," said Travers. "Suppose this elastic had been stretched from side to side right round the top rails there, about a foot from the stair, and fastened with this drawing-pin. Suppose the phone bell went and the man up there came down to answer it? What would you call that?"

Cane still stared. Then his mouth opened but Travers spoke first.

"What I've told you, keep to yourself. Now you'd better be going for I'm using that phone to call up Scotland Yard."

"You mean . . . ?"

"All sorts of things," said Travers enigmatically. "Later on when I come to the office, I may be able to see you and give you your chance."

"You mean . . . it was murder?"

Travers shook his head but his smile had a world of meaning. Cane gave a last stare, then turned and bolted down those stairs as if heaven lay before and the devil behind. Maybe his brain already whirred with thought like the whirr of the giant presses. Pole's letter for the midday edition and the streamer headlines—

MURDER ON MONDAYS

So much for the headlines of the midday front page splash. But that splash should be mere ground-bait. In the six-thirty the headlines should let out their full triumphant shriek—

MURDER ON MONDAYS!
GREATEST PROPHECY OF THE CENTURY!!
T. P. LUFFHAM WAS MURDERED!!!

CHAPTER II
TRAVERS WHIRLS ROUND

"Just a moment, Mr. Cane!"

At the very door Travers's voice was calling the young reporter back. Cane came bounding up the stairs again.

"Your prints will be needed when the Yard people come here," Travers said. "Just wipe your fingers on that dirty wall, will you, and press them on this envelope. You and I might have handled no end of things up there."

Cane had stared for a moment, but he soon jabbed down his prints. He turned to go, hesitated, then put his question.

"Would you mind t-t-telling me, sir, what I may say and what I mayn't?"

Travers thought quickly. "You can guess it was murder and no more. What we found and how you know you're not to mention. When I see you I'll give the word to go ahead, by which you can assume it definitely was murder. Which reminds me. Let your editor know I may be a few minutes late."

"Th-th-thank you, sir." Cane's face was beaming. Then suddenly he was bolting downstairs again, only to halt once more on the bottom landing.

"Would you mind t-t-telling me, sir, what it was you found up there when you didn't want me to move?"

"A footmark," Travers said. "More than one, in fact, and the sole worn on one side. They weren't Luffham's because I looked at his shoes in the bedroom. I don't think they were the charwoman's—"

But Cane had gone. Travers heard the quick words he snapped to the constable at the door. The last rush of feet came from the far pavement and as Travers reached for the phone he could smile at Cane, and youth and its infinite possibilities and rich enthusiasms. And he wondered what school Cane had been at and how, with a voice and a face like his, he had gone into crime reporting of all things—and on the *Blazon*.

* * *

Travers dialled the Yard. Wharton was temporarily engaged and while he waited Travers was smiling to himself at some quaint anticipation of the new encounter. He could see the face of the old "General"—as the Yard knew him—and hear the very snort that would blow out the Chester-Conklin moustache when the first words fell on his ear.

"Yes. How are you, Mr. Travers?" came Wharton's voice at last. He was always punctilious and polite to Travers, for whom in spite of much laboured irony he had a colossal respect.

"Pretty fit—between murders," Travers said. "There's one been done here, I think. You'd better come along at the double."

The snort came as expected. "What's the idea? April Fool's Day?"

"Martlet Street—constable on duty at the door," Travers said tersely. "A man found dead and I think it's murder."

Wharton grunted a something and hung up. Travers was still smiling as he went down to the door.

"Keep it under your helmet," he said to the constable, "but Superintendent Wharton is due here at any moment now." So much by way of flattery and oiling the springs of conversation.

The constable's eyes opened.

"Something fishy turned up then, sir?"

"You never know," said Travers. "You were here from the start this morning?"

The constable, it turned out, had been in the very street when the charwoman came running out and it was he who had called up his superiors.

"What happened then?" Travers asked. "I suppose a doctor was fetched?"

"Oh, no, sir," the constable said with a kind of informatory reproof. "Our own man came with the sergeant. I was with them while they examined him."

"About two o'clock, wasn't it, when your police-surgeon thought he died?"

"That's right, sir."

"And did any of you have a hunt round to see if there was anything—fishy?"

"Why should we, sir?" the constable said. "There wasn't anything fishy to look for."

"Exactly," said Travers as if he wholeheartedly agreed.

"What was done, sir, was to go through his pockets and then—" He broke off with a cautious look. "I didn't catch your name quite, sir, what the sergeant called you."

"Travers, my name is." He smiled genially. "Ring up the Yard and they'll give me a clean sheet."

"A friend of the General—of Superintendent Wharton—I think you said, sir?"

"Brothers in arms, so to speak," said Travers. "And you were saying that after you went through his pockets, you did what?"

"Well, sir"—the constable hesitated for the merest moment—"then they discovered some papers that said he was someone different to what he'd made himself out to be."

"Exactly," said Travers again. "And except you three, and the woman, no one has been up those stairs."

"No one, sir," the constable told him emphatically. "The inspector came and the ambulance, sir. Then there was a reporter and a photographer, from the *Blazon* I think, sir."

"Did any of them hang about on the top landing?"

"No one was on the top landing except the sergeant, sir, when he was telephoning." He gave Travers a shrewd look. But Travers was thinking about the sergeant and how if it were he who had rung up the *Blazon*, he was entitled to his graft. So the constable coughed. "Was there anything special on the landing then, sir?"

"Only the telephone, of course," said Travers with an arch look of his own, and left it at that. And then as he sat on the stairs and waited for Wharton his thoughts ran to young Cane again and the *Blazon* building. Cane would give Maylove the news in confidence and the roaring presses would be held up. Cane himself would be like a head of steam and when the word came to go he would be an explosion. Refreshingly unlike the hard-boiled school was Cane, but with plenty of drive of his own as even a fool could have told by the way he had bolted down those stairs. Cynicism and speed; those, thought Travers, were the hallmarks of the hard-boiled school. "Luffham's murdered. Fetch me a pint of his blood," the modern editor might say, and the old-timer would come back with: "Oh, hell, and I was doing something else,"—and fetch it all the same. Maybe Cane would come to that in time when the bloom was worn off. And as Travers dabbled with those sanguinary trifles a sound came and he cocked his ear and ran down the stairs again. A car had slipped quickly round the corner and was making for the wrong side of the road where he stood. Five seconds and George Wharton was getting out.

He nodded at the constable's salute, and caught Travers's eye. The two went silently up the stairs to the landing.

"Well?" said Wharton then. "What's it all about?"

Travers began explaining the purely personal reasons that had brought him to Martlet Street.

"Luffham, was he?" Wharton said. "First I've heard about it. I remember Luffham, of course. Got into some mess with a woman or something like that, and disappeared." He gave a quick, suspicious look. "You haven't dragged me round here just to tell me you've discovered that Clough was Luffham?"

Travers did some more explaining and then produced the elastic. Wharton whipped out his miniature ruler.

"Quarter inch. Sort of stuff sold by the mile every day." Then he peered at the slight tear in one end and put his glass over it. A grunt disturbed the ample curve of his vast, overhanging moustache. "Where's that drawing-pin?"

Then he grunted again, and puffed out his lips in a moment's thought.

"If it was stuck in a rail to hold the elastic, then the rail would be near the top to make the fall greater. This side would be the handiest. and so that the pin would fall this way." He handed the glass to Travers. "You're the giraffe species. You have a look. And keep those prints of yours off the rails."

Travers gave a polish to his glasses and set to work. In half a minute he had found the minute hole where the drawing-pin had been pressed into the rail. Wharton grunted approvingly, but as he moved for a closer inspection, Travers's hand fell on his shoulder.

"Don't tread there, George. There's something else that you might like to see. Got a candle on you?"

Wharton ignored the flippancy and produced his torch, then squatted down for a good look.

"Notice how the shoe was worn on one side?" said Travers, trying to peer round Wharton's bulk.

"Haven't I got eyes?" said Wharton, still crouching.

"Then you've seen a few other prints as well," said Travers imperturbably. "What's left of them, I mean. Lucky for us that charwoman was as careless as she was and bad luck she wasn't a trifle lazier."

Wharton got to his feet.

"Now then, before I ring up for everybody to come, let's talk this quickly over. I can read your mind like a book—"

"God forbid!" said Travers hastily.

"Your idea's this," Wharton went on, "and you can correct me if I'm wrong. Wait a minute, though. Who else has been up here besides those on the first job?"

Travers repeated the constable's words.

"All right then," said Wharton. "This is a smallish boot and no cop ever wore it. Besides, there's only the one set of marks and they follow round the right way to fit in with your idea—which is this. Someone had got to know that Clough was Luffham. He was here last night for a friendly chat and when he left he saw himself out. Perhaps there was some agreement between Luffham and himself that he was going away to find some piece of information that Luffham wanted, and which he would phone up. But he slipped back quietly and affixed that elastic—"

"Having a perfectly good excuse if Luffham heard him."

"Just so. He put it right round those two top rails and fastened it loosely with the drawing-pin. You only need a touch to upset a man's balance. Then he went to a call-box and duly rang Luffham up. Luffham came out to answer the call; caught his foot in the black elastic, and crashed down. But as the other man knew, the pin wasn't in so tight but that the force of the kick against it and the spring of the elastic wouldn't loosen it. Out came the pin and rolled away. The elastic uncoiled itself with its own spring and went away across the landing. The evidence had in fact disposed of itself."

"Most admirably put," said Travers. "And neither the elastic nor the pin would be likely to cause comment. The mere fact that they were left shows that the murderer never came back and never had any intention of coming back." His eyes all at once opened and his fingers fumbled at his glasses. "I've thought of something else that makes it even more damnable. The man, whoever he was, must have known all Luffham's domestic arrangements. The one to see the elastic first would be the charwoman, and the way he'd work it out, he calculated that if she did see it, she'd simply say, 'Hallo! this looks like a piece of elastic. Might come in handy for something.' But for the fact that it went into that corner, she'd have pocketed it."

But Wharton had not waited for the end. He was already dialling the Yard and Travers stood by while he gave his long instructions.

"I don't think we'll go upstairs yet," he said when he hung up. "There might be some more of these worn prints, if our theory happens to be right. Tracing that phone call is the first main thing. By the way, did Luffham in his prime make any noted enemies?"

"Hundreds, I expect," said Travers. "Public men of his type always do. But that line of research is a bit far-fetched, don't you think?"

"You never know," Wharton said. "There's that scandal that broke him, for instance. Why shouldn't there be something in that?"

"Well, finger-prints and even these shoe marks aren't going to be much use to you if you're going back all that far," Travers told him. "This is an amateur's job and a modern one, and a pretty clever one at that."

"Why shouldn't something have been stolen?" Wharton challenged him. "Besides, we've got the charwoman to talk to, haven't we? Then there's that place where he used to get his meals. They'll know there if there was anyone he used to meet."

"Yes," said Travers, and gave a curious hesitating smile as he shook his head. "I have a confession to make, George. It was from the editor of the *Blazon* that I heard about Luffham, and as soon as I said I'd be coming round here, he very courteously sent one of his men—Cane, their crime-reporter—to meet me. These are his prints. You must understand, of course, that all of us then thought the death merely some sort of accident plus heart."

"Yes?" said Wharton impatiently.

"Well, the point is that Cane and I found together all the things I've mentioned. I sent him off, but we've got to face the fact that he knows it's murder. I've told him he's not to say a word about the method employed, so all the *Blazon* can do is hint that it was murder and challenge a denial from the Yard."

Wharton breathed a bit heavily for a minute and Travers waited for the outburst. But one last grunt and the General gave a nod.

"Unfortunate, of course, but it can't be helped. Cane did you say his name was?"

He wrote it on the envelope on which were the prints and looked up to see Travers smiling.

"Well, what is it now?"

"I've just remembered something else," Travers said. "Cane has written two detective novels at least. I expect he's the same man because they're from a crime-reporter's angle. Tristram Cane his name is."

Wharton shot him a look. "Tristram? What the devil should anyone do with a name like that?"

"Now you're being prejudiced," Travers told him, "but I suppose it can be accounted for if you work it out."

"Oh?" said Wharton, and smiled with a grim irony. Travers, as he had often said, could account for anything. Two minutes' thought and he could explain the larynx of Balaam's ass or the gullet of Jonah's whale.

"Yes. For instance, Cane's about twenty-four or -five. Say he was born at the end of the Edwardian era. Edwardian—which means the last lingering of the Victorian. Sad romance, George, and Tennysonian lawns and blighted love. Knights of the Round Table and all the rest of it. Now do you see it?"

"As far as I'm concerned you're talking damned rubbish," Wharton told him.

Travers smiled. "Well, what about this? Young Cane's father died at his birth. Cane may even be a posthumous child. Therefore the sorrowing mother—Cane was wearing a black armlet, by the way, so she's probably died recently too—called her son Tristram. Sorrowful in other words, George, as you as a French scholar know as well as I."

Wharton grunted. "What's that got to do with what we're here for?"

"You never know," said Travers and then his mouth opened blankly. "By Jove! I'd almost forgotten. Look at this. Found in the waste-paper basket up there."

Wharton had a look and gathered little.

"Ferdinand Pole," said Travers. "He's very well known in Fleet Street. Writes detective novels and founded a society not unknown to you perhaps—the Murder League."

"Yes," said Wharton, and frowned.

A noise of cars and voices was heard in the street below. The camera and print men had come and Wharton had a hasty word.

"Can you tackle this man Pole yourself? I mean he's your sort. Most tactfully, of course."

Travers beamed amiably. "Never say *can*, George, always say *will*. It adds a touch of flattery and buoys one up with hope."

In a moment the tiny downstairs space was crowded. Travers shook hands with an old friend in Chief-Inspector Norris, waited until the landing was uninhabitable and then made an unobtrusive exit.

But long before he turned into the Strand he was thinking of Ferdinand Pole. He had never met the man but he knew him by repute as a thruster, and a certain correspondence had given ample confirmation. That was on the very day when *Kensington Gore* was published, for Pole, in his capacity as president, had countersigned with the secretary an invitation from the Murder

League, most flatteringly and indeed oleaginously worded, for Travers to become a member. Travers had courteously declined, Pole had renewed the attack and then Travers had retreated out of range.

And Pole lived at Marsham Chambers, scarcely a stone's throw from where Luffham had died. By no means birds of a feather, the two—and yet one never knew. Maybe young Cane might have taken the dropped hint and hunted up Pole, but if he had mentioned the card outright, Travers hoped to Heaven the thing had been shrewdly done.

But as Travers stepped out of the lift in the *Blazon* building, Cane was waiting on the top landing. His face was all excitement.

"Everything all right, Mr. T-T-Travers?"

"Yes," said Travers. "What I said and no more. A fact to hint at, but no evidence."

"Yes, sir, I understand." Then Cane's beaming face sobered. "I had a very discreet word with Mr. Pole, sir. He knew Luffham years ago. He says he hasn't seen him since."

Travers nodded, wondering how Cane could have run Pole to earth so quickly. Cane's voice lifted again. "The editor's waiting for you, sir, if you'll see him now."

Travers was ushered in. A fussy little man with plump belly and badger hair that showed a trace of auburn was still holding forth to Maylove.

"Ah, Mr. Travers." The editor came forward. "I don't know if you and Pole know each other."

"Spiritually but not in the flesh," smiled Travers, who had started as if Pole—pot-belly and all—had been a ghost.

Pole shook with a spirited hand and his shrill little voice was all unction.

"Everybody knows Mr. Travers, of course. Great pleasure to meet you, Mr. Travers."

"I must have a talk with you some time," Travers said. "Where can I get hold of you?"

"Pardon me," said Pole, and hunted for a card. Travers took it with gloved hand and stowed it away.

"I shall be here till three," Pole went on. "If you happen to be here then we might adjourn somewhere."

"Very good of you," said Travers. And then Maylove was taking Pole's arm and leading him to the door. Travers heard the farewells and the editor's last words.

"Immediately after lunch, then. And you will have the scripts ready."

"Now, Mr. Travers," Maylove said. Cane was still in the room and he waved the two to chairs. "In strictest confidence I believe you have done us a tremendous service, for which we are enormously grateful."

"In the same strict confidence," said Travers, "may I hope you won't make too much use of it."

Maylove chuckled. "I understand. But about yourself and Luffham. Do you feel equal to writing an appreciation? Say in the course of the next half hour?"

"Good Lord, no!" Travers told him. "Give me twenty-four hours and I'll have a shot at it. It's an insult to Luffham to rush him over in thirty minutes."

Maylove smiled tolerantly. "You literary top-notchers are too punctilious. Still, if you won't, I have another man in mind." He picked up a printed "pull" of Pole's soon-to-be-famous letter. "This might interest you."

Travers read a few lines, polished his glasses and began again. Once he let out a "Good Lord!" and more than once he raised a polite eyebrow.

"Well"—Maylove leaned back in his chair—"what do you think of it?"

"Ingenious—but erratic."

"But near enough to the truth?"

"As near as all speculations," said Travers guardedly.

Maylove nodded. "Now let me come to the point. That letter is the front page splash of our midday edition. Mr. Pole is getting some of the Murder League experts to write up each day those unsolved murders he mentions. The publishers of detective fiction are collaborating and we are having what might be called a Thriller Week. So much for that. The point is, will you as one of our most famous living literary men and criminologists, take charge generally?—just a mild supervision for this one week? Name your own price. If you can't do more, let us use your name."

Travers staggered at last from his blushes. That Fleet Street should regard him as a criminologist was incredible. In those cases he had handled with George Wharton his light had been hidden beneath a bushel, but what he forgot was that modern bushels are rarely lightproof. So he pleaded pressure of work with a half dozen deft excuses and ended with the promise to write up the Romney Dyke affair.

"Well, we're grateful for that much," Maylove said as he rose. "Cane here, whom you know, had been hoping that he might be your liaison officer. By the way, weren't you at Halstead, Cane?"

Cane flushed. "At Millborough, sir—not Halstead. I believe a distant cousin of mine was at Halstead."

"Sorry, my mistake," said Maylove, as if it didn't matter a damn either way.

"Millborough's a very fine school," put in Travers, with a sympathy for Cane's confusion. "A young nephew of mine happens to be there. I've a very high opinion of Millborough."

"Drop in whenever you can," Maylove said, and the door closed on him and Cane. Then out came his head again and he was calling to a passing reporter. "Jackson, give Mr. Travers a midday copy."

Travers stood at the lift-head. A paper was put in his hand and he rammed it mechanically into his overcoat pocket. Cynicism there might be but the speed was there beyond question and Travers was feeling like a man who has unexpectedly looped the loop.

Wharton was on the landing watching a camera man taking a flash. At the sight of Travers's lamppost figure he came down the stairs. Travers gave him Pole's card.

"His print's on it, George. The same issue, I'd say, as the one found here."

Wharton called up to Norris, who took it over.

"The first card had four smudges on it," Wharton said. "Yours, Cane's, the dead man's and an unknown. Lucky for us if this is the one we want. What did you get out of him?"

Travers explained. Wharton grunted and remarked that three o'clock might be soon enough. His own news was all negative. No prints found but Travers's, Cane's, the dead man's and the woman's. The woman, said Wharton, was a fool. She had never known the telephone go or seen a soul in the flat, and Luffham had never spoken except to give orders or hand over her pay. They knew his bank, but the manager knew him only as Clough. The telephone call at two a.m. was untraceable, for it must have been an automatic registration as a local call. The restaurant had been found where he had taken dinner the last two years, and the proprietor had never known him dine other than alone or seen him in conversation.

"Routine is what we'll go on with for a bit," Wharton said.

"Somebody may have seen the murderer early this morning. People never really go to sleep round this quarter. We might start an enquiry into that old scandal."

Norris popped his head out of the upper door and called a startling something before he disappeared again.

"That's the print we're looking for!"

Wharton raised his eyebrows. Travers frowned.

"Pole said he'd never clapped eyes on him for years!"

"A half truth most likely," said Wharton. "He mayn't have clapped eyes on Luffham but he may on Clough."

Travers nodded.

"You turn him inside out this afternoon," said Wharton. "That's the sort of thing you can do as well as myself, and I'll say it to your face. Find out if he was a teetotaller. There wasn't a second glass, the charwoman says. Luffham's prints were on the only one and on the bottle." His face took on a calculated anxiety. "Well past your lunch hour, isn't it?"

Travers laughed. "You flatter me, George, when you want a job of work done, and you show concern for my stomach when you wish to be rid of me. When I theorize you ridicule and when—"

He had thrust his hands into his coat pockets and now he brought out the folded paper.

"Here's the midday *Blazon* Maylove was so anxious for me to have . . . Good Lord!"

His eyes were blinking at the streamer headlines—

MURDER ON MONDAYS

From an oval inset there regarded him the features of Ferdinand Pole, set for the occasion in a repose that was meant to be cannily intellectual. In a neat framing Pole's letter shouted with heavy type while in a lower artistic scroll was a foreword above the signature of Tristram Cane.

"Good Lord!" said Travers again. "And never a word about Luffham. Oh, yes, there is, though. Just a stop-press para."

"Here, let me have a look at that."

Wharton took the paper from Travers's fingers, grunted, stared and grunted again. Then he adjusted his antiquated spectacles, shot a look at Travers over their tops and began a methodical reading of Pole's letter. Then he spat.

"Damn the *Blazon!*"

Travers gave a tepid chuckle.

"Humbug and flapdoodle! Lies—most of it. Knows the ins and outs of the Trunk Murder, does he?"

The General glowered grimly at the features of Pole, and once more nodded.

"Turn him inside out, do you hear?"

"By all means, George," said Travers mildly. "But not before lunch."

From the outer door he glanced back to see Wharton with his eyes still glued to that front screaming page of the midday *Blazon.*

CHAPTER III
AN HOUR WITH POLE

JUST BEFORE three o'clock, Ludovic Travers once more ascended the lift in the *Blazon* building and stepped out to the spacious landing. Once more Cane seemed to be on the lookout for him, for he and Travers met at the enquiry office.

"Mr. Pole won't be more than a minute or two, sir," he said. "Perhaps you'd like to wait in here."

No sooner were they inside the small annex than Travers regarded the young reporter with a look of kindly approval. In the morning Cane's dress had been of the haphazard variety, neat enough but lacking distinction; but since Travers had seen him last he had found time and occasion to rig himself out anew from crown to heel.

"Things prospering young fellow?" Travers said with a twinkle.

Cane flushed, and came near a titter. "You see, I don't know who I may have to meet, Mr. T-T-Travers."

"I know," and Travers, "All the Fleet Street kings are bringing tribute and you're the High Chancellor." His hand fell on the other's shoulder. "Pardon an old man making a bit of fun. This business is giving you a pretty big chance. Grab it with both hands."

Cane nodded. "I'm trying to make a good job of it, sir."

"Of course you are," said Travers, and then gave a dry smile. "I imagine you're going to make such a good job that your senior—Stowe, isn't his name?—will be somewhat annoyed when he reads today's issues—if they reach him."

"I'm not dreaming of trying to cut out Stowe," Cane said. "He's always been pretty decent to me, Mr. T-T-Travers, and it's just bad luck that it broke while he was away."

"In England, is he?"

"In Switzerland, I think, sir."

Tuke went by then, morose and badgered as ever though his mouth alone showed it, for his eyes were inscrutable behind those dark glasses. He was in his shirt-sleeves, as usual, and had a hand full of clippings.

"Oh, Mr. Tuke!" called Cane. "I thought you might like to meet Mr. Ludovic Travers. This is Mr. Tuke, the news editor, Mr. T-T-Travers."

Tuke had turned belligerently but at the sight of Travers he smiled.

"How d'you do, Mr. Travers. I know your name, of course, but I've never had the pleasure of meeting you. You're doing the Romney Dyke Case for us. Tomorrow, isn't it? You'll excuse me going away. Up to the eyes as usual."

Off the news editor went. Travers recovered from the starting knowledge that the evening must be spent in writing up that Romney Dyke affair.

"I'll see if Mr. Pole is ready now, sir," Cane was saying.

"Oh, about that," Travers said quickly. "I do hope you didn't misunderstand me this morning when that card was found and I so airily suggested it might be worth enquiry. Mr. Pole has no connection whatever with what happened in Martlet Street. You do understand that?"

"Certainly, sir," Cane said, and looked somewhat hurt.

"Of course you do." Travers smiled so delightfully that Cane's fact was aglow again as he went off to find out about Pole. Travers was feeling a kind of avuncular pride in him. There was about him a something the least bit wistful, and Travers, prompt to theorise as ever, imagined a son orphaned at birth, and a mother's darling who had come at long last to a he-man's estate and was standing squarely on his own two legs.

Cane returned with the information that Mr. Pole would not be more than a minute.

"He and I happen to be going the same way," Travers explained, "and we might as well go together. Where do you live yourself, in case I happen to want you at any time?"

Cane wrote down the Highbury address, which was less than no time away if one took the tube from Covent Garden.

"I may be seeing you later." Travers held out his hand and some new kindliness glowed at the sight of the grateful face.

"Please don't think me too personal, but I've been making up all sorts of romantic stories about you, young man."

"Have you, sir?" said Cane, and flushed.

"Unpardonably rude of me," Travers went on, "but I'm an inveterate theorizer. If I were a backer of horses, I'm positive I could infallibly announce the Derby winner."

"An expensive bit of theorizing, wouldn't it be, sir?" grinned Cane.

"You never know," said Travers. "But about yourself, if I may go on being rude. I wonder if you'd mind telling me when your father died."

The smile of anticipation went from Cane's face. His mouth gaped for a ridiculous moment, then his cheeks flushed scarlet. His lips moved, then he shook his head, and at last the words came stammeringly out:

"It was in the war . . . I think Mr. Pole is coming now, sir."

Then he fairly bolted. Travers watched him for a regretful moment, knowing a bad brick had been dropped. Maybe there had been some deep tragedy in the father's death, and the idle chatter had touched some grief on the raw. But as Travers moved off in quick pursuit, Pole's voice was heard, and Cane had altogether disappeared.

Pole and Travers fell into step, or perhaps it was that Travers shortened his stride to suit the mincing patter of his companion. As they walked they chatted on nothings, with Travers keeping carefully from the things he was most anxious ultimately to hear preferring indeed not to force the pace but to let the other bare his mind by an avoidance of one topic or the intrusion of another.

"Ragazzi's, of course," said Pole as they passed the well-known restaurant, and there was something calculating in the patronizing wave of the hand. "We—the Murder League, that is—meet there once a fortnight. Just talk, and tea."

Travers expressed a polite interest. A yard or two on, at the corner of Pintail and Lapford Streets, Pole chuckled cheerily and gave another wave of the hand at the now closed doors of the bank.

"That's where I keep my overdraft."

Once more there was a complacence in words and gesture, and Travers was certain that Pole was an enormous distance from financial embarrassment, but just when he was about to use the opening for a subtle mention of murder, Pole was halting before a new, imposing block of service flats.

"Not the ideal neighbourhood, but in the centre of things which suits me admirably. Perhaps you'll allow me to offer you tea. They do you very well here."

"I'm sure they do," Travers said. "No tea, however, but I'll certainly come in. Curiosity with me has become one of the major virtues."

They went past the porter's desk and the empty lift to a wide stairway.

"Only a flight up," Pole said. "That's what I like about this place. Nobody to spy on your comings and goings."

Travers was pricking his ears at that. Pole prattled on.

"Not such palatial affairs as those flats where you live, at St. Martin's—but they serve. If it isn't a rude question, what rent do you pay there?"

"I'm afraid I avoid paying any," Travers said.

Pole stared, and he smiled.

"Oh, no. I'm not a wanderer by moonlight. It just happens that I own the whole block. No merit of my own. I merely happened to inherit."

"My hat!" said Pole. Instinctively his manner became more subdued and his tone took on a certain deference. "One step here, Mr. Travers. I'll switch on the light. Rather overcast today, don't you think? Now let me take your hat and coat."

The living-room was large, and with furnishings not too ultra. And, as Pole explained, some of the things were his own, such as the bookshelves and the writing-desk.

"And the parrot?" smiled Travers.

Pole gave his little cackle of a laugh, and beamed amiably at the parrot. It was a grey African in a cage beneath the main window, and no sooner did he approach than it gave a kind of ruffling to its feathers.

"Is that the kitchen? Is that the kitchen? Breakfast for one. Breakfast for one."

Travers was startled, for the voice might have been the pompous squawk of Pole himself. Pole merely cackled merrily as he whipped a sateen cover over the cage.

"Wonderful, isn't he? Not that we want to hear him now. All the same I can assure you that that bird can carry on a conversation between two people. All my friends come up here to listen to him. I've refused forty guineas for him."

"I can quite believe it," Travers said. "Somewhat disconcerting though, to hear a voice quite so human?"

"That's nothing," Pole said. "If you came here two or three times and had any peculiarity of speech, he'd have it off absolutely pat."

Before they set down he showed the bedrooms and the small study. Travers saw and praised, and Pole once more mentioned tea.

"You won't think me a toper," Travers said, "but I wonder if I might have a tiny whisky. Half an inch and a splash. I'm feeling just a bit jaded."

"My dear sir?" Pole got out decanter and siphon at once. "I'll join you, I think. I've had a tiring day myself. Just been writing an up-to-date obituary of that poor devil Luffham." He brought the whisky and soda. "You knew it was murder? But, of course. You were round there, didn't I hear?"

"Just taking a look," Travers said. "Amateurs are a red rag to the police bull. You knew him then? And as Luffham, or Clough?"

"Here's the best," Pole said, raising his glass. "About Luffham we were talking. It was about a year before he dropped out that I saw him last. When I heard the news and how he'd been masquerading for years as a hairy old hermit, you could have knocked me down with a feather."

"It's a pity you didn't know him as Clough. There'd have been a fine story there."

"I'll tell you something," Pole said. "A few years back I got together some material for a short life of Luffham. Then I aban-

doned the idea. Thought even the brilliant Luffham was a trifle démodé—so to speak. Still, my material came in handy for
the *Blazon* today."

"You don't happen to know the true history of his dropping-out?"

Pole threw out his chest.

"But I do! I'm one of the few men living who do."

His voice shrilled somewhat more primly while he related at
length the ghastly, salacious thing. Travers was shocked, and incredibly distressed.

"You're really sure of your facts?"

Pole looked dignified.

"You knew Braigne, his second master? Well, Braigne married my only sister. Dead now, poor chap! and she too. I tell you
that if Luffham hadn't been given the chance of dropping-out,
he'd have been jailed. A spot more whisky?"

"Thanks, no." said Travers, still sadly shaking his head.

"I do wish you'd see your way clear to changing your mind
and joining us in the Murder League," Pole said, with a kind
of flirtatious humility. "Your name would carry a tremendous
weight—not that we haven't got some very fine people already.
A few coming-ons, of course, who got in on the ground floor."

"Yes," said Travers, wondering where to steer the talk. "You
have some very admirable people."

"You know Petrie Cubbe, our secretary?"

"Cubbe? Cubbe?" Travers thought hard. "He writes detective
novels, doesn't he?"

"We all do," Pole told him with an arch reproof.

Then Travers smiled and was all at once leaning back in the
chair. His eyes closed and he raised his hand.

"Don't stop me. I'm just remembering something. Ah, yes!"

*There is about the works of the greatest masters a rare, elu-
sive quality which can best be described by the single word—
haunting. John Bunyan had it, Hardy had it, Emily Bronte had
it, and I have found it in the prose of Masefield. That same rare,
haunting quality we find today in the work of Petrie Cubbe.*

Before the eyes of Travers opened, Pole laughed. It was a shrill, belly cackle as if he was tickled to some hilarious bursting point.

"My dear Mr. Travers! Really too funny. You read the advertisements, I see." Then he went off again. "The really funny thing is that you should be reciting it to me. I wrote that myself!"

Travers stared.

"I'm Mortimer Pugh, the reviewer!"

Travers was momentarily speechless. The strange contortions into which his face was twisted must have been taken by Pole for mirthful appreciation.

"We all know Cubbe," he said. "The League is one of his enthusiasms. Cubbe has done no end of work for the League." The smile became roguish. "You didn't discover the haunting quality?"

Travers coughed gently. "Not to any recognizable extent."

"Maybe you weren't looking for it in the right spirit," Pole told him roguishly. Then his face straightened to a kind of magisterial complacence. "Modern publicity requires modern methods. Personally I'm out for any publicity which brings results. Authors have got to live, you know."

Travers almost added the obvious, "Why?" Then he became arch instead.

"You mean you'd do anything short of committing murder?"

"Murder?" Pole chuckled. "Why draw the line at murder?"

"No, but reasonably seriously."

Pole finished his longish tot, set the glass down, and frowned in Gargantuan thought. Then his fleshy lips took on an ironic twist.

"You appeal to me as a writer of detective novels, perhaps. Well, what I say is, if I ever did commit a murder, I'd combine business with pleasure. First of all I'd make my murder the safest thing known." He cocked an important eye. "Have you read my *Three Bags Full?*"

"A very clever book," said Travers.

"Well, you'll admit that there was a murder that would have baffled any detective force in the world. That would be nothing if I were ever really on my mettle." He smiled as his mind surveyed what Travers hoped was the past. "A fine feeling of power—what?—to practically boast to the police that you've done a thing and then tell them in so many words to go to hell?"

And then he looked Travers clean in the eye with what seemed so stark a challenge that Travers was startled and his fingers went to his glasses.

"That's the sort of murder I'd commit, my dear sir. I'd remove someone who needed removing, do myself a good turn at the same time, and stick my fingers to my nose at the police."

"You terrify me," Travers told him, but with an uneasiness that was not the humorous assumption it appeared. "You almost convince me you've had experience already!"

Pole gave an airy shrug of the shoulders.

"And suppose that sort of thing got in your blood," Travers went flippantly on. "A man like you, to whom safety is such a certainty, might become a new Jack the Ripper."

"Nothing so crude," Pole said and uttered his epigram before it quite made sense. "Murder is an art when it has art—I should say, finesse. Not that there aren't quite a number of people whose departure I shouldn't regret. A certain actress, for instance—but we won't talk of her now. You're not going? Sure you won't let me have tea sent up?"

"Most kind of you," said Travers, "but I really won't. I've just remembered a certain appointment. Some time perhaps you'll allow me to come again—to hear the parrot."

"The parrot?" Pole reared up momentarily, suspecting maybe some double meaning. But Travers was holding out an urbane hand.

"Good-by. Very nice to have had this chat. Perhaps you'll dine with me towards the end of the week when you're a less busy man. The parrot's name is?"

"Charlie."

"An excellent name," said Travers. "Do let me come some time and hear him talk. And talking far from seriously, he isn't by any chance a member of the Murder League?"

Pole chuckled, then sobered.

"My hat! there's publicity in that. It might be worth considering as a *jeu d'esprit*. Every gossip writer in London would leap at it."

Wharton would be at the flat as arranged and as Travers walked homewards he knew that things were working themselves out with too smooth a simplicity. Pole was a hot-air vendor; an exhibitionist, in fact, and the immediate problem was one of two things. When he had talked so confidently about baffling the police, had it been merely hot-air or had he been in complacent earnest? And when Travers weighed up the evidence, it seemed that a third factor entered—that sneering, truculent look that Pole had cast when he made his boastful statements.

So at the moment Travers was inclined to believe that Pole was the man, and then again he was shaking his head. The fact that he was so admirable a suspect proved according to the exasperating experience of years that he was the last man to suspect; so when Travers walked in on Wharton, his air was somewhat chastened.

"You see, George," he explained to Wharton, "I can't make out several things. He knows well enough that I have a certain standing with you people—the law, if you like. Was he blowing a kind of defiant bugle? Was all that stuff he came out with—incriminatory, most of it—a sort of ironic challenge? If so, and he's the murderer, we know two things. First of all, from what he said to me, he did himself a good turn by rubbing out Luffham—and a good turn other than publicity. That means we may have to delve down into past history. The other thing is that he's cocksure. He knows that what he's done is dead plumb safe."

"I'll use your phone if I may," Wharton said, and got hold of Norris. The Inspector would find Pole probably still in his flat and he was to question him tactfully about the card.

Wharton came back to his chair. "Facts. They're the things I want. Let him wriggle out of that card business and then we'll see. The fact that he's not a teetotaller proves nothing. He says he knew Luffham and up to the moment he hasn't an alibi. I've known people hung after worse starts than that."

Travers winced. Death and hangings and all the bloody impedimenta were out of his line. Indignation there might be at the foul or wanton, but his delight would have been in murders without corpses and retributions unknown. The grim pursuit was the thing for him—the quick theory and the neat deduction.

"Ichabod, George," he said. "The glory's departed from Luffham now I know what that scandal was. For me he's merely someone who represents the problem. He's no more than a caretaker or a dead dustman. But what I'm betting you—two new hats, for instance—is that Pole, if necessary, will have a perfect alibi for two o'clock this morning."

"I'm not betting," Wharton said, but nodded exasperatingly as a last word.

He stayed on for tea and Norris. The Inspector was along sooner than expected.

"What do you think?" he said. "He swore blind he'd never seen Luffham or Clough for years and as good as told me I was a liar about the card. Talk about a fighting-cock? He's a regular little bantam."

"What happened then?" asked Wharton.

"He as good as told me I could go to hell." There Travers caught Wharton's eye. "So I thanked him and told him I might be seeing him again, and just as I was wondering whether to take the lift or walk down the stairs, out he came. Reckoned he could explain the card. It appears he's a lot in that publisher's office next door and he's always handing people cards there. So according to him one of his cards must have been dropped and Luffham must have picked it up. Else, so he said, why was it in the waste-paper basket?"

Wharton grunted.

"Then he turned all genial," Norris went on. "Asked me to step down stairs with him and see the porter—the same one who'd been on duty up to six o'clock and was doing a double shift to oblige a pal. This porter said Pole came in last night at just before midnight and didn't go out again."

Travers smiled drily. "In other words—a perfect alibi."

"I'm afraid so," admitted Norris. "All his windows overlook Lapford Street and you can't imagine him climbing out."

"Squared the porter perhaps," said Wharton.

"That won't help us, sir," Norris told him. "What the porter swears is evidence." He nodded grimly. "But I haven't finished with him yet by a long chalk. I'm now trying Rote and Grumby's to see if one of their people was about the place early this morning and heard anything."

He went off and Wharton with him. Travers found a notebook with the details of the Romney Dyke affair and began to write. At six o'clock he was still writing, and Palmer came in with the evening papers.

Travers smiled as he reached for the *Blazon*, wondering what had been let out about Luffham. Across the front page were the midday streamer headlines—

MURDER ON MONDAYS

and below it, standing out from an unmissable frame, a copy in miniature of the midday edition. Below that, new headlines shrieked:

WE CHALLENGE SCOTLAND YARD

Travers nodded noncommittally and cast his eye on the first column.

T. P. LUFFHAM WAS MURDERED ANOTHER MONDAY MURDER

HAS ENGLAND A NEW JACK THE RIPPER?

But when Travers had skimmed the upper half of that front page he was acknowledging a piece of journalistic enterprise. The murder of Luffham was presented as a thunderclap confirmation of what the midday had offered as speculation. A vague note of the sinister was in it all, with a touch of fear that would frighten in lonely places, and an urgency that demanded action. As for Tristram Cane, he had played the game. While the murder was claimed for an incontrovertible fact, no word of evidence was there to bolster it.

And then Travers's eyes fell on a row of portraits at the page bottom, their line broken by a special oval inset that framed a face curiously familiar. It was—and yet it couldn't be! But when with a blush he read the words beneath, he knew it most certainly was.

LUDOVIC TRAVERS

the world-famous writer and criminologist who will analyse tomorrow for our readers a murder that has much in common with that of Luffham—

THE ROMNEY DYKE MURDER

Travers hooked off his glasses, blinked for a bit, then laid the paper gently aside. He winced as he saw Wharton's eyes on that front page and heard his comments. At the moment he knew he would never dare face Wharton again, and as his eyes rose to the phone, he had the sudden fear that the bell would shrill and the General's voice come blasphemously booming.

So Travers was a coward and pushed the bell for Palmer.

"I'm going on working in the study," he said, "and no matter who calls or rings, I'm out. If Superintendent Wharton should ring, however, you might say I left a message—that about the newspaper article I'm being most discreet."

Palmer got it pat and Travers went into hiding. It was well after ten o'clock when the work was finished and he could emerge for supper.

"Did I hear the phone, Palmer, or did I not?" he said.

"Mr. Wharton, sir," Palmer told him. "I gave him your message, sir."

"What'd he say?"

"I didn't quite gather it, sir."

Travers made a wry face. "He uttered noises?"

"Well, yes, sir." Then Palmer produced the phone pad. "He added, sir, that something most important had turned up, sir, and there was some mention of a bet, sir—about two new hats. It's all on the pad, sir."

For the rest of that night Travers was tortured by a dozen curiosities. With them was a depression, for the case had promised well. Now, if Wharton really had his hands on Pole, it was over before it had hardly begun.

CHAPTER IV
MURDER GONE MAD

TRAVERS BREAKFASTED at eight. At half-past the phone went and Travers knew that Wharton was about to read the riot act. But it turned out to be Tuke, and Travers spoke to the news editor himself.

"Oh, yes, it's ready," he said. "I'll bring it along myself if you like. Be there in ten minutes."

"Well send a messenger and save you the trouble," Tuke said.

"Not at all," said Travers, who was itching to enter once more the Blazon building. "Wouldn't dream of it. In ten minutes then. Good-by."

So Travers and the manuscript cut through to the Strand. At a quarter to ten Tuke was bringing Travers into the news room.

"We're very different from the morning papers," Tuke explained. "They'd have all day to work in; we've got about two hours. Also we're thinking of building the midday round this article of yours."

"Luffham finished with?" Travers asked.

"After today he will be," Tuke told him, and waved a vague hand. "It'll all peter out by Thursday, unless something breaks."

Then as Travers's eyes wandered interestedly round the room, and through the haze of tobacco smoke he was discerning even the far corners, the outer door swung and a breezy voice broke in on the hum of work.

"Morning, everybody! How are you, Fred? How are you, Cane?"

Tuke rose startled to his feet, and the newcomer progressed through a chorus of greetings.

"What're you doing back, Tom?"

There was something the least bit hostile, Travers thought, in the news editor's greeting, and his mouth had a hard suspicion that was far from a welcome. Stowe came breezing over, and his voice had so marked a cockney accent as to fit in amply with the perkiness.

"Morning, Bill. Just popped along, that's all. You didn't think I was going to be left out of all this, did you?"

"But how'd you know?"

"Pal of mine wired me the tip," Stowe said. "I hopped the first train from Lausanne to Lyons and flew the rest. Just got here." He rubbed his hands. "Now we'll begin to hear things hum."

He looked about thirty, and his face, as Travers saw it, had the go-getter's beefiness. As a confidence crook he would have been in the front rank, for though he oozed with self-satisfied and self-possessed confidence, there was an honest simplicity about him as of a boastful boy.

"How's Rhoda, Bill?" Stowe was saying. "Getting along all right?"

"Pretty slowly," Tuke said, and his tone was a shade more gracious. "She mentioned you the last time she wrote."

"I sent her a card from Geneva only yesterday," Stowe said, "Give her all the best from me, though, when you write."

He had cast an enquiring look on Travers.

"Oh, Mr. Travers," Tuke said. "This is Tom Stowe, our crime-reporter."

"I know Mr. Travers," Stowe said, and to Travers's somewhat blank look, "though he mayn't know me. How are you, Mr. Travers?"

His grip made Travers wince. Tuke was at work again and ignoring the pair of them. Travers made a brief conversation:

"How was Raertens looking, Mr. Stowe?"

"Raertens?" said Stowe blankly.

"The frontier station," said Travers. "It's a favourite spot with me."

"Oh, of course," Stowe laughed. "Looking just the same as ever." Then he gave a sudden, cautious look and the words that followed were too matter-of-fact. "How long did you usually have to wait there?"

"A quarter of an hour, I imagine."

"That's right," Stowe said. "That's all we had to wait. You'll excuse me now, Mr. Travers. There's some dope I must look over."

As Travers made a slow exit, he saw from the corner of his eye Stowe and young Cane in animated talk, and the sight brought a quick depression. Then he smiled drily to himself at his own hackneyed caption—YOUNG CRIME-REPORTER MAKES GOOD. That had been his hope for young Cane; now Stowe was at the helm and Stowe was not the kind to share publicity. Still, Cane had done himself no harm. A junior he might remain, but the next detective novel he wrote, with a bit of *Blazon* backing, should find its readers waiting. It might even be—and there Travers smiled with a characteristic touch of quiet amusement— that Pole might invite him to join his performing sea-lions of the Murder League.

"Morning, Mr. Travers. They told me you were here."

Travers looked up startled to see Pole before him.

"Sorry," he said, "to look so surprised, but you're making quite a habit of popping up just when I'm thinking of you."

"You were thinking about me?" Pole was absurdly anxious.

Travers smiled. "Yourself—and Charlie. How is my talkative friend, by the by?"

"Oh, very fit," said Pole, and smiled with a queer relief. Then the anxiety came again. "Could you spare me a private minute? I have a cubby-hole of my own here that I'm occupying during the week. Something about which I'd very much like your advice—and help."

Travers followed him to the little office and hardly was he seated than Pole was wading in.

"Something most amazing happened after you left me yesterday!"

The story was the visit of Norris, which Travers had heard from Norris's angle. Travers expressed a hypocritical indignation and concern.

"But that's nothing, my dear fellow," Pole went on, voice shrilling and hands vibrating. "You hear what happened later. You know the lie of that flat where Luffham was killed?"

"Reasonably well," Travers said.

"Well, above the living-room is a sort of attic office that's used by the London traveller of Rore and Grumby. Bert Quiff—you know him well, of course. Best man in the trade at selling books. That's why Percy Rore keeps him, though he's always going on the blind, Well, Quiff had a real day out last Saturday and kept it up all Sunday, and about ten o'clock he suddenly remembered he was due for an important conference on the Monday morning and had no end of stuff he hadn't got ready, so—it's his own tale I'm telling you—he says he sobered himself up and let himself in and went up to that room of his to work. And this is the amazing thing—or at least it isn't, the way I explain it. Quiff says he heard voices beneath him and wondered who the devil it was, so he put his ear to the floor and listened. What do you think he swears he heard? *My name mentioned.*"

"Good Lord!"

"Yes, but it was someone talking to me! Someone who addressed me as Pole!"

"There are other people of that name, surely?" said Travers. "But did he hear the man speak? The man who'd been addressed as Pole?"

"No," said Pole. "He says he only listened for a minute. And now I'll tell you my idea. Quiff was still drunk—at least, as drunk as he ever is. I'd seen him and spoken to him on the Sunday evening as he was going into the *King William* in Burton Street. Therefore what he did when he got up to that office of his, was to go sound asleep and dream the whole thing. And that's what I told Superintendent Wharton."

"The Yard saw you, did they?" said Travers, and raised an eyebrow.

"They did," said Pole tersely. "I insisted on being confronted with Quiff, and we went in the office and up to that room in Luffham's flat."

"And what was the upshot?"

"The upshot?" Pole's smile took on a truculence that had in it something pathetic and unreal. "The upshot, my dear sir, was that I reminded them of my alibi and informed them that they could do what they damn well pleased. I also hinted that I might make public use of it if they worried me again."

"Did you, by Jove!" said Travers. "But what was it you wanted my advice about?"

"Well"—he broke off the gesture as a new thought came—"I'm not worrying myself in the slightest. The law may be an ass but there's such a thing as one's own knowledge of one's self."

"I know," said Travers. "To quote from the same source, you feel yourself so armed in honesty that Wharton's no more than a puff of wind."

"Exactly!" said Pole. "But what I would like is for you—as a great personal favour, of course, and in the strictest confidence between ourselves—to give me the private tip if you happen to hear anything. You'll admit that after that amazing discovery of my card—of all people's!—in the room, and now this preposterous story of Quiff's, they may act without due discretion. As a public man I want no scandal."

Travers smiled. "But, as Ferdinand Pole, you wouldn't mind the publicity."

"Well"—Pole smirked—"I'm not altogether denying that." Then he gave a peek through the window. "Hallo! they're out of conference already. Thank you very much indeed, my dear Travers. You'll let me know how the wind blows?"

"And send you the very straw," Travers told him. "Don't bother to move. I know my way about by now."

Maybe Pole thought he had been a bit ungracious. "I wasn't hinting for you to go, but you know what newspaper offices are like. By the way, not a word of course to our friends—the, er—myrmidons."

The guarded hint was for the benefit of Cane who stood across the landing waiting possibly for Travers. Travers gave a mysterious countersign. The law should be kept duly in the dark.

He was feeling quite himself again as Cane joined him at the lift. The two went down together and had it to themselves.

"Bit of a jolt for you, your chief turning up?" Travers said sympathetically.

"I don't know, sir," Cane told him. "Stowe will handle things better than I, and I haven't done so badly so far."

"That's the way to take it," Travers said and lingered for a moment at the outer door, wondering just what to say. For in spite of those fine sentiments young Cane had uttered, a look had been on his face which was not difficult to read. It was the look of one who tries to be a good loser but fails because of some inherent temperament. Cane's tongue had said that Stowe was a good man to handle the splash; Cane's look and the petulance of his very smile had said that Cane himself could have handled it better.

And then it came to Travers that such a feeling was no more than human, and some pious priggishness of his own was sitting in judgment. Maybe too he could still lend Cane a hand.

"Would it do you any good," he said, "if the floodgates were let loose on the Luffham affair?"

Cane stared. "You mean if I could say I was there? And say what we found?"

"That's it," Travers said. "But no mention whatever of my name. However, we'll leave it like this. If you hear nothing from me in the next hour, you can go ahead. I take it Stowe doesn't know a thing except what was published?"

"No one knows, sir, not even the editor."

"Good," said Travers, and gave a farewell smile as he moved off.

"Th-th-thank you, Mr. T-T-Travers," Cane was saying, but Travers was scurrying off to avoid his gratitude. As he sat in the taxi that was carrying him towards the Yard, he was still somewhat perturbed about the young reporter, because perhaps he had romantically endowed him with all the virtues. There was no question of a cloven hoof, but merely a faint flaw in a fine surface; and then Travers began to think about Pole and Cane was forgotten.

Wharton was in his room. He shot a look at Travers over the tops of his glasses.

"Morning, George," began Travers. "Sorry I didn't take your message personally last night. Just been to the *Blazon* office though, where Pole nobbled me and told me all about things." He shook an uneasy head. "What perfectly unscrupulous things papers are."

"Well, you weren't forced to walk into the hyena's den?" said Wharton.

"That's libellous," Travers said. "Besides I'm not sure that hyenas have dens. But it's most annoying I admit. I'm inveigled into writing a purely objective article and they make me a buffoon." He had been filling his pipe and now he passed over the pouch. "Try some of this. And by the way, you must get the *Blazon*. I've done you awfully well in it."

"You don't think I want their publicity, do you?" said Wharton, but already feeling for his pipe.

"Not publicity, George—merely scant and overdue justice," said Travers severely. "I think the Commissioner should be delighted. Moreover those like yourself who can read between the lines will observe that I've given Pole a very adroit kick in the pants." Wharton grunted, lighted his pipe and handed back the pouch.

"What'd Pole tell you?"

Travers gave Pole's version. Wharton admitted it was substantially true. Travers took off his overcoat and drew in the chair like a man who proposes to stay.

"Tell me your impressions of Pole, now you've seen him at close quarters, George."

Wharton pursed his lips. "I think he's a bit alarmed. I had the idea we'd found out more than he thought we would. Purely an impression, of course, and possibly very wide of the mark."

"He was very slightly uneasy this morning," Travers said, "or he'd never have nobbled me. Yet I don't know. The complacence was still there. Most men would have been white to the gills if the police were questioning them seriously about murder. He was still practically sure he was safe. Not smugly and defiantly sure, as he was with me yesterday afternoon, but sure enough."

Then Travers drew the chair in still closer.

"And I wonder if he hunted me out to tell me his attitude because he was dead certain I'd pass things on to you people? He puzzles me. Frightens me too, a little bit."

Wharton grunted.

"Will you take me seriously if I do some theorizing?" Travers asked, and then remembered something, "But before I begin, are you thinking of making public the details of Luffham's murder?"

"They're being communicated straightaway," Wharton said. "I expect there'll be a whole crowd of reporters down below by now. Not that I've got much faith in it. Someone may remember who bought the elastic but it's a chance in a million."

Travers was glum for a moment, knowing that fine scheme for helping young Cane had miscarried. The bright and breezy Stowe would handle those details for the *Blazon*.

"Now what about this theory?" Wharton was saying.

"It's just this," Travers said. "Pole is an egomaniac. He's got a third-class brain but agile ideas. His mania is publicity. He wants the world to be talking of Ferdinand Pole, and he's been fed on cheap flattery and the little power he controls. I won't go into details, but I refer to the Murder League and his nasty little pen as the worst type of biased, vindictive, back-scratching reviewer. The little success he's achieved has given him the idea he's really someone who counts. Perfectly seriously then, why shouldn't he have engineered the whole of this business? He's the one man adapted to it? He fits in?"

"Facts?" asked Wharton.

"Well, he wrote the letter, which was purely for his own publicity. Then there's the evidence you have against him—proven or not. Then there're the boasts he made to me; though they of course may have been mere blether. And one last fact. Undoubtedly a man of his kind who must make a study of murder could devise and work out the perfect crime."

"Anything else?"

"Yes," said Travers. "Having in mind the evidence against him in the Luffham murder, doesn't it strike you that the murder was uncannily apposite for Pole? Didn't it clinch the *Blazon* publicity at the one perfect moment?"

"Yes," said Wharton. "Admitting most of that, but—well, it strikes me as murder gone mad."

"Precisely! Madness or mania. Egomania, in fact."

Wharton was reaching for the overnight edition of the *Blazon* and running his eye over the front page.

"At the moment I don't agree at all, and everything's too vague. But to pin down your theories, let's see who else might have profited. The proprietor of the paper? Lord Tabard, that is? Too far-fetched. The Murder League? Too far-fetched again. But what about your friend Tristram Cane?" and his finger jabbed down on the signature below the Cane column.

"Far-fetched for several reasons," Travers said.

Wharton brought up his heavy ironic artillery.

"Now don't go and tell me that he's not the type. All my life I've heard that particular argument. There is no murder type."

"Don't I know it?" Travers asked mildly. "Of course Cane might commit murder. So might I and so might you—given the particular mental stress. There's no community from that sort of thing. Even a duchess may suffer from hiccoughs. In fact I'd say that the murder of Luffham would have suited Cane admirably!"

Wharton gaped.

"Yes," said Travers. "Cane gives one the impression of gentleness, but he's got brains; Luffham's murder might be called the work of a man who hates blood but wouldn't mind committing a dirty, underhand murder—not that Cane's necessarily underhand. But he didn't commit the Luffham murder."

"Why not?"

"Well, how could he and Luffham have come into contact? They'd nothing in common. They were different generations. Still, leaving out all that, Cane didn't write the letter, which was the work of Pole. Therefore he wasn't aware of the existence of the letter at two o'clock on the Monday morning, when Luffham was killed. Therefore the publicity in his case was sheer luck."

"Wait a minute. Suppose it was sheer luck, in a way. But what if the luck was Pole's? What if Cane killed Luffham for a private reason, but being all the time unaware of Pole's letter?"

"If Cane murdered Luffham for a private reason, then the one thing necessary for him to do was to save his own neck. The murder had to appear suicide. When Cane was sent round there with me, he had his great chance. He had a dozen chances to pocket the elastic which was the only vital clue to murder. He made no attempt to do so. In fact he was utterly at a loss to know why I picked up the elastic at all."

"Hm!" went Wharton. "That's conclusive enough. And who else might be likely to profit?"

"Well, there's Stowe."

"Stowe? Who's he exactly?"

Travers gave full details.

"No use worrying about him then, if he was abroad," Wharton said. "Not that all the damn nonsense we're talking isn't a sheer waste of time."

Travers drew in still closer.

"And what if Stowe wasn't abroad!"

Wharton frowned. "What's the idea? You just said he took a train to Lyons and flew back here."

"No, George, I said *he said so*. Then some imp of cussedness prompted me to ask questions. You see, he was looking far too spruce for a man who's had a hectic journey like that. I don't know quite why, but I had the idea he was telling his story too tersely. He's the sort of one to seize a chance to spread himself—but he wasn't profiting from the occasion. So I asked him what Raertens was looking like; you know, George, that wonderful show place where you halt on the frontier, with all those marvellous wood carvings that decorate the station. He said it was looking the same as ever. And then he wondered if he'd made a slip. He asked me how long I usually had to stay there and I told him the truth. 'Quite so,' he said. 'That's just about how long I had to stay there.' But the point is this," and there Travers produced a clipping from his pocket-book. "If you'll read that—taken by the way from the *Telegraph* of yesterday morning—it says that all lovers of Raertens will be grieved to hear the station was completely gutted by fire on the Sunday evening and so fierce was the heat that rails were twisted and traffic had to be diverted."

"Oh," said Wharton grimly, and then, "I see. So he may have been in England all the time?"

"Or even in London."

"Yes," said Wharton. "And how would he fit in?"

"This way," Travers told him. "And that brings me to my real theory. Stowe and Pole worked out the letter between them as fine publicity for Pole and superb copy for Stowe. So that there should be no suspicion of connivance, they held the scheme up till Stowe was ostensibly away from the office. But he was lying handy so as to be on the spot and take over as soon as the story broke. But in the meanwhile Pole—whose idea the whole thing was from the start—had done what he had all the while intended, He did that perfect murder of his, which set the publicity flaring sky-high. Stowe, definitely alarmed because the murder had been altogether too apposite, promptly turned up to find out what the game was."

Wharton frowned. "I like it. But I don't know. It's as full of holes as a sieve."

"So's wire-netting," Travers told him promptly. "But a ten-ton tractor will go over it, even when it's laid on sand."

The phone went. Wharton lifted the receiver, and at once was giving Travers some secret sign.

"The editor of the *Blazon?* Yes, put him through."

Another raising of the eyebrows and he was speaking. But Travers gathered little except that it was about a letter, and Wharton was being most polite. Then the General's last words made it clear that he was going at once to the *Blazon* building. And no sooner did he hang up than he was getting to his feet. His face had a tolerant smile.

"The usual crank letter just reached the *Blazon*. Same old gag. Someone saying he did the murder."

"Sure Pole didn't write it?"

"You never know," said Wharton. "The editor swears it's genuine. And he says the chap who wrote it proves that it's genuine. That's why he'd like to see me or someone from here."

"You can give me a lift is far as the Strand," Travers said. "But I suppose, by the way, this obliging gentleman didn't enclose a photograph?"

Wharton grunted. "Not exactly, but he says he's a man of sixty and has a most pronounced squint."

CHAPTER V
THE MAN WITH THE SQUINT

TRAVERS READ that letter in the midday edition, and the *Blazon* published it admittedly without comment.

SIR,

I was interested and amused at all the talk in your paper about Murder on Mondays, because I am the one who did Luffham in and I was also the one who did three of the other murders.

Years ago I was a sufferer from the brutality of the law which refused to right a wrong and sided with money and influence against me, which made it plain that if anyone wants justice, he would have to take the law into his own hands. Monday has always been my lucky day and that was why I always executed justice on a Monday.

You will not publish this letter as you will take it for one of the letters that are always written after a murder. so I will say no more, except that if you do publish it I will give facts to prove my words. I can do that with impunity as my murders can never be discovered. I am not afraid of saying that I am a well-preserved man of over sixty and have a most pronounced squint in one eye, which is not noticeable because of the dark glasses I wear.

Yours, etc.,

London   JUSTICE.

Travers drew his own conclusions, and when Wharton called in after lunch, asked what his views were.

"I don't think it matters," Wharton said. "The test will be what he discloses next time he writes. If he knows anything about the Luffham murder that we don't, or about any other murder, then it's genuine."

"What about paper and writing?"

"Common or garden paper and writing very neat and careful," Wharton said. "It was slipped into the letter-box and marked urgent. Not a print on it that hasn't been identified."

"The letter's full of conceit," Travers said. "It also has a definite underlying vulgarity. Unless Luffham had become a remarkably queer fish, the man who wrote it was the last sort of person to be on terms of friendship with him."

"Well, we'll wait and see before theorizing," Wharton said. "I had a most interesting time in the *Blazon* building, by the way. I made the acquaintance of Stowe. A regular self-made one that, and cockney as they make 'em."

Travers tapped the front page of the midday.

"He doesn't write it though. Quite a good effort of his, this column. If you run your eye over it, you'll see he's put Cane's nose completely out of joint. Cane isn't even allowed to say he was there when the elastic was found. It merely mentions him as a *Blazon* reporter. Did you see Cane?"

"Yes," said Wharton. "Quiet-looking young fellow. And now if you're not too busy, I'd like you to step out with me and make an experiment. Pole won't be there by now."

It was a testing of Pole's alibi, Wharton explained as they came in at the top of Lapford Street. Norris thought the night alibi unassailable: Wharton had other ideas.

Pole claimed to have come in at half-past eleven. Til midnight the front swing doors were open. After that time, assuming that Pole slipped out again, he would have had to push a bell to arouse the hall porter who would then have let him in. The porter swore he had not done so.

"That doesn't say he hadn't a key of his own," Wharton said. "If the porter was asleep he could have tiptoed by him to the stairs, across the carpet."

"No other means of getting out and in?"

"Have a look at the lay-out," Wharton told him. "There's only the one main entrance, and that service entrance, and both on Lapford Street. The first floor flats, like Pole's, have no back windows at all. If Pole used a flat on the second floor, and so got out of a back window, it's a sheer drop and he'd have had to use a rope ladder when he got out and kept it dangling for when he got in—which isn't feasible. The same applies to his own front windows, and they overlook the street which is light as day. Besides, all this Covent Garden area is wide awake at two in the morning."

"The porter admits to having been asleep?"

"Why shouldn't he have been?" said Wharton. "His job was to wake up when the bell went." He moved on towards the main entrance. "By day it's easy. You go up to Pole's flat and try. If you're caught, say you're just going."

Travers took a peep through the doors. One or two residents were about but there seemed no sign of the porter. The lift was automatic but he walked boldly past it and up the stairs. When he turned back the porter was in the hall, but in a minute he had gone again, and out came Travers to the pavement.

"What'd I tell you?" said Wharton. "I suppose they reckon the Yale locks on the flat doors are good enough in ordinary times."

"How's it help?" asked Travers. "I mean, my going up to Pole's flat just now?"

"It doesn't," Wharton told him. "It might be good evidence all the same. I'll wager that in a court of law the porter would swear that the hall is supervised all day. You've proved it isn't."

"And what now?"

"Routine—unless our squint-eyed friend is genuine." And routine was slow work. Nothing had happened about the marks of the worn sole and no one had yet been found who had seen or heard a suspicious thing in Martlet Street at the time of the murder. As for Quiff's evidence, Wharton was inclined to discount it. Admitting that even with one's ear to the crack of his office floor little but a murmur could be heard, the fact remained that whereas he claimed to have heard the mention of the word Pole, he had heard nothing of the crash of Luffham's body down the stairs.

Travers and Wharton parted in the Strand.

"If our squint-eyed friend does send a letter in the morning." Wharton said, "I'll let you know." He tapped his breast pocket significantly. "That'll be the time to hand this letter over to the experts and make it say things."

In the morning that letter arrived at the *Blazon* office by post, and it bore a Holborn post-mark. Travers, duly called up, saw the two originals in Wharton's office at the Yard. The latest effort ran thus:

SIR,

As you printed my letter, I am sending what I promised. Luffham was a swine in spite of what people thought who didn't know him like I did, which was shown by what happened when they kicked him out of Halstead, which was what it amounted to. He did the foulest thing a man could do and I got him for it. How I met him is nobody's business but mine, and how I gained his confidence either.

For proof I did it, let the police try out this. According to the accounts in the papers, a piece of elastic was fastened round the rails with a drawing-pin on the outer side, and the hole made by the pin was found. I say that I originally intended to put the pin there, and did so, and then I realized that when the pin sprang out, the elastic would spring back and hit the wall and remain on the stairs. So I put the pin on the wall side, with the ends of the elastic inwards, by which means the elastic sprung back to the landing, where I guessed naturally it would be found, but not taken any account of. The chances were that it would spring to a dark corner where it would not be found till a new tenant took the flat. As proof of all this, if the clever police will examine the rail on the wall side, they will find the second hole made by the pin.

"And he was right!" Wharton said, interrupting Travers's reading. "There was the hole, just as he says. But the funny thing is—but you read on and see for yourself."

With regard to the other information which I promised, first the Vickers Street stabbing. The knife was bought at that ironmonger's in Morral Street but not from a male assistant. It was a young lady who served me.

Travers screwed up his eyes in thought. Wharton told him to go on reading.

Next the Hackney shooting affair. The revolver, which was never found, was thrown by me into the River Lea, opposite Manifold's timber works, where no doubt it still is.

"Read the next," said Wharton grimly. "Then I'll do a bit of summing up."

As for the catgut that was used in the Hyde Park strangling affair, that gut was not bought from any music shop but was a new gut I had by me, and which was intended for the weights of a grandfather-clock.

I shall also add that my affairs take me abroad a lot and as I am leaving England in two days' time, I shall be writing no more letters, but as I have given ample proof of my genuineness, there is no more to say. I may be back in London on Monday.

Yours, etc.,

JUSTICE.

"Notice anything?" fired Wharton.

"Only about the Hackney affair," Travers said. "That took place ten years ago. Any hot-air merchant could claim to have thrown a revolver anywhere. Who's going to dredge the shifting mud of a whole river?"

"Exactly. Now take the catgut. There are three main uses as far as the man in the street knows: for stringed instruments, clocks, and tennis rackets. You couldn't strangle anyone with a string that came out of an old racket, so that leaves two guesses. In Gilham's book"—it was on his desk and his knuckles were rapping it-"it says enquiries were made at music shops, though the gut might have been used for either a clock or a 'cello."

"Gilham handled that case, didn't he?" It was Chief-Inspector Gilham, he meant, whose book of reminiscences Wharton was then consulting.

"Yes," said Wharton. "And the Vickers Street stabbing case. With regard to that, have a look here. Gilham distinctly says it was discovered later that the knife was sold over the counter by the young woman at the cash desk who took charge while the owner and a salesman were at dinner. You might call it a revelation, in fact, that Gilham was making. Something that wasn't known to the public at the time."

"What you're getting at is this," said Travers. "The writer of the letter wanted to establish a claim to having committed three murders, so he bolstered up the claim with spurious evidence; namely, one lie about a revolver, and two chosen extracts from Gilham's book—and all three making most convincing reading for the uninformed."

"You've got it," said Wharton. "And the logical deduction is that he didn't commit any of those three murders. Then why did he claim to have done so?"

"Because he did commit the Luffham murder," Travers said. "All this Justice bunkum and claims to have committed the other three murders are red herrings to throw us off the trail; to make us look for quite a different person from the one we want."

"That's it," said Wharton. "Therefore Luffham's murderer wasn't a man of sixty."

"And he hadn't a squint."

"Exactly." And then Wharton leaned forward, peering away over his spectacle tops. "But are you realizing that this second letter is just the kind of thing the *Blazon* readers would gulp down?"

"You mean it emanated from the *Blazon* itself?"

Wharton gave a shrug of the shoulders. "Everybody there swore it was genuine, and Pole among 'em. Each volunteered a specimen of his handwriting." He gave another shrug. "Still, the fact remains. They tell me there's little doing in Fleet Street at the moment, and this letter certainly keeps that *Blazon* splash alive. And how many people will buy the *Blazon* tomorrow, just to see what Justice has written next?"

Travers gave a Whartonian grunt and began polishing his glasses. The *Blazon* was a joke, a fact admitted shamefacedly by its ardent supporters, whose zigzag courses were shaped by the gaudy, erratic compass of Lord Tabard. That second letter was indeed the perfect *Blazon* letter, and yet Travers was shaking his head.

"Why speculate, when there's one staring fact? The man who wrote that letter was the man who committed the Luffham murder. Get a psychology expert to work on it, George, and try to see the mind that produced it—when you've given him every bit of evidence you've got. Get the handwriting experts on it and then have a conference of all of you."

"That's roughly what I was intending," Wharton said, and gave a dour shake of the head. "Instinct's a funny thing. I can't get away from the idea that this is all cheap publicity to bolster up that paper." His finger jabbed down fiercely on the letter again. "What about that last line? *I may be back in London on Monday.*"

"I know." said Travers. "It's just too round a peg in too round a hole. But what are you doing about the letter publicly?"

"What am I doing?" Wharton grimaced. "I'm having the *Blazon* announce most prominently that Scotland Yard considers the letter a practical joke in the worst kind of taste. Not only are we ignoring the letter but we're regarding it as an insult to our intelligences. And why? I'll tell you. The exhibitionist, egomaniac, call him what you like, who wrote this is out for the limelight. The best way to provoke a person of that kind is to ignore him. Hurt his vanity and he'll begin screaming. What we want is another letter or two from our friend Justice. Let him scream enough and we'll be listening to something that'll hang him."

"Very sound," said Travers. "And suppose this last line in the letter turns out to be a prophecy? Suppose Justice is in town on Monday and commits another murder?"

Wharton gave another shrug of the shoulders. As far as he was concerned apparently, sufficient unto the Monday was the murder thereof.

But the Wednesday went and there were no further letters to the *Blazon*. As for the progress in the Luffham murder made by Chief-Inspector Norris beneath the benevolent eye of Wharton, it was so slow as to be indiscernible. The handwriting might have been anybody's, and the psychology experts had given Wharton a pretty problem with regard to the mind behind its careful lettering. If the letter was the hub of a wheel, then the theories were like spokes, and as each spoke-end radiated new spokes, Wharton was furnished with sufficient theories to last him the rest of his inquisitorial days.

But the *Blazon* was undoubtedly happy. The splash might be petering out but its offspring were very much alive. With its tongue in its cheek it could gently dissociate itself from so shocking a breach of good taste as treating murder as a joke; with its fingers to its nose it could keep up a pertinent enquiry as to what the Yard was doing, and with an enlarged Correspondence Column it could go over past ground and speculate about the future. Where the old streamer headlines had clamoured:

MURDER ON MONDAYS

there now appeared each day what was in fact the summary of a new and less clamorous splash:

WILL THERE BE MURDER ON MONDAY?

British humour has always in it something perverse and paradoxical. In its springs and origins is something so fantastic and unaccountable, that it was no wonder that THE MAN

WITH THE SQUINT became a public and hilarious joke. Poulson and Pry in their famous act in the latest Palladium Crazy Week, introduced a special verse into their newest song-hit—*Do As Auntie Tells You*—the said verse beginning—

> Let us give you a hint,
> If a man with a squint
> And wearing big specs of a very dark tint . . .

while on the Friday night, Giggling Gilbert, the B.B.C.'s pet comedian, sprang a new song on a listening nation—

> I don't want to be murdered on Monday.

The *Megaphone*, in its Saturday cartoon, depicted a certain European dictator in smoked glasses, through which could be seen a remarkable distortion of one eye, and as for those experts in back-chat—costers, taxi-men and charwomen—a new witticism was in the air, with: "Who do you think you are? The man with the squint?" and retorts of the same devastating nature.

For Ludovic Travers the glory had almost departed. Each day he would scan the main editions of the *Blazon* with the hope that the man with the squint might have been provoked into some indiscretion. But there was never another letter, and as for the Yard enquiries, they were proceeding with a patience too laborious for even a simulated excitement. But on the Saturday Travers was proposing to vary his week-end by a visit to Halstead and a hope of unearthing a something vital about Luffham. On the Friday towards tea-time, he was strolling along Martlet Street with the hope of inspiration, when he ran into Pole. The Pooh-Bah of crime was most effusive, and Travers, at a temporary loose end, accepted an invitation to tea at the flat, whither Pole was bound.

"Sorry I had nothing to report to you," Travers said. "But that business of yourself and the police was nothing but the usual routine enquiry work."

"I wasn't worried," Pole said largely. "China tea, by the way, or Indian?"

"Just your usual," Travers said, and walked across to Charlie, over whose cage the sateen cover was hung. While Pole was speaking down the tube, he drew the cover off, and he and the parrot regarded each other for a moment or two. Then the bird drew near and Travers put out a tentative finger.

"Ah, making friends?" said Pole blithely. "I shouldn't scratch him though. He's liable to give you a nasty nip."

He uttered a cajoling word or two in some parrot of his own devising. Charlie's voice broke startlingly in:

"Hello? Hello? Is that you? Is that you?"

"His famous telephone conversation," whispered Pole, and beamed approval. But then Charlie decided to defer the exhibition, for however much Pole coaxed him, no further speech was forthcoming.

"Some other time perhaps," Pole said, and was whipping the sateen cover over the cage. Then in that last second Charlie spoke again, as if sorry for his reticence.

"Thank you, Mr. Powle. Thank you, Mr. Powle."

"Good Lord!" said Travers. "Now who is that he's imitating? Surely not Stowe of the *Blazon*?"

"Stowe it is," said Pole, and waited a moment for more words before finally covering the cage. "Didn't I tell you? Stowe's been up here two or three times this week, and Charlie's got him to the life. A slightly cockney accent, don't you think?"

"Say a perky suburbanese," suggested Travers.

"Well, yes," granted Pole. "A clever fellow Stowe, in his way. A bit of a rough diamond but a first-class journalist."

"You've known him for some time, I expect?"

"Not at all," said Pole. "I never clapped eyes on him till last Tuesday."

No sooner did he leave Pole's flat than Travers was ringing up Wharton.

"The fact remains," Travers said, "that Pole and Stowe do know each other now. Whether or not the friendship's of longer standing is up to you to prove."

"We're most likely asking Stowe a question or two very soon," Wharton said. "Arising out of that holiday in Switzerland. He wasn't on the 'plane lists and I'm expecting any minute to hear he didn't stay at that hotel in Lausanne which he mentioned to me."

"I wouldn't mind being there," Travers said. "When's it likely to come off?"

"Monday," said Wharton. "And if you're going to say anything about Monday murders—don't!"

Travers came back to town fairly early that Monday morning. He rang up the Yard but Wharton and Norris were out, but just about midday the phone bell went and Palmer reported that a Mr. Cane was on the line.

"Hallo, young man," smiled Travers. "What's the trouble with you?"

"I just wondered if I could see you anywhere, Mr. T-Travers," Cane said. "Only a little personal matter."

"Come along here," Travers told him. "Come along now. Come and have lunch, in fact . . . Oh, round about one o'clock. Where are you speaking from? The *Blazon?* . . . Right, any time now, and we'll be ready for you."

Travers warned Palmer to order an extra service lunch and two half bottles and settled down again to his work in the inner room. It seemed hardly a few minutes before Palmer was tapping at the door and announcing Mr. Cane was in the dining-room.

"Here you are then?" was Travers's greeting. "Take that chair, won't you? And do let me give you a sherry."

"Thank you," Cane said, and somewhat self-consciously took the indicated chair. "I'm afraid I'm a bit early, Mr. T-T-Travers."

"Nonsense," Travers told him. "It's only a few minutes short of one o'clock. Let's go in the other room after all, while Palmer sees to the meal."

Before the talk had got under way, Cane had to go back for his handkerchief which had been left in his overcoat pocket. By the time he had broached that personal topic, Palmer was announcing lunch.

What was on Cane's mind, however, was a departure in the very near future for New Zealand, where he had a distant relation with whom he had never lost touch; but before taking so vital a step he would like, he said, to hear what Travers thought about it all.

"I'll talk to you like a Dutch uncle," Travers said. "Tell me perfectly frankly. Is this an old idea or is it a kind of blighted ambition?"

"You mean about Stowe coming back and cutting me out," Cane said, but said it very nicely. "It isn't that, sir—honest it isn't. I've th-th-thought quite a lot about it. I'm not the Fleet Street t-t-type, sir, and I know it."

Travers laughed at him. Those two articles he had written had been first-class stuff. Still, if his heart was set on New Zealand, there were few finer places for a young man.

"And of course you'd go on with your writing?"

"Oh, yes, sir," Cane said. "I've got some money of my own and I shouldn't be t-t-tied down."

So through the meal they discussed the ins and outs. Travers, somewhat puzzled as ever why he should be made the depository of another's secrets, was unaware as ever of the qualities that invited them. But Travers was always the perfect listener, delightfully mannered and supremely well-informed. For all his disregard of die-hard convention and his occasional quaint mannerisms, one recognized in him the man of taste and breeding, and of insight and sympathy, with whom confidences would be safe and from whom advice would be a kindly, heart-felt thing. All that was why young Cane began at last to talk of himself, though his very first disclosures gave Travers a quick wonder.

His father had been killed in the war when he was still a very small boy, he said, and it was in Travers's mind then to come cautiously to the reason why Cane had been so perturbed when in the *Blazon* building he had been asked about his father. Then the thought went and Travers listened, for the young reporter's story was one that stirred new thoughts of help, and Travers had also a certain shame for a romantic theory he had thrust on George Wharton—of a heart-broken mother and a posthumous child.

Cane had left Millborough early, he said, for things had gone wrong with his mother's investments and has contribution was needed for the home, the pension being little enough for people in their station. An introduction had landed him in Fleet Street, on the staff of a paper he preferred not to mention, because he had apparently been a kind of butt. Then he went to a literary weekly and from there to the *Blazon*. He spoke warmly of his mother, and all he owed her and the sacrifices she had made. Travers nodded.

"Well, I begin to see now what's at the back of your mind about this New Zealand business," he said. "But suppose I could get you an introduction to something much more congenial in Fleet Street, would you be prepared—"

The telephone went. Before Palmer could appear, Travers was hopping up with an apology and answering it himself.

"Yes, speaking," he said, and "Good Lord! you don't say so! . . . Yes, in ten minutes or so . . . Right. I'll be there."

As quickly as that it was over, but he stood for a moment or two in thought as he hung up the phone. When he turned, Cane was still sipping his coffee, eyes on the pleasant fire. Travers came over and clapped a hand on his shoulder. Cane looked shyly up.

"You'd better cut along back to the office," Travers told him gravely. "Something's just broken, as you call it."

Cane was getting to his feet. "Broken, sir?"

"Yes," said Travers. "Something's happened. Laura Delayne's been murdered."

"Laura Delayne." His eyes were bulging. "Why, that's terrible!"

"I know," Travers told him. "It also happens to be murder on a Monday."

CHAPTER VI
THE VOICE OF JACOB

THAT POST-WAR caravanserai known as the Harbinger Hotel lay handy for the hub of town where the Strand ends, and had its own seclusion that overlooked the river. Ludovic Travers walked through the swing doors unquestioned, decided that Room 27 must be the first floor, and made his way, still unquestioned, through the busy foyer to the stairs. Following the numbers on the doors he came to the corridor end and then turned into a cul-de-sac, where a window overlooked the Embankment. A man stood there on duty and he knew the room was the one he sought.

But whatever privacy the police were making for the sake of the hotel management, that room was busy enough, with Wharton's men working like ants. Wharton himself stood with his back to what looked like two tables placed end to end, surveying the scene and who should be with him but Tom Stowe. At the sight of the newcomer the General shifted somewhat and Travers saw that on those twin tables was lying the body of a woman covered with a sheet, with the head alone visible.

"Here you arc then," said Wharton quietly. "You and Stowe know each other I believe." He was turning at once and looking down at the body. "Did you ever meet her?"

Save for an unbreathing quiet there was nothing of strangeness or distortion on the dead face of Laura Delayne. As she lay there in what might have been some pose of sleep, her face had indeed a gentleness it had lacked in life, and the calm poise of breeding; and her silver hair made a placid aureole about the high forehead and the thin cheeks.

"I saw her once lately," Travers said. "About three weeks ago, it would be—in *Mortal Instruments* at the Harmony Theatre. An almost terrifying performance."

"That's right," broke in Stowe. "Embittered spinsters, those were her parts. No one to touch her in them. Doesn't look that part now, though, poor old girl. Almost handsome, I'd call her."

There seemed something unusual, Travers was thinking, in Stowe's staccato chatter.

"Stowe knows quite a lot about her," Wharton said.

"Not that's any good to you people, I don't," Stowe told him. "Seems a rotten thing too, Mr. Travers, raking up the old girl's bad points."

"Which were what?" Travers asked gently.

"Oh, a notorious cat," said Stowe. "She used to keep herself to herself, if you know what I mean. Wasn't one of the regular ducky darling sort. Thought a lot too much of herself, people said. And mean?—I'll say she was. Tight-fisted as they make em. Might have had a nice little flat, for instance but always lived here to keep expenses down."

"You mean, proud of her talents?" asked Wharton.

"No, not that. Proud of her family. Proud of being a lady, if you know what I mean."

"And what were her family?"

"Search me," said Stowe, and gave a shrug of the shoulders.

"What did it, George?" asked Travers.

"That," said Wharton, and pointed to the black-handled, tri-angular-bladed knife. "Stabbed through the back ribs and died before she knew it. Menzies says it was just after midday." He turned to Stowe. "Do you mind telling Mr. Travers just how you got mixed up in it?"

"Certainly," Stowe said briskly. "It was like this, Mr. Travers, as I was telling Superintendent Wharton here. Just before one o'clock when I was having a bit of lunch in our restaurant up-stairs, I was called to the phone. One o'clock exact, it was, when I actually took the message. Someone—I didn't know who it was—saying I was to go as quick as I could to where we are now."

"You'd no idea who it was?"

"I was just going to ask, when he rang off. So I came along here and that's all there is to it. I couldn't get an answer so I reported it downstairs. The manager opened the door with his key and there she was, lying on the carpet by the door, just over there, with the knife in her back."

Wharton broke in with a kindly gravity that would have been an unctuous geniality but for the presence of death.

"Now Mr. Stowe's bursting to get back to his paper, so we won't keep him here any longer. Any time we want him, we know where to get him."

"That's right," Stowe said, and was turning to go. "What may we publish about this?"

"Anything you like," Wharton told him, "so long as it's the truth, and you keep us out of it."

They watched him go. Travers gave a shake of the head.

"I thought he seemed the least bit nervous. Now I know why."

"Yes," said Wharton. "A bit fishy, that yarn of his. There isn't a crime-reporter in London who wouldn't have given an ear to have been rung up like he says he was." He reached up and Travers inclined a listening ear for the hoarse whisper. "I've got a man on his tail!"

He moved across the room and left Travers for a minute or two to himself. It was a large, airy room with a dressing-room annex, and the dead woman's belongings gave it a character of its own. For it was not smothered with florid photographs flamboyantly autographed, and play-bills and programs and framed notices that seem the essential adjuncts of what had been partly her world. On the main table were two photographs only, and in silver frames—of an actor who had been one of the first to be knighted and an actress who was the widow of a once famous actor-manager. Two charming but old-fashioned water colours flanked the table, and there was a delightful period bureau which Wharton himself was then examining. In the air was a faint scent as of musk and lavender, so that Travers was suddenly recalling his mother's room and a bureau there, and the scented contents of mysterious drawers.

There was a tap at the door and a black-coated man of middle age looked in. Wharton brought him across and introduced him as the manager.

"It was exactly eleven o'clock when the call came," he told Wharton. "All our operator did was to put the caller through to here."

"Anything noticeable about the voice?"

The manager shook his head. "You forget the quantity of calls we have here. The operator thinks it was a woman, but she wouldn't swear to anything."

"Then what happened?"

"Miss Delayne rang down for breakfast at about a quarter past eleven. Usually she would have it round about midday. When the maid brought it up she was dressed but in her dressing-gown, if you know what I mean, and she asked to have the room quickly done out, as if she was expecting a caller. I may say that was done and the maid was out of the room by the time Miss Delayne had finished breakfast, which she took in the dressing-room there—or the boudoir, as she used to call it."

"Did she say anything about not being disturbed?"

"Why should she?" the manager said. "The room was finished with and in the ordinary course of events she wouldn't be disturbed. The papers were brought up, as you saw, and usually she didn't go out till about three, except on matinée afternoons."

"No lunch?"

"No lunch," echoed the manager. "Tea occasionally, and dinner at six. Miss Delayne was an old and valued resident, and we were happy to make special arrangements to suit her wishes."

"Nothing suspicious seen or heard?"

"So far I've unearthed nothing," the manager said. "Unfortunate, I admit, that the one room which adjoins hers should have been temporarily unoccupied."

They drew back for a minute while the body was removed and the twin tables replaced by the wall.

"I think you said she'd been here quite a time" Wharton said.

"Just over ten years," the manager said. "When she was resting she kept up just the same times for everything as if she were working and when she was on tour she kept these rooms on."

"In fact, they were her home," said Wharton "Many callers, had she?"

"Very few," the manager said, "but those she had were what I'd call distinguished." His finger went out to one of the framed photographs. "Sir William had tea here occasionally. I believe he was actually here the day before he died."

"Indeed," said Wharton, suitably impressed. "And did the dead lady ever talk to you about her personal affairs?"

"Never." His tone was most emphatic. "She was very reserved, and, of course, I didn't ask for it or expect it. Always very nice, of course. A lady in every way, in fact."

A plain-clothes sergeant came over then with something he wished Wharton to see. The manager departed with expressions of gratitude for the private way the police were handling things. Wharton assured him that the police would be away and gone, and by the back way, before the afternoon was out.

"Now what's all this?" he said to the sergeant, and adjusted his antiquated spectacles.

All this was a cheque book, with the counterfoil showing a cheque drawn on self on the first Tuesday in the month—and for two hundred pounds.

Wharton grunted. "Over a fortnight ago. Any prints on it?"

"Only hers."

"I'll take that myself," Wharton told him. Then the telephone went and he put it in his inner pocket.

"Yes," he said, "put him through . . . Yes . . . Indeed? . . . Capital! . . . I say it's capital . . . That's all right. It'll keep till you get here . . . Right. Good-by."

He gave a backward nod to Travers and moved off towards the dressing-room door. Travers followed him through.

"That man of mine who was trailing Stowe," Wharton said. "He's on something, he says. Heard Stowe talking on the phone to the man who rang him up—the man he told us he didn't know."

"Good Lord!" said Travers, and stared.

Wharton nodded mysteriously. "He ought to be along here in a few minutes, then we'll know all about it. Now then, what's the best way of finding out all an actress's private history?"

"Ring up her agent—if she had one," Travers told him.

"There's a file of stuff that looks like an agent's in there," Wharton said. "You handle that for me. You're more in the know than I am. I'll have the line held and anything that comes for me can go to that next room."

Keptmanns appeared to be the agents and Travers got them at once. Ben Keptmann said he had heard a rumour that Miss De-layne was dead and now he was coming round at once. Travers told him it would be waste of time. The police would notify him about the private papers that might concern his firm, and in the meanwhile they would like some information.

But when Travers had heard all that Benny Keptmann had to say, he could merely grimace at Wharton.

"Five years they've handled her, ever since she broke into the talkies. They don't know a thing about her private life; whether her name was her real one or a stage name, or what her stage history was. She was well established, of course, when she came to them. Creese and Blackman handled her before that. You have a word with them and I'll carry on." Archie Creese had no immediate information, and Travers hung on while he made en-quiries. In two minutes Creese had something to report.

"Just after the war she came to us," he said. "To the best of my knowledge she had no agent before that. Of course you know where she made her name?"

"No," said Travers. "Where was it?"

"Why, with Wightman's touring company."

"Yes," said Travers, "but there hasn't been any such thing since the war—and Sir William's dead. How can I get informa-tion about how she came to join them?"

"Don't know," snapped Creese, and then: "Wait a minute, though. Try old Percy Standard. Hang on another tick and I'll give you his address."

Standard, so Travers gathered, had been manager of the Wightman companies that had toured England and the Colo-nies in Shakespeare and the classics. Before Travers could do more than take down the address and offer thanks, Wharton's man was back. Wharton followed him up a minute later and the three adjourned to the inner room.

"Now what happened?" Wharton said. "And take it steady."

Daggon took it steady and his tale was this. He picked up Stowe as he left the hotel and Stowe had never a suspicion that he was being tailed. And he was looking for something of whose existence he seemed aware but of its whereabouts uncertain. It turned out to be that old series of telephone booths along New Christchurch wall, and he made for the spot straight as a die as soon as he caught sight of it. Daggon was in the adjoining box, facing outwards with ear against the woodwork, and ready to shift at the sound of a passer-by.

"I heard him distinctly say, 'Is that you, Mole—or Pole or some name that sounded like that.' "

"We'll call it Mole," said Wharton.

"Then someone went by and I had to draw back. When I got my ear there again he was fairly letting rip. 'I tell you it *was* you!' he was saying. Then I heard something about meeting him, and the *Blazon*, so out I nipped before he finished. Then I picked him up just past the steps and followed him through to Fleet Street. He was tearing along just as if he'd got bad news. As much as I could do to keep up with him, sir. Then soon as he'd gone in the building, I slipped in too and got the same lift. When the attendant asked what floor, I told him, 'Mac.' There's always a Mac somewhere about in a newspaper office, sir."

"And damn nigh everywhere else," Wharton said. "And what then?"

"Then a very awkward thing happened, sir, that put the kybosh on me. Soon as he stepped out of the lift, a fattish sort of gentleman, like a doctor or a city man, was waiting for him, and Stowe gave him a nod and went off with this city gent trailing him. I was on the same game too, and just as I nipped behind a pillar and Stowe and his pal went in some private room, I saw another man who looked as if he was interested. One of them that work on the paper he was; you know, sir, in shirt sleeves and arm full of papers. A tall, surly-looking man in dark specs. He was snooping to see what the other two were up to so I stayed put. Then he came along right by the room where they'd gone in, just as if he was always going that way, and when he drew alongside he gave a squint round and clapped his ear to the door. There was I, sir, lying doggo, and him with his back to me not five yards away, and his eyes down the corridor to see if anyone was coming. Then when I judged he was going to move I stepped out and met him natural-like. He asked me what I was doing there so I said I was looking for a compositor called Mac. Then he told me to buzz off downstairs and enquire there. Which I did, sir, and that was when I rang you up."

"Pretty good work so far," Wharton told him. "And what happened next?"

"Nothing, sir, except that I hung about till this city-looking gent came out and I tailed him to a block of flats in Lapford Street. By the way he walked in I reckoned he lived there, so I came back to report."

"Anxious-looking, was he, when he left the *Blazon*—this city gent?"

"Anxious." Daggon snorted. "His face was all red, sir, as if he'd been having a rare old dust-up with someone. Muttering to himself and going on, he was."

"Good," said Wharton. "Now go and post yourself in the locality of his flat in Lapford Street and if he comes out, tail him again. His name's Pole, by the way, not Mole—but keep that under your hat."

"Well?" said Wharton, and raised his eyebrows. "Didn't I tell you there was something fishy?" Then he nodded and his face flushed with a quick anger. "Murder on Mondays. You aren't telling me this was just another coincidence? I tell you I'll get to the bottom of this if it costs me my job."

He had glowered so fiercely that Travers drew back and was fumbling for his glasses. The General's growl became a final rumble.

"Looks too easy, that's all that's wrong with it. Pole's our man. He rang up Stowe to come here." He shook his head. "I knew from the first it was all part of the same game; that's why Norris is going to handle it. And who was that other man who was watching Stowe and Pole at the *Blazon* office?"

"Tuke, the news editor," Travers told him. "Maybe you met him when you were there. But I shouldn't worry him if I were you."

"And why not?" glared Wharton.

"Well, I'd formed the idea some time ago, from earlier acquaintance than yours, that Tuke didn't care a lot for Stowe. I'd say he was merely snooping for his own reasons connected with his job. You don't want to let too many people in on what you're likely to have against Stowe. If he gets a hint that you're interested, he'll have too much time to think."

Wharton grunted.

"But one thing I'd like you to tell me," Travers went on. "Why all this enquiry into Miss Delayne's earlier years?"

"I'll tell you," Wharton said. "Soon as I was rung up and told what had happened, I grabbed a reference book and looked her up. It said she had learned her art in the hard school of Shakespeare repertory and had made her London début in 1914, and it then gave her list of parts to date, including film work. That's merely a quick synopsis, of course. But what intrigued me was that there was no mention of what her real name was."

"Why should she have another one?"

"Why?" said Wharton and began a new glare. "Isn't Delayne an obvious stage name? Besides, when I looked up everyone else of her standing, there were the two names given, if the stage name differed from the real one. And didn't Stowe tell us, and didn't the manager tell us, that she was proud of her pedigree? Yet there wasn't a word in the book about where she was born and educated, which you can bet your life she'd have plastered all over the place if there wasn't something fishy about it. And didn't they say she was secretive and kept herself to herself? Besides, we've got to go into it all some time, so why not at once?"

"That all seems logical enough," Travers said. "I've heard the usual gossip about her from time to time—her sharp tongue and squabbling, for instance. But if you're trying to trace all the enemies she's made ever since the day she first acted a part, you're surely planning a pretty big job?"

"What am I paid for?" fired Wharton, and then frowned for a while in thought. "Look here," he said at last, "you take this cheque book and slip along to her bank. It'll be closed but you'll see somebody. Then go to the *Blazon* building and see the operator who took the one o'clock message asking for Stowe. Hear what the voice sounded like. Norris may be along at any minute, and if so I'll catch you up."

"Just a moment before I go," Travers said. "I'd like to have everything clear in my own mind. Miss Delayne had a telephone message, from a woman probably, at eleven o'clock. It made her get up and have breakfast well before her time, and she had the main room tidied. What I'd like to put to you is two things. Why shouldn't a woman have done the murder?"

Wharton shook his head. "You're running on ahead. What you mean is that a woman might have called up here. That doesn't imply by any means that she did the murder. And your two reasons are that the downstairs operator thought the voice was a woman's, and that Miss Delayne wouldn't have fussed over tidying the room if her caller had been a man."

"You've caught me out," Travers told him admiringly.

"Nothing clever about that," Wharton said. "Ain't I a married man? Women say men don't notice things; it's other women they're always particular about."

"But there's just one other reason that makes me think the caller was a woman," Travers said. "A woman could have walked into the hotel, all wrapped up in furs and things on a cold day like this, and have stood much less chance of being identified, or of being questioned about her business, than a man."

"I don't know." Wharton shook his head. "I've had years of experience of crime of all sorts in hotels, and they're the easiest places in the world to walk in and out of."

As Travers left, Wharton's men were still at work on those two rooms, though it was well on in the afternoon. The bank had long been closed but with the approach of the quarter's balancing, the staff were working late. A clerk was at the side door and he hailed Travers as soon as he came up.

"Mr. Travers, sir?"

"Yes," said Travers. "How did you know me?"

"A message just came through to ask us to expect you," the clerk said and took him through to a private office. Travers showed the manager the cheque book and counterfoil.

"About ten pounds in cash was found in her rooms," Travers said, "so we wondered what she did with the rest of the two hundred. Perhaps you'll let us know how she took the money; denominations of notes and numbers."

The manager was out of the room no more than five minutes.

"If it had been a customer less well-known than Miss Delayne we mightn't have been able to help you," he said. "She took the money in pound notes—what I might call two ordinary clips."

"Which looks as if she wasn't keeping them."

"Yes," the manager said. "That certainly looks like it. If she'd been keeping them she'd have had tens and fives. But something else I'll call your attention to. Miss Delayne when in town was methodical in her habits. She would draw cash and pay in monies on a Monday afternoon. The afternoon before she drew this cheque for two hundred, she retained ten pounds cash for current spending, which I'm told was about her usual sum. It's no business of mine to draw deductions, but it certainly looks as if the two hundred was something unexpected."

The information seemed important and Travers rang up Wharton there and then. Wharton said Norris had come but there was no chance of getting away. The operator at the *Blazon* was being held for Travers's arrival, and Wharton would be staying on at the hotel to hear what happened.

The operator required no setting at ease, and Travers in any case was no formidable representative of the law. It was impossible, she said, to keep track of calls, but she remembered something of this one because firstly it came during a comparatively slack time, and also she knew Mr. Stowe personally. The voice that had asked for him had had a high-pitched quality. Questioned deftly by Travers she admitted that shrill and peevish were admirable descriptions.

That was in an annex to the main foyer downstairs, and as Travers stepped out, whom should he see but Pole himself, making for the lift. Travers whipped back.

"This is most frightfully confidential," he said to the operator, "and if there's any talk it might cost you your job, but a man's just going upstairs and I'm trying to catch him up. You follow us and listen, then come back here and wait for me."

Pole, by an amazing stroke of luck, was still waiting for the lift. Travers greeted him boisterously. Daggon was at Pole's elbow, and caught the hint to sheer off.

"If it isn't Pole! How are you, my dear fellow? Still harassed with work?"

Harassed, Pole certainly looked. His smile was feeble and his hand-grasp weak.

"Work's all very well," he said, and the words were plainly no more than a sparring for time. Then he looked up. "Could you possibly see me for a minute or two? Anywhere to suit yourself. I shan't be here more than ten minutes."

"Delighted to," smiled Travers. "At my place, shall we say? And in half an hour?"

"That's very good of you," Pole said, and oozed gratitude. "I wouldn't bother you, only it's something really vital—to me, that is."

Travers gave him a cheery nod as the lift bore him upwards, then turned and followed the disappearing figure of the operator.

"You know who that was?" he asked her gravely.

"Yes," she said. "I know who it was."

"Then if you want to keep well away from trouble, forget the last ten minutes," Travers told her. "But before you do so, tell me if the gentleman's voice was anything like the one that asked for Mr. Stowe."

She moistened her lips, then her eyes rose to his.

"It was him," she said. "I'd know that voice anywhere. He was the one who asked for Mr. Stowe."

CHAPTER VII
POLE HAS AN IDEA

TRAVERS GOT WHARTON on the phone at once. Wharton said he was pleased, though it was no more than clinching of evidence.

"Listen to this," Travers said. "Pole's scared stiff about something and he's asked to have a heart to heart talk with me. At my place, George, in five and twenty minutes from now. You come along at once and listen unofficially."

Wharton said he had something in mind that was better than eavesdropping. He was having Pole and Stowe on the carpet that very evening.

"Don't do that, George," Travers said. "I've got quite a good scheme—an experiment, in fact. And I've got a vital question to ask Pole. You remember when I was giving you an account of how he spread himself to me that afternoon and talked of doing himself a good turn? Remember he said there were all sorts of people he'd like to remove—*including an actress* . . . Oh, no; he didn't say what actress. You're expecting far too much for the money . . . Right. You'll be along by the time I'm there."

When Wharton arrived, Travers had Palmer in and explained the scheme.

"What I'm proposing is this, George," he said. "You'll be here and just in the act of leaving again when Palmer shows Pole in. Now when Pole sees you—after a few well-chosen words of mine especially—he may decide to talk to us both. If he doesn't then you leave this room but go to the service door where Palmer can let you in to hear what goes on. I'm playing no dirty trick on Pole in any case because I shall tell him I'm too far in with you people to listen to pure confidences."

So that was arranged and Palmer was instructed to watch out for Pole's arrival.

"Anything new turned up?" Travers asked.

"We've found her will," Wharton said. "I expect it's the final one, though it's dated a couple of years back. Everything to theatrical charities except five hundred pounds to a Reginald William Wightman—address I've forgotten—as an expression of gratitude to his late father."

"That fits," said Travers. "William Wightman, as he was then, ran those pre-war touring companies that gave her her first chance. This would be his son." He found a reference volume and looked it up. "That's right. His only son."

"I've also been in touch with the theatre," Wharton said. "An understudy's going on tonight, of course, but it's her dresser I wanted to talk to only they couldn't run her to earth. She ought to turn up, though, by the time I leave here. And I want to have a good look over the dressing-room."

The faint sound of the lift was heard. A minute, and Palmer was announcing Pole.

"Do come in," Travers said. "And don't trouble about Superintendent Wharton. He's just going."

"How are you, Mr. Pole?" said Wharton, and shot out a welcoming hand.

Before Pole could get in a word, Travers was talking again.

"I'm not going to treat you with any courtesy, George. Drop in even if I'm not here, just as you always do. But perhaps it wasn't important?"

Wharton grasped something of the idea, and pursed his lips in thought.

"I'll pop in a bit later when Mr. Pole has gone."

"Please don't go on account of me," Pole cut in. "As a matter of fact"—he was all nerves and stuttery for a moment—"well, the fact is . . . I mean if Superintendent Wharton can spare the time, I'd like to talk to him too. I mean if Mr. Travers doesn't mind."

"Good Lord, no!" said Travers. "Take a seat. Take that one there. And have a sherry. Cigarette?—or do you prefer your own?"

He bustled about with so much abandon that quiet, when it finally came, had the ease of a family circle.

"Cosy enough here," said Wharton, stretching his legs to the fire.

"Most comfortable," agreed Pole, and gave a little clearing of the throat. "What I want to mention is something that's really very, very important." He shook his head like a mild man roused at last to desperate action. "I believe there's a conspiracy against me. A conspiracy to implicate me in a murder!"

Wharton, who had put on his spectacles to add comfort maybe to the local colour, shot a look at him over their tops. Travers was looking flabbergasted.

"Oh, I know it sounds preposterous," said Pole, now in full swing, "but I tell you it's been getting on my mind. I'm convinced it's true."

"But, my dear Pole," began Travers suavely. Pole cut him off dead.

"But you hear the evidence. And you too, Superintendent. I want you to hear it. I tell you it's been getting on my nerves so that I haven't been able to think or do anything." The shrill voice lowered and he leaned forward, wagging an impressive finger. "I'll tell you something that perhaps I oughtn't to. Do you know that Stowe was rung up at the *Blazon* building at one o'clock today by someone purporting to be myself, and told to go to the very room in the hotel where Miss Delayne was murdered!"

"Purporting?" said Wharton. "He used your name?"

"Oh, no," Pole said quickly. "At least I don't think so. How he managed it I don't know, but he imitated my voice so perfectly that Stowe took it for granted it was me speaking. Then he rang off—whoever it was."

"That's a remarkable thing to happen," said Wharton, and grimaced in thought. "You haven't got a brother or anyone who speaks like yourself?"

"Nobody, my dear sir. I haven't got a relative living, that I know of." Then he gave a dare-devil titter. "Lucky for me, in a way, that I can produce evidence to the effect that at one o'clock I was otherwise engaged than in ringing up anybody. At that very time I was actually coming through the hall of the flats where I live. Just as I walked in, my own clock struck one—and it was dead right. What's more, when this business arose I took the precaution of asking the hall porter if he remembered me coming in, and he said he did. He agreed it was about that time."

"A spot more sherry?" said Travers, and while he replenished Pole's glass, shook his head with a smile that was dolorous and whimsical. "You're treating all this far too seriously. Let's look at it in a different way. You won't think me rude if I make a remark that's occurred to me? I assure you it's merely my own brand of humour."

"Say anything," Pole told him. "That's what we want in a situation like this. Plain talk, and plenty of it."

"Oh, this isn't plain," said Travers; "it's merely personal. For instance, the alibi you've just quoted; would you regard that as a fool-proof one if you used it in one of your books?"

"Used it? Oh, I see." He frowned. "Well, what's wrong with it? Where's the flaw?"

"You're not going to be annoyed with me? Well, then. Let's assume I read that alibi in a book; an assumption which removes the personal element altogether. I'd have said, 'Hallo, this won't hold water.' The whole of the phoning could have been done in a couple of minutes. There's a call-box right against that block of flats and the phoning could have been over a second or two after one o'clock, and the person who phoned could have been walking into the hall. Clocks only half a minute out are popularly assumed to be right. The perfect alibi would have been for synchronized clocks and the porter's to have struck the hour at the same split second with your own. Moreover it would have to be proved that the clock at the *Blazon* office was also right to a split second with the other two."

"What's a split second among friends?" broke in Wharton with a hypocritical chuckle. "Motive is the thing in murder. Mr. Pole had no motive. He didn't know the dead woman."

"I've never actually spoken to her in my life," Pole said.

"Exactly!" said Wharton, with a beam of triumph. "But let's get back a bit. You were talking of conspiracy. One act doesn't make a conspiracy. I take it you've got other evidence?"

"Plenty. And you're the one man—if you'll forgive me for saying so—who ought to be interested. I think there was an attempt to implicate me over the Luffham affair."

"Just how?" asked Wharton mildly.

Pole was sitting bolt upright and his look was positively belligerent.

"I've come to the considered conclusion that someone was impersonating me with Luffham. I believe that Squiff actually heard Luffham address my impersonator as myself."

"But, my dear Mr. Pole, that's fantastic." Wharton waved a helpless hand. "As Travers here would say, Would you dare to use such a device in a book of yours and expect it to be credible?"

"I've a Roland for that Oliver," Pole came back at once. "You cannot deny, Superintendent, that there've been cases in your own experience which, if you'd read them in books, you'd have regarded as utterly preposterous."

"Pole's right enough," broke in Travers. "But any other evidence of the conspiracy?"

"Yes," said Pole. "I believe that card of mine was planted for the police to find." He shook his head. "That's all—and it mayn't seem much to you. To me it's overwhelming evidence, though I haven't had time to sift it yet. I only tumbled to it late this afternoon."

Travers refilled Wharton's glass and freshened up Pole's.

"I'll make another rude contribution," he said. "You don't think there's anything in the fact that you put yourself up to be shied at? You did write that Murder on Mondays letter, you know."

"Shied at?" said Pole, with a quick indignation. "The letter was one thing and murder's quite another."

"Now you're taking me too seriously," smiled Travers. "But Superintendent Wharton is a friend of mine and incredibly discreet. May I therefore mention—as between friends—a something that scared me badly when I heard of the murder of Laura Delayne? You had said to me that if ever you committed a perfect murder or a series of murders—"

"Purely in fun."

"Quite so, but let me finish. You said if you did these murders you'd do yourself a good turn at the same time. You'd polish off a few enemies, for instance, and you specially referred to an unnamed actress. Now as soon as I heard of Laura Delayne's murder, for a moment I almost believed that out of the scores of actresses of standing, she might be the one to whom you had referred."

But Travers's voice had been tailing lamely off. Over Pole's face there had flashed such a wave of crimson, and he was at such a sudden startled loss, that Wharton's eyes were fixed on him, and Travers's heart gave a quick leap.

"I'll own up," Pole managed to get out. He shook his head, snapped his eyes and slowly pulled himself together. "It's nothing—really—but I did actually mean her when I spoke to you, Mr. Travers. You see, I wrote her a play; one that fitted her like a glove. Everyone who read it said it was the very thing for Laura Delayne. So I rang her up and she agreed to read it. A week later she sent it back with the most insulting letter that's ever been written to any playwright in the whole history of the drama. I've got the letter and you can see it. It was as if she'd been spending her time in composing a letter that contained more bitter insults to the line than anyone could imagine. It said she returned my most amusing play—amusing, mind you!—and said that when I'd learned the elements of what was a serious craft, she would be happy to read something else of mine. Then there was a postscript, mentioning a possible chance for the manuscript with the Children's Hour of the B.B.C.!"

"How utterly distressing," said Travers. "But you've sold the play since?"

"Of course I haven't. Didn't I say it was written for her—and round her?"

"You mentioned this grievance of yours openly?" asked Wharton.

"Among my friends—yes." Pole's voice had a new note of belligerence. "It was more than a grievance. It was a deliberate insult. I had the right to spread it about, and warn people against her—so to speak."

"Quite so. But you never went to see her?"

"I didn't even write to her. I treated the whole thing-and her too—with the contempt deserved."

"Well," said Wharton, with a shrewd thrust of his own, "there have been times, Mr. Pole, when you've instructed the Yard not only how to suck eggs but how to hatch 'em. Now I most humbly suggest that you've a problem of your own which—if it were mine—I'd find perfectly easy of solution."

"A problem?" He was staring intently.

"Yes, the problem of the Chief Conspirator. Go over the whole list of your enemies—if an old-time professional may advise you—and when you're sure you've got all their names down, make a new list of those who knew you were an authority on Luffham. Sift them out again through the sieve of those to whom you handed a visiting card, bearing your own prints but not his, because he was wearing a glove perhaps. Keep on sifting through the finer meshes of those who knew your grievance against the dead woman, and those physically capable of imitating your voice"—he gave an elaborate shrug of the shoulders—"and the answer's your man."

"The man with the squint, perhaps," said Travers with an assumption of gravity.

In that moment there was some peculiar quality of stillness in the room, and again Travers saw on the face of Pole what was a rare flash of illumination. Then Pole frowned, and the frown went and his eyes narrowed. A set smile came to his face but he was shifting on his seat like a man who is anxious to be away and gone.

"I'm afraid none of us believe that yarn of the man with the squint." He got to his feet. "I'll do what you say about that problem of mine, Superintendent".

Wharton beamed amiably. "Learning the old dog's tricks? Well, let me know the results."

"I certainly will." He hesitated, opened his lips, closed them, then opened them again. "I might have some news for you that will surprise you." And then again it seemed that he was aware of having let out too much, for once more the set smile came.

"I'm most grateful to you, and to you, Mr. Travers. And I apologize for having taken up so much valuable time."

So Pole went, and no sooner had the door closed on him than Wharton's face lost all its amiability.

"Did you see that look on his face? There's something he knows that I'd give a month's pay to find out."

"Yes," said Travers. "He knows the Chief Conspirator."

Wharton gave a snort. "You don't believe all that blether, do you? He was bluffing, bluffing from start to finish. Laughing up his sleeve, the same as he told you he'd do."

"Oh, no," said Travers.

"Well, what then?"

"What?" Travers began polishing his glasses. "I believe the *Blazon*—chosen deliberately for the purpose—has had foisted on it some mad stunt that has gone beyond the bounds of mere publicity. I believe, as you do, that Pole is a connecting link in some amazing scheme, which has two or more principals. I think Pole is the main organizer and has taken every step to make his own position secure. All the same, he's uneasy. I bet he knows the original scheme has got out of hand. Things are happening that he hasn't bargained for, and they've scared him. Or they had scared him up to the time he came here this evening. Now he's got his pluck and his wits back. He believes he can handle the situation."

"You don't think there's anything in that man with the squint business?" Wharton's tone had an anxiety.

"I don't know what to think," Travers told him. "As soon as I mentioned the subject, he seemed to have an idea." His mouth gaped. "George, we ought to have had him followed. He's left here with something on his mind that he's got to do—and do quickly."

"Yes," said Wharton. "That's a bad slip. He'll be going back home though, and we'll pick him up from there. Give him five minutes and he'll be settled."

But he remained on his feet all the same and began slowly filling his pipe.

"Mightn't that young friend of yours—Cane—have been in this? You mentioned two or more confederates?"

Travers shook his head.

"What connection is there between young Cane and Miss Delayne?"

"They rhyme, don't they?" His face straightened again. "You were saying?"

"Why should he murder her? And not only that, he's got an alibi, and I can swear to it."

"You?"

"Yes," said Travers. "Young Cane's tired of Fleet Street and he's joining a relative in New Zealand. I should say he isn't sure yet, but he rang me up from the *Blazon* office round about twelve o'clock asking if I could spare him a minute. If he'd had murder in mind my answer might have spiked his guns, because I might have told him to come round at once. But his manner was perfectly normal, and if he did the murder later, then Menzies was woefully wrong about the time."

Wharton shook his head. "Did you ever know Menzies wrong? And about the congealing of blood?"

"That gives me a further answer then. We agreed that Luffham's murder might have been a Cane murder—a tip-and-run murder; the murder of someone who hated blood. The same person didn't commit both murders."

"I'm not so sure," said Wharton irritatingly. "But your friend Cane might have imitated Pole's voice to Stowe? Why, his own voice has a kind of high-pitched quality that isn't too unlike Pole's own."

"He's got a very nice voice," said Travers mildly. "But he didn't do any imitating, George. Cane lunched with me in this very room, and was here long before and long after that call was made." He smiled disarmingly. "Sorry. I ought to have told you that first of all."

But Wharton dodged defeat and was dialling Marsham Mansions.

"That Marsham Mansions. . . . Can you tell me if Mr. Ferdinand Pole is in? . . . Yes, I'll hang on. "He hummed to himself

while he waited, and the tune, of which he was profoundly ignorant, was Giggling Gilbert's latest—*I don't want to be murdered
on Monday*. Then his gaze fell from the ceiling. "He isn't? . . . I
see. . . . It doesn't matter. Good-by."

The receiver went back with a snap. Wharton stood for an
indecisive moment, then came slowly across.

"You were right. Wherever he's gone, he went straight to it.
Still, he'll keep. When we want him, we'll just reach out and
pick him up—like that." He grunted. "He'll have a few more ro-
mances ready by that time."

"I've been thinking, George," Travers said. "If he worked out
all that conspiracy tale he was telling us, then he's the cleverest
actor you and I have run across. For instance, go back to what
Daggon heard in the telephone booth. Stowe was saying that
Pole *did* do the phoning; therefore Pole was protesting to Stowe
that he didn't do it. Then take the next sequence—when I caught
sight of Pole waiting for the lift at the *Blazon*. Pole didn't see me.
There wasn't need for acting, in fact, and yet his face, as I saw it,
had a look of worry. Again, what need was there for him to talk
to you just now? He didn't know you were aware of the fact that
he was supposed to have telephoned Stowe; in fact I'd say Stowe
assured him that you had definitely not been told."

"If the man's mad—"

"Not mad, George—pardon me. An exhibitionist but most
certainly not a homicidal maniac."

"Damned if I can understand you," burst out Wharton. "Not
so many days ago you were sure he was the one we wanted. He'd
made up his mind to commit a perfect murder and he'd done
it, and he'd boasted to you that he'd never be caught. In fact,
he handed you much the same line of talk as he was handing to
both of us in this very room ten minutes ago." He gave one of
his most irritating, contemptuous grunts. "All air; all theory—
that's what everything is. Give me facts. Give me a foundation
and then I'll build. What's the good of air?"

"It's a fine thing to fly on," Travers told him drily. "But if you
want facts, what about gathering a few from Standard, and the
dresser, and the dressing-room?"

"All in good time," said Wharton. "I'd like to use your telephone first. A quarter of an hour and I'm with you."

So Travers drew up to the fire and left him to his telephoning. Palmer brought in the evening papers and as Travers took them he saw on the front page of the *Record* an obituary of the dead actress. There, in fact, was an idea. Among all the obituaries must be some hint of her early years which seemed to Wharton so important.

But when Travers had read the three obituaries, that in the *Record* alone contained more than a hint. All three were known facts of Laura Delayne's career, tricked out and amplified with journalistic padding and surmise. All three had references to her reticence and unobtrusive pride of birth—that in fact she prided herself on being a lady; all of which was in some ways amusing but far from informative. The *Record* alone had something resembling facts.

> With her, it is understood, died the last representative of an old county family. In stage circles there were stories and rumours which Laura Delayne herself would neither affirm nor deny; that, for instance, she was cut off by her family when she insisted on choosing the stage as a career; that her parents both went down with the unfortunate *Titanic;* that there was in consequence no reconciliation, and that the tragedy embittered her life. Certainly it can be said . . .

Wharton finished with the phone and Travers called him over.

"Have a look at that, George, and see if it helps."

Wharton read it. "I think it's just padding," he said.

"So do I," Travers told him. "All the same, a list of married couples of a certain age who went down in the *Titanic* might help a good deal."

Wharton was hoisting on his overcoat.

"Let's go and get some information first hand. We can always sift the newspaper yarns." The words brought an idea. "What've your friends the *Blazon* got to say about things generally?"

His eye fell first on the picture of Stowe. A grunt came and he read with a heavy irony:

"Murder of famous actress. *Evening Blazon* discovers the body. Mysterious telephone call brings crime-expert to scene of tragedy."

The sneer went as his eyes rose to the streamer headlines. The old war-cry was installed again, and in type only slightly less heavy, came a couple of supporters:

MURDER ON MONDAYS
KILLER ABROAD AGAIN!!
WHERE IS THE MAN WITH THE SQUINT???

"Damn the *Blazon!*" said Travers, and hastily explained. "Just saying it for you, George, as we're in a hurry."

Wharton ignored the facetiousness. He was nodding to himself as he laid the paper down.

"The man with the squint," he said. "That's what's intriguing me. Wonder if he'll write anything tomorrow morning?"

CHAPTER VIII
CONCERNING AN ACTRESS

PERCY STANDARD'S VILLA lay no more than two minutes from the exit at Golders Green, and he was at home. An unmarried daughter, herself a woman of sixty, kept house for him. Standard himself looked more actor than manager, with his silver halo of hair, and his thin, eager face, and old garrulity.

"A terrible thing indeed, sir," he said to Wharton. "Years and years of life she had before her. She and I didn't always see eye to eye, sir, but a grand actress she was, and a credit to the profession. Not of the oldest school, sir, but of the old school—if you know what I mean. What the great ones had, sir, she had—gesture, presence, voice, everything."

"How old would she be?"

The old man was reaching for his evening paper. Travers cut in.

"The papers can't be relied on, I fear. And without being personal to Miss Delayne, I might say that only the supremely great can afford to disclose their ages."

The old man seemed grateful for that fine flow. Travers was in harmony with his mood:

"Perhaps you're right, sir. But let me see now. It was in . . . in . . . yes, it was in 1909 that she first came to us. At Nottingham, it was—"

"And how old was she then?" put in Wharton.

"How old, sir? She was a woman then, sir, but quite a girl. Not more than twenty-four, in actual age."

"Surely not," said Wharton, and did some lightning calculating. "Why, that would make her only fifty!"

"That would be about right, sir," the old man told him quietly. "Her hair whitened early and she wasn't ashamed of it, like this generation. There's an adornment, sir, in silver hair."

Wharton nodded. "Only fifty—and I'd have put her as ten years older. And now, Mr. Standard, will you tell us about how she came to join you?"

"How, sir?"

"Yes, where she came from and so on."

He shook his head. "The Guvnor himself brought her along, sir, at Nottingham." His eyes closed. "Let me see now. We were doing Macbeth that night—"

"Yes, but didn't he say anything about her to you? Who she was and where she came from?"

"Never a word, sir. He was the master, sir, and I carried out his instructions—and glad to do so, sir. I understood she was a friend of his, sir, and had talent. The very same week, sir, she played Lydia Languish, Sir William himself being Sir Anthony Absolute. The part didn't suit her, sir, and I ventured to remark as much at the time. But she had talent, sir; oh, yes—she had talent." His hand rose in an ample gesture. "The next year at Nottingham, the town rose to her Lady Macbeth."

"Indeed," said Wharton. "But surely you must have gathered something during your association with her? Didn't she ever speak of her home? Didn't she have letters?"

Old Standard shook his head.

"What about her accent? Couldn't you gather from that what part of the country she came from?"

He shook his head again.

"Tell me any of her friends who happen to be still living."

"She was not one to make friends, sir."

Wharton made a motion of helplessness. "Didn't she have any love affairs?"

"She took no interest in that sort of thing, sir. You see, she was never what you might call beautiful. Hers was what I'd call presence. Personality, they call it nowadays."

Wharton clicked his tongue. "And she never let anything fall by which you could make even a guess?"

"One moment." The old man was raising his hand. "I remember one incident . . ."

Best part of five minutes the story took him, and what it amounted to was that on a certain occasion a member of the company had spoken slightingly of Ipswich and Silly Suffolk. Laura Delayne had turned on him and rent him in a furious minute, then the flare of anger went and the matter was never alluded to again.

"Well, that's something," Wharton said, and expressed his gratitude. But time was pressing and no further information was coming, so Wharton left instructions where the old man could send what further vital memories occurred to him.

"A fine old character that," said Travers, as they hurried back to the tube again.

"Chattering old fool," said Wharton. "For our purpose, that is. What we'll do, though, is get hold of that Reginald Wightman—Sir William's son. He might add something."

When they reached the Harmony, the curtain was due up in five minutes. With the new situation caused by the tragedy, Harry Blenn, the manager, was in a minor panic, and the two stood by till the curtain rose.

"Sorry keeping you waiting," he said, "but everything's all over the place. Some hell of a happening, wasn't it?"

"You haven't any ideas on who might have done it?" asked Travers, who knew Blenn pretty well.

"Me? My God, no!" At once he was fussing again. "What was it you wanted to see? If it's her dresser, I've got her waiting for you in her dressing-room. Mrs. Dart, her name is. The room's there and you can do what you like in it. Now if you'll excuse me, I'll buzz off. See you later."

Wharton grabbed him just in time. "Any chance of using a phone for a few minutes?"

"Sorry, old boy. I doubt it," Blenn said. "Come along with me and we'll see."

Wharton waved a backward hand for Travers to carry on. Travers found his way to what had been Laura Delayne's room.

"You're Mrs. Dart?" he said. "The late Miss Delayne's dresser?"

"That's me, sir. I've been with her ever since the show opened here."

"We'll sit down, shall we?" Travers said. "And don't let my questions bother you at all. Just answer them simply, the same as you might do the man from the Prudential."

She was a middle-aged, matter-of-fact body, but that made her smile.

"I don't reckon them sort'd ever get any answers from me, sir."

"Perhaps I'll have better luck," Travers said. "Now to show how utterly ignorant—and harmless—I am, I always thought that an actress of Miss Delayne's standing had her own dresser who went with her everywhere—on tour, for instance.

"You're right, sir," she said, "but I'll explain. Miss Delayne's own dresser died just before this show started and I'm what you'd call her regular dresser now. If she'd been going on tour—which she was, poor dear—I'd have been going with her.

"That's splendid," said Travers, who now knew the quest hopeless. "What'll be the best thing to do is to let you know what's behind the questions."

But when Mrs. Dart had heard the guarded details she had no information whatever to impart.

"She never let a word fall to me, sir, not about her home, sir, nor her parents, nor nothing. She never was one to talk, in a manner of speaking, though no one wanted to work for anyone better. But never a word about anything private, if you know what I mean." She gave a little theatrical shrug of the shoulders. "I used to throw out a hint sometimes, in my own way, sir; not for curiosity but just to make conversation, if you understand me. Might as well have been talking to that there table."

"I know," said Travers. "Always a very secretive lady. And never by any chance, I suppose, did you hear her mention Ipswich?"

"Ipswich?" She shook her head.

"Suffolk then. Any part of Suffolk."

"Suffolk?" She screwed up her eyes in thought. "Now just a minute, sir, while I try and recollect. Lowestoft's in Suffolk, isn't it, sir?"

"Well, most of it, I believe."

"Well then, sir, this is what I heard her say. Last September my sister was taken ill who lives in Lowestoft, and I went to see her over the week-end. She's better now, nor that that matters. Well, when I got here on the Monday, she asked me—Miss Delayne, that is—how my sister was. Very kind that way she was—least to me. Then she said which way did I go and what places I went through; regular sort of interested she was. Then I said as how perhaps that was her home; Suffolk, I meant, where I'd been through; and then she cut me off proper sharp, so I didn't say no more about it. Forgotten all about it, I had, till you mentioned it just now."

As that was all that Travers could extract, Mrs. Dart was kept no longer, and departed with a tip that brought her to an incipient curtsey. Travers surveyed the room.

Now there was nothing noteworthy about that room or its contents. It was up-to-date, with a corner wash-basin and running water; its lights were well placed; it had the latest thing in electric stoves and a radiator in addition, and its dressing-table and wardrobe had ample space. But in personal touches it was utterly lacking. The furnishings were plainly the property of the management, even to the chesterfield suite in its linen covers.

All that might be the private property of the dead actress was a water-colour that hung above the electric stove, and recalled to Travers's faint memory the pair of pictures that had been in the hotel room.

Wharton came in and Blenn with him.

"Gone, has she?" Blenn said. "Getting on all right? And got everything you want?"

"Everything," said Travers. "But this picture here. Did it belong to Miss Delayne?"

"That's right," Blenn said. "Far as we can make out, it's the only thing of hers there is here—I mean, outside the usual. Anything else I can do for you, old boy. If not I'll buzz off again."

"Busy fellow that," Wharton said. "I managed to use his own phone though. Young Wightman will be ringing me here at half-past. He's only just of age, so Blenn tells me. His father married twice, and he's the only one. One of the bright young people in the movies, Blenn tells me. Just got back from America."

Travers was having another look at that water-colour.

"What happened to those two pictures that were in the hotel room?"

"They're at the Yard," Wharton said. "Everything she had of her own is at the Yard. Why?"

Travers begged the question.

"Funny, don't you think, that she should have so few things of her own, and yet three pictures? Have a look at this one, George, and tell me what you think of it."

"What do I know about pictures?"

"Don't be awkward," Travers told him. Wharton shot him a look, hooked on his antiquated spectacles, and came over. Travers's brain, as he knew, moved in its own eccentric grooves. Behind his flippancies, his enthusiasms and even his misgivings was always a something that might be a startling truth.

"Looks rather pretty—to me," Wharton said. "A nice little piece of English countryside. It isn't valuable, is it?"

The tone had been so hopeful that Travers smiled.

"Ten bob would buy it in an auction room. Less perhaps."

"What do you think of it yourself?" challenged Wharton. "You're supposed to be an authority."

"Heavens, no," remonstrated Travers. "Not on material like this. Still, let's use the wits God's given us. It's the faded Prussian-blue and sepia school, a sort of burnt sienna symphony. Done by a talented amateur, about fifty years ago."

Wharton stared at what had sounded like so much Sherlock Holmes exhibition patter.

"The lady's name being Gladys," he said, "and one who could never stand rice pudding."

"Scoff all you like," said Travers amiably. "The fact remains that you ought to have known it was painted in the eighties."

"How do you make that out?"

"Look," said Travers. "Observe that figure of a mother, leading a small boy by the hand, and introduced to break the line of the hedge. What about the clothes they wear? Aren't those the clothes of the eighties?"

Wharton took a look over the tops of his glasses and grunted something about every man to his trade. Travers laughed. Then Wharton was all at once pushing him on one side.

"Here, let me have a look at that picture."

His glass was out and he was running it over. Then he grunted impatiently, hooked the picture off and took it under the light.

"Have a look there," he said, finger-marking the place. "I make it L.D."

"L.D.?" said Travers, and stared. But Wharton's eyesight had not betrayed him, and Travers shook his head.

"She didn't paint it herself. She couldn't have done."

"Who said she did?" chuckled Wharton. "Why shouldn't her mother have painted it?"

"It doesn't fit," Travers told him. "She didn't want her name known, yet she had a picture with initials on that were her mother's. And they're her own initials. There's something too easy about it, unless she thought the signature initials wouldn't be read."

"As much as I could do to make them out," grumbled Wharton. "Say what village it is. That's what we want to know—not theories about initials."

Travers frowned. "Sounds easy, George, but it happens to be the hardest part. You could find lanes like that all over England. The cottage is merely a thatched cottage. There's no distinct architecture about the top of that mill just above the trees there."

Blenn stuck his head inside the door.

"You're wanted, old boy. That call of yours."

He disappeared and Wharton followed hard after. Travers had retained the glass and spent the next five minutes going over the picture inch by inch. When Wharton came back he was still at it. Wharton himself was clicking his tongue exasperatedly.

"Says he doesn't know a thing. Never knew his father to mention any of Miss Delayne's private affairs. He hasn't got a relative in Suffolk and he's never heard his father mention any."

"I'll take this picture if you don't mind, George," Travers said. "I've got an idea. Could you by any chance bring the other two pictures along to my place some time later?"

"Heaven knows when it'll be then," Wharton said, and recited a list of things he had to do. "And if I don't get a meal soon I'll be down and out. All I've had since breakfast is a slab of bread and cheese, one glass of beer—"

"And two tots of admirable sherry."

"Sherry, was it?" said Wharton, and left it at that. "Suit me better if you could come along to the Yard. Eleven o'clock suit you?"

"Admirably," said Travers, who was a bird of night. "Palmer may be coming with me, by the way."

"Palmer? What's he got to do with it?"

"Don't know yet," Travers told him, and left it in his own exasperating way at that.

But Travers bore that water-colour home to St. Martin's Chambers and when the main meal was over and Palmer brought in coffee, he kept him back. Palmer had been valet to Travers's father and had doubtless seen the infant Ludovic in his first pram. He was a man of much tact, considerable—if jumbled—reading, and of unexpected talents, and Wharton thought a lot of him for more than once he had shown a shrewd and homely insight that had done the Yard much service.

"Sit down, Palmer," Travers said. "Glass of port or a kummel?"

"Neither at the moment, thank you, sir," said Palmer.

"Well, sit down and make yourself comfortable. Light your pipe. Try some of this." He left him to it and fetched that water-colour. "Let me see. You're not a Suffolk man, are you? You're Essex."

"Essex, sir, is correct."

"But you know a good deal about Suffolk?"

"Yes, sir," said Palmer, and deliberated for a moment, pipe in air. "Ellen, you may remember, sir, married a Suffolk man."

"That's right," said Travers, who was well aware of the fact. Ellen, Palmer's sister, had been second nurse to the same infant Ludovic. "And you stayed with her from time to time after she was married?"

"Very frequently, sir. And your late father, sir, shot a good deal at Ringham Hall. And at Mewford, sir. I always accompanied him, sir."

"Take a look at this," Travers said. "See if it's a place you know. Don't miss the mill in the left-hand corner, behind the trees."

Palmer put his specs on, frowned considerably and examined the picture from various angles. Finally he shook his head.

"No, sir. I can't say it's anywhere I know."

Travers nodded. "It's a bit vague, I admit. Nothing to cling to."

"This is a picture of somewhere in Suffolk, sir?"

"I'm hoping so," Travers told him. "What it may come to is sending it to a curator at Ipswich museum." And as Palmer began getting to his feet: "Wait a minute. We haven't finished yet. You and I are due at Scotland Yard in half an hour's time. Now get me an atlas, will you? No, better get me the motoring map to include Suffolk."

Palmer brought the map and then waited for a hesitating moment.

"Scotland Yard you said, sir?"

"Yes," said Travers. "Does that strike home to your conscience?"

"Conscience, sir?"

Travers chuckled as he waved him away. And while he examined that map of Suffolk and memorized the essentials, he kept thinking in some queer, amusing way of Charlie, Pole's parrot.

"How are you, Palmer?" said Wharton and held out his hand. "I don't know what Mr. Travers wants you for but make yourself at home."

"These the two pictures, are they?" Travers had a look at both, then selected the larger. In its foreground were grazing cattle, and a path that twisted down through meadows and the middle distance, where a village lay in full sun. Behind it were distant woods and the faintest line of hills. "Excellent composition," he said, and handed it to Palmer. "Recognize it at all?"

Palmer showed immediate interest. "Do you mind if I put on my glasses, sir?"

He held it to the light and at last put it gravely down.

"That's Tarrfold, sir. It's twenty years since I saw it. sir, but it's Tarrfold."

Travers's face was one huge beam. "George, he's got it! She asked that dresser particularly about places on the railway route from Liverpool Street to Lowestoft. Tarrfold lies just off the railway. She was thinking of the trains she used to hear as a girl."

Wharton came over for a look. Travers was thrusting the third picture into Palmer's hands. This time it was of a long stretch of meadow or parkland between woods. Sheep grazed there, and in the middle distance were ornamental gardens, and above the woods to the left the chimneys and part of the roof of what might be a Queen Anne house.

Palmer had a look, then rubbed his lean old chin.

"This beats me, sir. I believe I've been in that very ride, sir, but I can't be certain. It's there, sir, but I can't get it out."

"Have another look at the one you saw first," suggested Travers.

"Ah, sir!" said Palmer then, and gave a look of triumph. "There was a mill at Tarrfold, sir. I know this lane now, sir. I know it well."

"Magnificent!" Travers turned to Wharton. "Wonder if Palmer could think back twenty-five years ago and tell us who lived at Tarrfold Hall?"

"Tarrfold Hall, sir?" He rubbed his chin. "Yes, sir. I remember that perfectly. Sir Henry Vallor lived there, sir."

Travers's face fell. He was dead certain that the owner's name would have begun with a D.

"Think back again then," he said, "and tell me if you can remember any important family who lived there, whose name began with D."

But that was beyond Palmer's capacity. Tarrfold, as he explained, had been for him no more than a place through which he had walked, and in it he knew no living soul. Travers thought for a moment, then turned to Wharton.

"You anxious to follow all this up?"

"Am I not?" said Wharton tersely.

"Then I'll do it, if you like," Travers told him. "I don't suppose there'll be a lot on here tomorrow, so I'll take the Rolls and Palmer and unearth what I can."

Wharton gave a nod of approbation.

"I'd like that man of yours—Daggon," Travers said. "Tell you what. I'll call up here at half-past eight sharp in case you have anything else for me."

Travers was staying on for a few minutes and Palmer went. Wharton shook hands and thanked him, and uttered his usual jest.

"Very kind of you, Palmer. Any time you get nabbed, send for me and I'll bail you out."

Wharton had nothing new to report. In the morning, he said, he was having a word with Stowe.

"His manner wasn't very guilty when he was with us, in the room with her," Travers ventured, and, seeing Wharton's look: "Oh, I'm not saying he isn't the type!"

"An excellent trick of his," Wharton said, "to have done the murder, and then got himself rung up, pretended it was a call to go to the hotel and so have got all the credit and publicity for discovering the body."

"I'd think about it, George," Travers told him. "Something tells me you'd be a bit too premature, tackling Stowe. You tell me more about it in the morning."

But when Travers came along in the morning to collect Daggon and hear the latest, there was nothing said about Stowe. A letter had reached the *Blazon* and the contents had just been phoned through.

Sir,

Your paper is asking the question, Where is the man with the squint? The man with the squint said he might be back in London on the Monday, and the world now knows he was.

I would like to call attention to two things. The first is only known to the police, and is that they will notice the resemblances between the killing of Laura Delayne and the Vickers Street stabbing. The other thing I recommend to the police is a study of the little word *blackmail*.

Yours, etc.,

Justice.

"What do you think of that?" said Wharton. "Don't it beat cock-fighting? Same kind of paper, they tell me, and the post-mark Holborn."

"Blackmail," said Travers reflectively. "Things begin to fit. That cheque she drew for two hundred pounds."

"Don't I know it?" said Wharton. "You're the one who's going to throw light on this. If you were a man of mine I'd say, 'Don't show your face here till you can write a biography of Laura Delayne!'" He grunted. "Cradle to grave. You know what I mean."

"Yes," said Travers. "I'm afraid I do. And it's a tall order. Perhaps it's as well if we say good-by."

Wharton chuckled and reached for his coat.

"Not for a bit. You might as well give me a lift in that hell-wagon of yours as far as the *Blazon*."

CHAPTER IX
OUT OF THE PAST

As HE DROVE that morning through the busy suburbs, Travers was on good terms with himself. Enquiries into the two murders were going feverishly on, with scores of men on routine work, delving into this and raking up that, and of that vast inquisitorial machine Travers felt himself a not unimportant cog. For while others hunted for they hardly knew what, his own course lay clear, and distance from the crimes was lending enchantment to the chase.

Palmer took the wheel when the suburbs were passed, and Travers moved back to Daggon, and showed him the water-colours and explained the situation.

"A family whose name began with a D," said Daggon. "The mother used to go about sketching and the daughter used to go in for theatricals. And all we want is to see if Laura Delayne lived down there and then get anything we can about her. That doesn't look too hard to me, sir, not if her people were gentry."

"You get what we want," Travers told him, "and you're on a fiver—hard or not."

He took the wheel again. Ipswich was passed, and Woodbridge, and Palmer began to prick his ears and look about him. Tarrfold was getting near, he said, and soon a direction post showed only three more miles. A busy little place it was, according to the reference book, with seven hundred population. When the first houses came in sight Travers pulled up for enquiries.

"There seem to be two pubs, Daggon," he said. "The *Bullfinch* comes first and we'll drop you there. We'll go on to the *Three Bells,* and if nothing turns up to stop you, you come along there for lunch at half-past twelve. Here's a small contribution towards expenses."

The *Three Bells* was more hotel than inn, and it stood back from the road with a kind of park for the car. Travers had taken pains with his dress that morning, and the Rolls was impressive and so was Palmer, and the landlord who had watched the parking, touched his forelock as the gentleman came in. Travers rejoiced to note that he was a man of sixty at least, and that lunch could be had, and that an old-timer or two was in the bar.

"You might see what my man wants," he said, "and in the meanwhile give me a tankard of bitter. You'll have one yourself, perhaps, and—" A wave of the hand suggested the other five occupants of the room.

"Just a visitor, sir?" the landlord was soon saying.

"Yes," said Travers. "The fact is I'm engaged in looking up a family who used to live about here some thirty years ago. A distant relative, you might almost say."

"And what might the name be, sir?"

"There you have me," Travers told him. "I'm really enquiring about a young lady who left here about twenty-six years ago. She was then about twenty-six years old. That makes it easy to remember. Twenty-six years old and left here twenty-six years ago. It's possible her name began with a D."

"Like Drew, or Dawson?"

"That's right," said Travers. "And remember the family was what might be called gentry."

The landlord turned to the room and the room buzzed in conference and argument. Travers at last broke in.

"If I might suggest it, gentlemen, why not take every D in the village you can remember. Work your way through. And see everybody has what he likes to drink, landlord. Working through's dry work."

A retired schoolmaster was among the company, and the landlord himself was a knowledgeable man, but even their efforts produced nothing. Travers brought out the two water-colours.

"We know these were painted by the mother," he said, "and if you look carefully in the bottom right-hand corner, you'll see the initials L.D."

The room identified both views in a flash. The years might have brought changes but one was the mill lane and the other the Hall from Copley's Corner.

"What about the Hall?" asked Travers. "Any lady with the initials L.D. ever lived there?"

A minute or two's discussion and the old schoolmaster submitted that the painter might have been a guest at the Hall. Nobody with a name beginning with a D had ever been in occupation.

"I wonder if this would help," Travers said. "The daughter—the one who left here twenty-six years ago—might have been an actress or very fond of the stage."

But nothing came of that. The bar clock struck the half-hour, there was an announcement that the gentleman's lunch was ready, and by the time Travers and Palmer were in the inner room, Daggon arrived. He reported bad luck.

"Nothing doing at the pub, sir, so I tried the almshouses right opposite. All I could get was a young lady and her sister—name of Smith—who used to get up things for charity. And they weren't even in this village at all—not exactly. Little Tarrfold, they call it; about a mile and a half on. Also they hadn't got no mother. She died donkey's years ago."

The meal had scarcely begun when a tap came at the door and the landlord reported that the room-still in impassioned conference after Travers's exit-had an idea. The schoolmaster came in and tentatively presented it.

"There was a family of gentry at Little Tarrfold," he said. "They don't fit in with all you told us, but the elder daughter—Lettice—was a great one for getting up theatrical shows in the district on behalf of charity. And she left the village about the time you mentioned. I can't guarantee that they were gentry exactly, but they were well-off or they wouldn't have lived at the Manor. Smith, the name was."

"Any members of the family still there?" Travers asked him.

"Oh, no," he said. "I only came here myself after the war, but from what I can make out, the father died and the two daughters kept the place on. Then something happened and the place was sold up and they went away. Some say it was nineteen hundred and nine and some the year after. I'm going home myself now, but if I get hold of anything else I'll let you know."

Travers returned due thanks and thought the clue promising.

"I've got an idea," he said to Daggon. "If the mother painted those pictures before she was married, then there's no objection to her married name being Smith. Soon as we've finished, we'll go along to Little Tarrfold and enquire."

And while the three discussed the situation, the more the hopes rose. If the name of the elder daughter was Lettice, the name might reasonably be her mother's—which gave half the initials, with the maiden name of the mother for the D. And Lettice Smith might well have changed that name for the more euphonious one of Laura Delayne. And then Travers had another brain-wave and asked the landlord the name of the local newspaper. It turned out to be the *Mellsford Advertiser* and of hoary age. Mellsford itself lay six miles on towards the Norfolk border.

"What we'll do is this," Travers told Daggon. "We'll go to the parson or sexton at Little Tarrfold and find out when the mother died. Then you shall go to the newspaper office and hunt their files for an account of the funeral, because it'll be practically sure to give the lady's maiden name. While Palmer drives you in to Mellsford, I'll be making enquiries in the village."

But when the car drew up before the tiny churchyard, Palmer ventured to suggest an inspection of the more imposing of the monuments. In two minutes Travers's eyes were opening wide, for on a stone cross beneath a straggling yew he read these words:

SACRED
to the
MEMORY
of
LAURA ALICE SMITH
(Born 1860 Died 1885)
Dearly beloved wife
of

THOMAS WIGHTMAN SMITH
of this Parish.

There was more to it than that, and below was the epitaph of the husband, buried in the same grave in the year 1907. His family name of Wightman proved beyond doubt that in Little Tarrfold lay the secret of Laura Delayne and the hotel murder.

Daggon left for Mellsford. Travers took a careful copy of the inscriptions and then paid a call on the vicar. Unfortunately he was a youngish man, but he had an elderly cook who was Tarrfold born. Most of her years of service had been spent out of the village, but she recommended a call on a Mrs. Crow, widow of a farmer, who in her earlier years had been housemaid at the Manor.

Travers passed the Manor on his way. It was a fine old house with spacious gardens, and could have been occupied only by people of considerable means. And, going back fifty years, it seemed not unreasonable to suppose that the young lady who afterwards became its mistress was of sufficient social standing to have painted, with the young ladies of Tarrfold Hall maybe, that delightful view between the woods.

Mrs. Crow was a massive woman of sixty-five; stolid, unimaginative and with a vocabulary incredibly small. Travers exerted every wile and expended his last ounce of patience, but getting information was a long, trying, catechizing business. Her great virtue was a submissive patience of her own.

She had never known Mrs. Smith, she said, but Mr. Smith was a very nice gentleman. She herself was at the Manor for a total of six years. After four of them, Mr. Smith died, and after two more the Manor was sold and the two daughters went away.

"The elder daughter was called Lettice?"

"That's right," she said.

"And the younger one?"

"She was Miss Maud."

It took a quarter of an hour to get details. Miss Lettice was the dominating one and the young housemaid had been in awe of her. Quite pretty, she was, and very nice when you got to know her. Miss Maud was beautiful and, Travers gathered, her father's favourite and something of a minx and a clinger. Miss Lettice had a temper of her own.

"They carried on the house all right when the father died?" asked Travers.

"Oh, yes," she said. "It didn't make no difference -not really."

"The same staff was kept up, indoors and out?"

"There wasn't no difference—really."

"Which means that they must have been left quite a lot of money."

But Mrs. Crow remembered nothing of that, except local talk. She remembered much however about the theatricals, and how Miss Lettice used to give a play in the drawing-room for all the staff at Christmas. Miss Maud, Travers gathered, was an unwilling helper. There was only a faint recollection of the visit of a gentleman of the name of Wightman—William Wightman.

"And why did the two ladies sell the Manor and go away?" Travers went on.

Mrs. Crow thought it was something to do with the quarrel.

"So they used to quarrel a lot, did they?"

"Not till they really quarrelled," she said.

Travers set to work patiently at a new quarrying and in ten minutes had the facts clear. There was a young gentleman, older however than Miss Lettice, who became a frequent caller at the Manor, and often in company with his mother, who was apparently a woman of advanced age. Then the gentleman got to spending quite a lot of time there, which was not too unusual in those days of young emancipation, and for a household which had considerable disregard of the conventions. Then at last word flew about that Miss Lettice was engaged. After that things seemed to have happened with dramatic speed, for there was a tremendous quarrel between the two sisters; Miss Maud left and never returned; the young gentleman was never seen again, and finally Miss Lettice sold the Manor and went too. Most people said she couldn't put up with the shame, for the general idea was that Miss Maud had stolen the affections of the young man, Miss Lettice had found it out, and then the young man and Miss

Maud had slipped off and got married. Mrs. Crow even suggested that Miss Maud's carryings-on with the young man had been something of a local scandal.

"I do wish you could remember his name," Travers said.

"I think I know now," she said. "I think it was something like Powell."

"Powell!" His eyes searched her face. "You sure it wasn't Pole?"

"Powell, it sounded like. I remember now it was Powell."

"And his Christian name?"

She shook her head. "I don't know what that was."

Travers smiled beseechingly. "But surely you know what Miss Lettice used to call him?"

"Oh, yes," she said. "Francis, that was what she used to call him and Frank, sometimes."

"Francis?" Travers moistened his lips. "Not Ferdinand?"

Mrs. Crow had never heard of such a name. All she could add about Mr. Francis Powell was that it was understood he was a London gentleman, and well off. Then when Travers began to recapitulate and fill in gaps, it appeared that the scene between the two sisters had been a violent one, with Lettice giving Maud an ultimatum to leave the Manor, and herself being away for the given time to allow her a free hand. When Lettice returned, Maud had gone, and a few days later Lettice went too, the Manor and its contents being sold later.

"Did Mr. Powell by any chance have any red in his hair?" Travers asked.

"Well, reddish it was," she said. And his height, it appeared, was the height of Ferdinand Pole, though she could do nothing towards identifying the voice.

It was after four o'clock when Travers finally left, and when he got back to the churchyard, the Rolls had been waiting an hour.

"Well, what did you find?" he asked Daggon.

"What her name was, all right," Daggon said. "Before she married, sir, she was a Miss Laura Dolan, the only daughter of a Colonel Dolan, who lived about ten miles from here." He grinned and his hand went out with a "Thank you, sir."

For Travers had heard the name and had heard little more, being busy with his note-case and disengaging a fiver.

Travers drove fast. On the edge of the inner suburbs he drew the car in at a kiosk and warned the Yard of his arrival in half an hour. The Embankment lights were glistening as the Rolls sidled in before the Yard, and Wharton was waiting in his room.

"Get anything?"

"Yes," said Travers. "Not quite all you wanted, but most of it. Maybe a little more—though that doesn't make sense."

Wharton had a stenographer in, and there was never an interruption while Travers told his story.

"Now then," he said, and waved to the stenographer to stay put, "let me see if I've got all this absolutely right."

His own notes in hand, he began.

"About the year 1880, Thomas Wightman Smith married a Laura Dolan. A daughter Lettice was born, and then a daughter Maud, and the mother died either then or soon after. Lettice grew up to be in charge of the house, and she had a liking for amateur theatricals. Maud was the prettier, was probably spoiled by her father, and was comparatively feather-brained. The father died and left the property between the two daughters, who were both of age. Later they made the acquaintance of a Mr. Francis Powell, who while engaged to the elder, was having an affair with the younger. The elder discovered it and there was a violent scene. Maud either was ordered out or was offered an arrangement by which she could go, and then Lettice went too. She changed her name to her mother's, with a slight difference—Dolan to Delayne—and went straight into professional acting under Wightman, who was a relation of the family. Neither Maud nor Powell has since been heard of."

"All in order," said Travers.

Wharton took the typed sheets and the stenographer left.

"What happened to Maud?" he fired at Travers.

"Lord knows," said Travers. "The idea was that she and Powell eloped."

"Then why did Francis Powell change his name to Ferdinand Pole? And why does the reference book state that he was traveling in Turkey in the winter of nineteen nine and most of nineteen ten? Then in the next year he was in India."

"You're taking an advantage of me," Travers said. "I haven't had time to refresh my memory over the book material. But why shouldn't he have taken Maud with him? I know he's down as not married, but that's nothing to do with it. He might have married her—and I'd say he certainly did—and then she died somewhere abroad."

"We've got him!" Wharton smashed his fist down on the table. "Said he'd never spoken to her in his life." He nodded, licking his lips like a Roman lion who has chosen his Christian. Then he gave a crafty look over his spectacle tops.

"Remember what you said about blackmail—"

"What you said, George," Travers reminded him mildly.

Wharton snorted the interruption aside.

"This afternoon I had a talk with that dresser. I worked my way round to the time when Laura Delayne drew that cheque for two hundred pounds; you know, asking if there'd ever been anything peculiar about her manner. What do you think I got out of her?"

He picked up a typed sheet with the information verbatim.

It was a Monday night and as soon as I clapped eyes on her I thought she was ill. "Good heavens, Miss," I said, and she took the words right out of my mouth. "I'm all right," she said, and then she didn't say anything for a bit while I was laying her dress out, and then all at once she said, "Have you ever seen a ghost?"—just like that. "Ghost, Miss?" I said, and then she cut me off all short like her way was and when I started talking again and tried to bring it round to the ghost, she told me to keep my tongue still because she'd a headache. When she come off last thing she was limp as a rag. Next day I asked her how she was and she nearly snapped my head off.

"There you are," said Wharton. "You know who the ghost was?"

"Pole, I imagine."

"Yes," said Wharton grimly. "Pole, whom we're now going to call on. Palmer can drop us at your place and we'll walk on."

Palmer drove and Travers began picking up Wharton's words.

"I can't get the hang of things, George. Pole's got money. Why should he want to blackmail her for two hundred pounds?"

"He'll tell us," said Wharton. "And what about that damned letter this morning? Why should this anonymous letter-writer have talked about blackmail?"

"A wild guess," said Travers. "After all, that talk about there being a resemblance between the murder of Laura Delayne and the Vickers Street stabbing, is the purest bilge. I've been thinking it over today, and there isn't a pennorth of resemblance, except that both were stabbings and both done with the same kind of knife."

"That part was hot-air for the benefit of the man in the street," said Wharton contemptuously. "The same kind of bluff we had in the other letter. But when it said the word blackmail it hit a nail on the head, just as it did when it revealed how the elastic was placed round those rails at Luffham's murder."

Travers shook his head bewilderedly. His brain was going round in circles.

Then just before the car drew up, Wharton became mysterious.

"I've got a little surprise for our friend Justice. Seen the *Blazon* this evening?"

Travers said he had had no time to see anything, except the bends in the road.

"I'll tell you all about it later," Wharton said. "Now what about going in to Pole's flat? Any particular excuse so as to keep him on a string?"

"Just an ordinary walk in, I think," said Travers. "You watch his face when he catches sight of us."

"You do the preliminaries," Wharton said.

So though the General remained within earshot, Travers it was who accosted the hall porter.

"Mr. Pole in, do you know?"

"Mr. Pole, sir? You wasn't wanting to see him, was you, sir?"

"I was rather," Travers said. "Why? What's the trouble?"

The porter became confidential.

"I don't know if you've seen him this afternoon, sir, or if you know anything about it, but he come in that door about twenty minutes ago, and blimey! if I didn't think he was going to peg out. He was all of a tremble and his face, blimey! it was whiter than that there paper. 'What's the matter, sir?' I say. 'I'm all right,' he say. 'That you're not,' I say, and then he got sort of snappy-like. 'You ought to have a doctor, sir,' I say, and I steadied him into the lift and took him right up to his room and poured him out a stiff 'un. Then about five minutes later he buzzed through and said he'd have a doctor after all, so I rang for one and he's up there now." He broke off, speaking out of the corner of his mouth. "Here he is now, sir. Just coming downstairs. The one in the—"

But Travers recognized the doctor as one who had lately been called in for Palmer's lumbago. The doctor gave merely a quick questioning look, then recognized Travers.

"Hallo," he said. "What are you doing here?"

"As a matter of fact I came to see Pole. Now the porter tells me he isn't very fit."

"He'll be all right tomorrow," the doctor said. "Said he had a pretty nasty shock. Didn't say what though. I've given him something and he'll be sleeping like a top." He turned to the porter and did some whispering, and then to Travers again. "I was just telling the porter I'd be along first thing in the morning. You coming my way?"

Travers said unfortunately not; gave a report on Palmer, and watched the doctor go. Then he caught Wharton's eye. The great balloon that should have been rocketing towards the heavens had collapsed like a dying pig, and two somewhat silent individuals made their way through the swing doors.

CHAPTER X
CLIMAX

They walked back to Travers's flat. Wharton said he had time for a sherry, and no more. Travers poured out the two tots and then delivered himself of a queer statement.

"George, there's a thesis I'd maintain against all the learned societies of Europe. Irony is the basis of all emotion."

The glass stopped short at Wharton's lips. He stared.

"What're you talking about?"

"This," said Travers. "At the moment I'm filled with a profound emotion, though the word perhaps is a misnomer. I have a feeling, and it's a frightening feeling. You've had it a hundred times, George; the feeling that something's going to happen. There's something horrible in the air and it's settled on my brain. And when I analyse it, I always find myself going back to Mrs. Crow. There she was, like some sloe-eyed, heavy-busted Hebe, singing of Troy and not knowing it. You see the irony? All this horrible business, intrigue and murder, was just some half-forgotten tale. Miss Lettice, she was talking of, and I was thinking of Laura Delayne."

Wharton shot him a look, took a belated drink, and set the glass down.

"I don't know what language you're talking in, but I recognized one word. And talking about irony, can you beat it, as they say? You and me ready to pop in on him and he goes and has a shock." Another look over the tops of his spectacles. "Wonder what gave him the shock."

Travers shook his head. Wharton was always firing questions and expecting answers like rabbits from a hat. And the point about Pole's shock was the very climax he had been working to.

"Some time in the morning we're going to pay this call," Wharton went on, "even if I have to bring a doctor in to keep him on his pins. A fine collection of lies he'll have ready for us."

"He won't be able to lie his way out of what we've found out today," Travers said. "But there's something I was thinking of on

my way back. That younger sister. There never was a reconcilia-
tion or there'd have been something left in the will. Or else she's
dead, as I put up to you before. But suppose she wasn't dead?
Suppose she was the voice—like a woman's—the hotel operator
heard at eleven o'clock that Monday morning?"

"Oh, no," said Wharton. "If I'd had the chance I'd have told
you. Norris spent quite a lot of time today with that operator,
and he's of the opinion that it wasn't a woman's voice. It had a
higher pitch than any normal man's, and she admitted that she
wondered herself at the time which it was. What we think is that
it was the same high-pitched voice that was supposed to ring up
Stowe."

"Oh, Lord!" Travers shook a woeful head. "I've some sanity to
keep. All this is whirling me round in circles."

"There's one simple way to account for it," Wharton said. "I
don't claim that it's a true theory, but it fits remarkably well.
Stowe did the first telephoning, imitating Pole's queer voice. He
had also arranged for Pole to call him up at the *Blazon* on something very different from any matter of murder. The operator
at the *Blazon* recognized Pole's voice, but Stowe made out that
Pole was telling him to go to the hotel."

"Let's get down to facts, George," Travers told him wryly.
"There isn't a thing we've mentioned tonight that doesn't con-
tradict every other thing—and itself. What was that trap you've
prepared for the man with the squint?"

"Ah!" said Wharton, and looked round for the evening papers. "Have a look at that."

Travers ran his eye over the front page of the late night *Blazon.*

"Story still hot, I see. Same old streamer headline . . . Ah, this
is it probably.

WE CHALLENGE THE MAN WITH THE SQUINT!

Oh, yes, and here's the thing you mean."

"Well?" said Wharton. "What do you think of it?"

"I think it's extraordinarily good. You annoy him by making
out that he's merely a sensation-monger who has always been

wise after the event, and shown his wisdom by revealing what everyone in the know was already aware of. As a final proof, he's challenged to reveal how he came to spot Luffham."

Wharton gave a nod of something very near complacence. "The whole idea is to keep him talking. You and I know there is such a man. Not with a squint necessarily—but the man who writes these letters and at the same time the man who either killed Luffham or was there when it was done." He got to his feet. "Round about ten suit you in the morning?"

"Splendidly," said Travers. "And what're you doing now?"

"Arranging for an army corps to descend on Tarrfold tomorrow," Wharton said. "If we have to interview every man, woman and child in Suffolk we're going to get the complete history of the Smith family. We're going on with the story after the quarrel."

"And with Pole?"

"Yes," said Wharton, and made a grimace that was almost diabolical. "We're certainly going to learn a few facts about Ferdinand Pole." And as he stepped into the lift he fired a final shot. "The man who changed his name. Have you thought of that?"

But the following morning Travers was still in the toast and marmalade stage of breakfast when Wharton turned up.

"Got the letter," he said. "Got the details, that is."

Travers rang for a second cup and Wharton had a freshener of coffee while the type-script was read.

SIR,

So you want to know how I came to discover Luffham when nobody else had any idea he was alive. But I see the game and I am not going to be caught in a trap as clumsy as this one is. This is my very last letter, because any sensible man with no ax of his own to grind must know perfectly that I am by now what I have claimed to be.

But I will tell you with pleasure how I came to spot Luffham. I was always one for prowling round at night and my attention was called to him in a certain restaurant where I dropped in for a meal, because of a certain trick of his that was well-known to us in the old days when he was a public character. I refer to that trick he had of running what I might call his hand, from wrist to forefinger, beneath his nose, just as if he was wiping his nose with his forefinger. I was informed years ago for a fact that his nickname was Snotty, but boys are malicious creatures, and the gesture was only a nervous one when he was hunting for words or ideas.

There will be no more letters from me. One more word to the wise and I say good-by to my public. I have no more executions in mind—at present. If I have to act again, my trade-mark is *Monday*.

Yours, etc.,

JUSTICE.

"The letter of a lunatic," said Travers, and sat back in the chair with eyes closed. "I can see Luffham doing that trick now. He had a moustache, and his finger used to ruffle it. Used to push his nose out of shape."

"Everybody aware of it?" asked Wharton. "Did the caricaturists use it?"

"Not to my knowledge," said Travers. "People who met him any reasonable number of times must have noticed it."

"Then the letter isn't worth the paper it's written on," Wharton said. "Besides, when Luffham went into exile he'd have taken pains to make an entirely new identity."

"I doubt it," Travers said. "A mannerism isn't a mannerism when its owner is aware of it. If Luffham had known the—well, the objectionable side of that trick of his, he'd have dropped it years before he fell out."

"Well, we're going to the *Blazon* to see the original," Wharton said. "You get hold of Pole at once and try to fix an appointment for ten o'clock sharp. Don't mention me."

In the act of dialling, Travers halted.

"If he's fit this morning he'll probably have seen that hall porter. He'll know I called yesterday evening, and he may know you were with me."

"You do as I say," Wharton told him. "Fix the appointment, and if he gets too chatty or curious, pretend the line's weak and hang up."

Travers got on with the phoning and Wharton could gather what was happening.

"Quite his old self again, wasn't he?"

"Almost," said Travers. "Very anxious, however, to know what was in the wind. You might have said he was wondering if it was an ill wind."

"It's going to blow him no good, you can bet your boots on that," Wharton said. "The trouble is what good it's going to blow us."

Ten minutes later he was examining that letter in Maylove's room.

"Same everything," he said, "except the postmark. W.C.1., this time."

"Perhaps that was the trap he was suspecting," Maylove said, "that you'd have all the pillar-boxes watched in Holborn."

"Make it all London while you're about it," Wharton said, and put the letter in an envelope. "Now for the next move. I think we'll say you've had an interview with the Yard and we're convinced the letters were a stunt. Say the time's not quite ripe to prove it, but we knew the whole thing was a fraud from the start."

"What about adding the *Blazon* interviewer saw in Superintendent Wharton's eye a hint that the perpetrator of the fraud might soon find himself in Queer Street for obstructing the course of justice?" That was Travers's suggestion.

"We'll get it written up all right," said Maylove, and pushed a bell.

"I'll get a rough draft down on paper," Wharton said, and began the job at once. Then young Cane came in with something for the editor to okay. He caught Travers's eye and there was an interchange of smiles. Wharton was oblivious to everything but the job in hand.

"Cane's leaving us this week," Maylove broke off to say.

Travers whispered for fear of disturbing Wharton. "You must be sure to come and see me first. When's it likely to be?"

"I don't know yet, sir, not when I'm going to sail, that is."

There was something amazingly friendly in the room at that moment, with the smiles and the exchange of confidences.

"Well, be sure you come and see me."

"I've heard from my cousin and I've sent another cable," Cane whispered, and then turned quickly to take the signed sheet from Maylove.

"Nice boy that," said Maylove, when the door again closed. "Thinks he's a misfit. When they think that, the sooner they go, the better."

"Here we are," said Wharton, and handed over his rough draft. "This may draw him out, and then again it mayn't. Now we won't take up any more of your valuable time." Then as an afterthought: "I'd like a word with Stowe if he's about. Just a little private matter, if there's anywhere we can talk."

That was fixed up in two minutes. Stowe seemed not the least uneasy as he took the two to an empty room; maybe because Wharton seemed in one of his most jocular moods. Stowe put chairs for them and offered his cigarette case. Wharton said he hadn't time.

"As a matter of fact," he said, "it wasn't anything to do with the Delayne murder I wanted to see you about. It was a personal matter."

"Anything I can do at any time?" began Stowe.

"Arising out of that holiday of yours in Switzerland."

Stowe stiffened.

"In these days of cruises and tours," went on Wharton, "you never know when it mayn't be useful to know the ropes—other people's ropes."

Stowe was wary, and he was puzzled.

"You had a good time, for instance, at the Gastner Hotel? It was one you could recommend?"

Stowe was relieved. He almost let out a breath, but he certainly beamed.

"Why, yes. They do you very well—very well indeed."

"Hm!" went Wharton, and appeared to notice that Stowe was still standing. "Sit down a minute. You're not in all that hurry."

"Well, I won't say as—"

"For instance, you've got time to tell us just where you did spend that holiday."

Stowe's eyes narrowed. "I'm afraid I don't get you."

Wharton was putting on his best paterfamilias manner.

"You see, you never were at the hotel, and you didn't return by plane. In fact, you were in England all the time."

"Oh?" He was the least bit scared, and Wharton's manner was puzzling. "And where in England do you reckon I was?"

"That," said Wharton, "I may be able to tell you at the proper moment." Then to Travers's surprise he slowly got on his feet. "When that moment comes, it may mean trouble for you. Isn't that so?"

Stowe was staring. For some reason or other he was taken by utter surprise. Then his eyes narrowed again.

"Well, what about it?"

"Nothing at all," said Wharton disinterestedly. "You're the one who's going to do things. You'll probably make up your mind to come and have a heart-to-heart talk with me, for instance."

He was already at the door, with Travers following lamely.

"Just a minute," burst out Stowe. "I'm not admitting a thing you've said. And what right had you to go enquiring into my movements?"

Wharton held out his hand. "Good-by. We'll go into all that when you come and see me. And don't make it too late. Why seek trouble when a few words could—" Then showman as he always was, he whipped round with a glare. "Or would you rather talk now?"

"I've got nothing to talk about," Stowe told him. "If you think you've got anything on me, all I can say is Go ahead."

But Wharton was already moving on towards the lift. Travers tackled him as soon as they reached the outer pavement.

"I wish you wouldn't spring those surprises on me, George. And what have you got up your sleeve against Stowe?"

"Not a thing," Wharton said. "I've owned up to nothing, I've proved to my own satisfaction that he's badly scared, and I'm now expecting him to talk. What's more, I've an idea that after what's just happened, he may wish to get into communication with somebody. That's why I've arranged for a man to be sitting on his tail."

"What if he phones?"

"The luck of the game. But what I'm expecting is that he may ring up Pole while we're there. Better hurry, hadn't we? It's practically ten now."

The hall-porter was a chatty individual who was plainly accustomed to taking liberties. He hailed Travers like an old friend.

"Morning, sir. Mr. Pole is all right this morning, sir."

"You've seen him?"

"Oh, yes, sir. I told him all about yesterday evening. Lift, sir, or will you walk up?"

"Walk, I think," said Travers, and caught Wharton's eye. Round the bend of the winding stairs he imparted his fears. "We shall find Pole rather too ready, I fear."

Wharton growled a something. Travers pushed the bell, and Pole was opening the door at once. He showed no dismay at the sight of Wharton, maybe because he was too busy with his own feelings, for he was looking far from himself. His cheeks, usually a flaky shrimp, were slightly yellow, and there were purplish bags beneath his eyes.

"Do come in," he said. Then, indicating the dressing-gown: "Excuse me receiving you like this, but as you know, I've been none too fit. Just a sudden indisposition."

He went on chattering away in a tone that was pathetically subdued, and there was an unreality about everything that was making Travers wonder. Why should Pole accept Wharton as a matter of course, and why should he be gabbling away with all that false geniality to hide a nervousness? Even Charlie was unusual, for his cage was swathed from the morning's daylight.

"They tell me you had a nasty shock," Wharton began. "You'll have to take care of yourself. A physical shock, was it?"

"A purely personal matter," Pole said. "It wasn't a shock at all—really, though the doctor insisted it was. A slight heart attack, I'd call it."

"Between you and me," Wharton went triflingly on, "I thought when I heard it, it might be the shock of seeing somebody you hadn't seen for years. Someone you thought dead. You know the kind of shocks we get?"

And Pole was getting a shock at that very moment. Then from somewhere a reassurance came, and a wonder. The gaping mouth closed and the eyes narrowed. Then he smiled—with an effort.

"Well, I don't know who I should see like that—I mean, thinking they were dead?"

Wharton swivelled his eyes lazily on him.

"What about Lettice Smith?"

There was no sallow on Pole's face then but a flare of crimson.

"You know," said Wharton. "Lettice Smith, who once lived at Little Tarrfold."

Pole's head was all at once in his cupped hands and Travers thought for a shameful moment he was going to blubber. Wharton was looking down amusedly, knowing that Pole was hunting for words. Pole looked up to catch his quizzical look.

"So you know then?"

"Oh, yes," said Wharton. "We know some remarkably queer things, that look like landing some people in Queer Street." His tone took on a magisterial abruptness. "Tell me why you told those lies about never having spoken to her in your life."

"It wasn't a lie. It was true!" Pole was shrilling the words at him. "I tell you I didn't know who she was till yesterday afternoon. That was the shock—when I found out."

Somehow in that second, Travers knew that another balloon had been punctured. Then a hope came, that it was the story Pole had prepared, and Wharton would prove it still to be lies. Wharton was waving an inviting hand.

"Well, ease your mind and tell us all about it."

Pole looked away. The theatrical prelude came.

"Do you mind if I mix myself a drink? I know it's early but I'd like something to steady me."

"Why not?" Wharton asked amiably. "That's the time for a tonic—when you badly need it."

Pole mixed the drink, took a long pull, and sat in the chair with fingers round the glass, like a somewhat shattered man of the world.

"I saw a certain picture of her," he said. "The one in the *Blazon,* and it was taken at some peculiar angle that made me hold my breath. I went all hot and cold, if you know what I mean, and then I knew it couldn't be true. Then I started putting things together, and her mother's name—and I fairly rushed out of here to the *Blazon.* On my way I passed the *Record* window with all those photographs in, so I went in. They know me there."

"Yes?" said Wharton.

"Well, then I knew for certain. They'd got some old photographs from somewhere—fifteen years old some of them." He shook his head, and all at once was leaning down with head in hands again. "That was when the real shock came."

"And you'd swear in a court of law that you'd never spoken to her for years?"

Pole raised his head, then drew himself up with dignity.

"I'd swear it anywhere."

"And you never suspected a thing when you submitted that play to her and she turned it down?"

"I tell you, No. Outside bread-and-butter I've no interest whatever in the stage. A friend of mine gave me an idea—I can give you his name—and said it would suit her. I wrote it and got opinions on it. Everything else I've told you."

Wharton nodded. "Well, let's go back a good few years. What happened when she found out?"

For a moment it seemed to Travers that Pole was really terrified. Wharton was looking away, and Travers wanted to call to him—and then something of the fright had gone and the face was watchful.

"Found out what?"

"About you carrying on with the sister."

"Carrying on?"

"My dear Pole," said Wharton. "Are you deaf or am I dumb? You know the meaning of carrying on?"

"Oh, yes," said Pole, and smiled sheepishly. "But there wasn't any—really. It was all jealousy. She wrote me a letter and said she never wanted to see me again. So I didn't see her again. I was piqued and almost before I knew it, I was abroad. When I came back after a year or so, I looked her up, but she'd sold the place and gone. After that I realized it had all been infatuation, so I merely proceeded to forget. I thought I had forgotten—till yesterday evening."

"And you've never heard of either of the sisters again?"

"Never. Not till yesterday."

His eyes were still with a strained intentness on Wharton's face. Wharton grunted.

"And why did you change your name?"

Pole gave a care-free shrug of the shoulders. "Professional reasons. I thought the old name somewhat effeminate—for an author."

"I see. And would you tell me how you first came to meet Miss Smith—as she then was?"

"Why, yes. I was staying with an old aunt at Ipswich, and my mother was with me. There was a performance for charity of some Shakespearean play or other—*As You Like It,* it was—and we all went. We were introduced afterwards; my mother and I called, then my mother died—and there you are."

Wharton got to his feet. "Well, it was certainly a surprise to you, finding out what you did. And if we want to dig down deep into—say—Little Tarrfold, you'll do all you can to help?"

"Why, certainly," said Pole.

"Don't stir," Wharton told him. "We can let ourselves out all right."

Travers smiled. "Sorry I haven't had the chance of explaining what I really came round for. Some other time, perhaps, when you're—"

Then suddenly he was darting forward, for Pole had staggered where he stood. Travers lowered him into the chair.

"My God, George, he's fainted!"

Wharton poured a quick brandy. Travers dashed water from the sideboard decanter. Pole was soon opening his eyes, but his face was deathly white.

"Take it easy," Wharton said. "You just were knocked out, that's all. Finish this up . . . That's right, now . . . Now lie back."

In a minute Pole was rousing himself and a faint colour was in his cheeks. Yet another minute and Pole was insisting that he was all right. There was no need for anyone to stay and if he wanted the doctor, he would ring. He would lie down quietly for an hour, and by then he would be himself. He had had attacks like that before.

At the end of Lapford Street Wharton held out his hand.

"You're not going straight back?" said Travers, surprised.

"Yes," said Wharton laconically. "I've had enough talk to last me for a bit. I'm going to lock myself up where no one can get at me—and think things over."

Travers was none too sorry for a respite, but the Thursday found him eager again, though with no wish to worry Wharton. A thick fog had descended on town, and he kept himself to the house, knowing that Wharton would ring in his own time. Then the midday *Blazon* appeared, and Justice seemed to have fulfilled his threat, for the taunts were not taken up and there was no letter.

The fog lightened that afternoon and while Travers took a stroll, Wharton rang up. All that Palmer had to report was that the message had been that there was no news. The Friday came and the fog with it, denser than ever. Wharton rang up soon after breakfast.

"Nothing doing at the moment," he said. "Nothing that would interest you, that is. Anything happens, you shall know at once."

"You sound a bit tired," Travers told him. "You must take care of yourself, you know, George."

Wharton mumbled a something, and then the name Stowe became audible.

"Haven't got a thing on him. He's just been going about his work as if he dreamt what I told him."

"Anything from Tarrfold?"

"Not a thing beyond what we can guess. Norris and everybody is up to the eyes and nothing coming out of it."

"Drop in and have a spot of dinner tonight," Travers said. "Any time you like, and we'll arrange accordingly."

"Maybe I will," Wharton said, and asked if it would be all right to ring up about it later.

So when the phone bell went just after four o'clock that afternoon, Travers was there by the time Palmer appeared. But the smile went startlingly from his face at the first words he heard.

"Yes . . . speaking."

"Message from Superintendent Wharton, sir. Will you go to Marsham Mansions straightaway, sir, and he's on his way there now. A Mr. Pole, sir, who he said you'd know . . . Yes, sir, he's been murdered!"

CHAPTER XI
CATASTROPHE

TRAVERS MADE his way through that fog like a man gone frantic. In its heavy, depressing darkness he felt a new descent of horror, and all the helplessness of a world from which the orderings of reason had gone. With Pole dead, theories were blown to smithereens, unless it might be that the last tragedy was the solution of the three.

In the hall of the flats one or two people were standing about as curious people will. Travers's long legs took the stairs two at a time. A constable stood by Pole's door, and the porter was there, and inside was a uniformed sergeant whom Travers did not know.

"Mr. Travers, sir? That's all right then, sir."

The body of Pole lay on the carpet, with cushion for pillow and bolsters propping the head. Travers heard the stertorous breathing and stared amazed.

"He's not dead!"

"No, sir," the sergeant said. "That was the fault of the porter who found him. He thought he was dead. Had a bit of sense, though, to go and ring up the Yard."

"Badly hurt, is he?"

The sergeant gave a snort.

"The doctor reckons he may snuff out before they can get him over for the operation, but he's the windy sort, sir, if you know what I mean. Didn't seem to me to know too much about it. He's just gone to arrange. Something went wrong with the phone or they'd have been here by now."

"Any idea how it happened?"

"Not the foggiest, sir. Don't even know what it was done with."

Travers moved over to where Pole lay. The cheeks had a deathly pallor but the light and the electric fire made curious colourings of warmth in the grey and auburn of his hair. What looked like a bandage pad lay where the back of his skull rested.

Travers shook his head, then straightened himself again and looked about him. The room had no sign of a struggle, so much was plain at first glance. And it had no sign of a visitor—no glasses for drinks and no remnants of tea. One chair alone was drawn up before the electric stove but there was no book, closed or open, to show if Pole had been reading. The bureau was closed, and the room had a look of perfect tidiness.

"Someone coming, sir."

Travers listened. Wharton's voice was heard on the stairs. Then came a second voice which the sergeant hastily whispered was the doctor's.

Wharton came in first, and the young doctor and two ambulance men at his heels. He looked badly shaken and gave Travers no more than a quiet nod.

"Can you people wait a minute before you take him away?"

"The responsibility's yours," the doctor said.

"I accept it," Wharton said curtly. "The living are more important than the half dead. What's your own opinion? Will he live or not?"

"Personally, I think he may. He's got a fighting chance, I'll say that. They're operating at once, that's all I know for certain." He was stooping and feeling the pulse. "He mightn't come round afterwards. All sorts of things may happen. If concussion sets in, for example."

"Then will you keep me informed from step to step," Wharton said. "I want to know whether I'm handling a murder or a murderous assault. Know where his keys are?"

The doctor found them in a case in the trouser pocket. Wharton took them over and accepted responsibility.

"Right," he said. "I've finished with him now. A lucky thing you haven't got more than a hundred yards to go."

He followed the small procession out and down to the outer door.

He came back to the room still looking like a man who has suffered a personal loss.

"Glad you got here," he said to Travers. "A nice thing to happen, wasn't it? Absolutely puts the lid on everything."

A lugubrious shake of the head and he got to work.

"What do you know, sergeant?"

"Nothing at all, sir."

"How'd you get here?"

"The porter caught my man outside, sir, and he called me from here."

"Seen or heard anything you'd like to call my attention to?"

"No, sir, I don't know that I have."

"I won't keep you then," said Wharton. "Fewer people we have cluttering up the place, the better. Leave your prints out there in case we want to check. And send that man of yours in here."

"What do you know?" Wharton asked the constable.

"I don't know as I know anything, sir. The porter out there, he fetched me and reckoned someone had been murdered—"

"What time?"

"Four o'clock to the dot, sir. St. Martin's was striking just as he hollered to me."

"Yes, what then?"

"Then I come up, sir, on my own, because he'd saved time by slipping along to the hospital. I saw the door open and him lying here like he said. So I rung my sergeant and by that time him and a doctor was back."

"Notice anything you'd like to tell me about?"

"Can't say as I did, sir."

"Right," said Wharton. "Stay on duty outside that door. You know nothing—understand? Keep everybody off who hasn't got proper business. Send that porter in and leave your prints outside for checking."

The porter came in, and he was not the perky individual of their last call, but a staider man of the best part of fifty, though his specs made him look older.

"You're an important man," said Wharton with a brusque geniality. "The star witness, in fact. And how'd you come to have so much sense as to do all the things you did?—phoning the Yard, and so on."

"Well, sir, I read a bit," the man said. "I know how things ought to be done. I've been reading up all this Murder on Monday business, sir—"

Wharton cut him dead short there.

"Name?"

"Brown, sir. Edwin Brown. Twenty-seven Oldbury Street, Islington."

"Wait for it," Wharton told him. "All the trimmings can come later. Tell us what happened this afternoon."

"This afternoon, sir." He rubbed his chin. "Well, sir, I brought up the jar of paste as Mr. Pole wanted it urgent -"

"Wait a minute! Wait a minute!" Wharton was raising a protesting hand. "Get this clear. Start off at the first occasion this afternoon when you and Mr. Pole had any dealings together, and then go straight on. Right. Off we go."

"Well, sir, the first time was when he buzzed me down to get him a jar of paste—"

"Time?"

"Three-forty to the dot, sir."

"How do you know?"

"By my clock, sir. I can check it any time I like by St. Martin's."

"Right," said Wharton. "Tell us just what Mr. Pole said and how he said it."

"He said, 'Is that you, Brown?' and was I busy. I said I wasn't, not if he wanted anything, so he said he was expecting someone to tea later on and would I slip across to Pflinger's—"

"That delicatessen shop about a hundred yards up?"

"That's the one, sir. He said would I slip along there and get him a jar of their sandwich paste—Number One Russian, they call it—and I was to pay for it, which I did, sir, and I brought it right up to him, and he give me the fifteen pence I paid for it and a tanner for myself."

"What was he like then? Perfectly normal?"

The bell shrilled before Brown could answer. Wharton had the receiver off in a flash. Travers watched the relief on his face as the first words were heard, then he was giving a quick thanks and hanging up.

"First stage through all right," he said. "Got him under the anaesthetic. He isn't hurt so bad as that doctor thought."

Brown went on with his story, and the brief interruption had given him time for thought, and thinking was none too easy a thing under the eye of George Wharton.

"Now you come to mention it, sir, I don't think he was quite himself. He seemed a bit fussy, if you know what I mean, sir?"

Wharton nodded. "I know. It was as if someone important was coming to tea and he was in a bit of a panic."

"That's just what it was, sir. So I put the jar down over there, sir, where it is now"—his finger was pointing to the modern tabular sideboard—"and down I went again. Nothing happened then, sir, till just on ten minutes to four. Then he buzzed down to me again and reckoned as how he was sorry to trouble me but that paste wouldn't be enough as some more people might be coming in, and could I slip off back and get another jar, which I did, sir."

"Pardon me," said Travers, "but are you absolutely sure that it was he—Mr. Pole himself, I mean—who was speaking to you that second time?"

"Why, yes, sir. Who else could it be?"

"That's all right," Travers said. "Just a little point I wanted to make. Go on with your story."

"Well, there ain't no more story, sir. I slipped across in a jiffy and nipped up here with that fresh jar. I tapped on the door and there wasn't no answer so I had it open with my own key and there he was, laying on the floor with his skull bashed in."

"Right," said Wharton. "You're a man of sense and a real good witness." He patted him so effusively on the back that Travers knew some cajolement was coming. "And now something strictly between ourselves. What you tell us shall never go out of this room but this wasn't the first time you'd slipped out for the residents here?"

Brown was regarding him warily. "No, sir, it wasn't."

"Although—strictly between ourselves—you were never supposed to leave the hall downstairs; except in—shall we say?—a case of emergency." Another clap on the back. "I'm not going to get you in any trouble. Why shouldn't you oblige people? I'd have done the same myself. But the real point is this: Has Mr. Pole lately been in the habit of sending you out?"

"I don't know that he hasn't, sir," said Brown with a cautious look. "As a matter of fact, sir, me and Ellis, the other porter, was talking about it only this morning. Not grumbling, you know, sir, because he always tipped you well for what you did."

"And how soon can you have Ellis along here?"

Brown used the phone there and then, and reported that Ellis would be along in under half an hour.

"That's all right," said Wharton. "Now you're to lie down on the floor in the exact position that Mr. Pole was lying in. Have a good look first and make sure you've got the exact spot."

Brown was making an awkward hand of it. Travers suggested that perhaps he might prefer to place some one else in the correct position, so Wharton had a print man in, and Brown was at once happier. The constable was called in to assist and at last the flash was taken. The body had its chalk outline, and Wharton called the other print man in. He had a word with Brown before he turned them loose.

"Go about your job as if nothing has happened. Any questions asked, you know nothing. Get that? You don't know a thing. And when Ellis gets here, you still don't know a thing. Tell him a gent wants him in Mr. Pole's room."

As Wharton drew aside with Travers to leave the print men ample room, the phone went again. Once more Wharton had the receiver off in a flash, and once more his face showed relief.

"Operation proceeding satisfactorily," he told Travers. "Still a bit tricky but they expect to get him round."

The print men brought out a table for their records and Wharton told them to tackle the bureau first.

"You and I are going to talk about this room," he said to Travers, as they drew back again. "Nothing about what's happened elsewhere. Just this afternoon, and no more. And tell me if I caught the drift of that question you put to Brown. You were implying Pole was getting him out of the way?"

"Partly," said Travers.

Wharton seemed a bit nervy still. He raised a quick hand.

"For the love of Heaven, let's make sure where we are. Pole expected a visitor and he didn't want Brown to see him. He didn't want anybody to see him." He broke off. "Just a minute. Nip off downstairs and ask Brown if he knows Stowe. Just describe him."

Travers reported that Brown had no recollection of Stowe. So many hundreds of callers came in, and friends with residents, that it was impossible to keep track.

"Then it may have been Stowe he expected," Wharton said.

"It may even have been Maud Smith," said Travers quietly.

Wharton's eyes opened, then he clicked his tongue. "What's the sense of raking up all that? Keep to this job or we'll get nowhere. Now where was I? Oh, yes. While Brown was getting the paste the caller came up. He was in one of those two rooms there while Brown was handing the paste over. He was here with Pole till ten to four. Then Pole rang down again to get Brown out of the way so that the caller could get clear."

"That was my point," Travers said. "Did Pole himself ring to Brown, or was it the man who attacked him—and after he'd attacked him?"

"I see." Wharton did some lightning thinking. "That implies two or three things. Pole must have told him—let's call him X, to save trouble—Pole must have told X the device employed to get X into the flat unobserved."

"Why not?"

"Also X must have been perfectly familiar with Pole's voice and perfectly confident in his own powers of mimicry."

"Why not?" asked Travers again. "I'll guarantee to imitate Pole's voice here and now with sufficient nearness to scare the life out of that porter downstairs."

Wharton grunted.

"But may I suggest something just as feasible," Travers went on. "X told Pole to ring up the porter and have the coast clear. No sooner had Pole done so than X smashed him across the skull. A second to make sure he was dead, and down X went and out."

"Yes," said Wharton. "That's almost certainly it. The body was lying just in front of the phone. Between it and the bureau."

"The wildest of questions," said Travers, "but suicide's quite out of all possibility?"

"Absolutely," Wharton said. "That was the first thing I asked that doctor who examined him. He'd had three or four murderous blows on the back of the skull."

"Then the murderer must have brought his own weapon."

"Why not?" said Wharton in his turn. "But wait a minute. As soon as X got in here, Pole put him in another room because Brown might have been up at any time. The pavements are wet from the fog and X's boots might have left a mark. We'll get a man and have a look. This study place looks the likeliest."

Travers looked on while Wharton and his man went over the carpet with infinite care, each square foot beneath the glass. Then the bedroom was tried, and there was never the trace of a footmark. Then the constable looked in to say that the other porter had arrived and was waiting. Before Wharton could see him, the phone went again.

Wharton blew out a breath as he replaced the receiver.

"Everything still all right. The operation should be over in another quarter of an hour. But he won't be round for a long while after."

Ellis was the perky individual who shared the porter's duties with Brown, and looked the sort who suffered from an itching palm. There was not much perkiness about him when Wharton had finished with the preliminaries.

"And now," Wharton said, "I want you to get your memory to work. No lies and no prevarications. You're getting into no trouble and what you used to make on the side by obliging people isn't worrying me a hoot. Start on the Tuesday, the day when Mr. Pole had his shock. You were on duty all that day. Did he send you out to do anything—get you off the premises, if you like—during that day? . . . didn't? Well, we'll go on to the next day. You were on duty then?"

"Yes, sir," Ellis said. "You see, we work turn and turn about. I was day duty till yesterday. From then I'm on nights for a week."

"Well, what about the Wednesday?"

"Yes, sir," said Ellis. "Wednesday, about one o'clock, he came down to the hall and asked me to slip out and buy him a midday *Blazon*."

"Anyone else in the hall while he was with you?"

Ellis said the hall was empty.

"And then Mr. Pole sent you out again somewhere else shortly afterwards?"

Ellis shook his head. Wharton thought for a moment.

"But perhaps you weren't in the hall all the time during the next half-hour or so?"

Ellis admitted frankly enough that he had a dozen jobs to see to, and that all day long he was merely in the hall and out.

"That's all right then," Wharton said. "Nothing that night?"

Ellis reminded him that Brown was on duty then.

"Yesterday then," said Wharton, but Ellis shook his head again. Then he volunteered the information that Brown knew something.

Wharton warned Ellis about promiscuous chatter, and sent him to relieve Brown. When all the questionings were over, certain facts had emerged, and Wharton set them down on paper.

Day	From	till Approx.
Wednesday	1.00 PM	1.30 PM
Thursday	9.00 PM	9.30 PM
Friday	3.40 PM	3.50 PM

"Those were the times when Pole had a visitor or visitors he wanted no one else to see. Two of the lengths of stay are pure guesswork. All three are after he'd had that shock. Now for the test."

The test was a questioning of Brown and Ellis to discover when Pole had first had the mania for sending porters out on errands. And as Wharton expected, Pole had first tried the trick on the Wednesday. Brown did say he remembered a previous occasion a fortnight or so earlier, but was unable to give full corroborative details.

"There we are then," said Wharton. "It seems to me an unanswerable statement to say that the visitor or visitors were a consequence of the shock. But for the shock he'd never have had them. If the shock was the discovery that Lettice Smith was Laura Delayne, how does it help?"

"As far as I'm concerned, it doesn't," Travers said. "I could put forward a dozen theories that I'd have no particular faith in myself. Why Pole should discover his old sweetheart had been murdered and then develop a mania for entertaining surreptitious visitors—well, it's beyond me. The only hope is that what you've discovered may fit in with something we haven't discovered yet."

"You're right," said Wharton. "We'll take a chance on his private papers now they've finished with the bureau. Found anything at all?"

But the print men had found nothing. Then yet again the phone went.

"Thank you very much," said Wharton. "I see . . . And shall I send two men along? . . . You're quite sure . . . I mean, the responsibility's yours and it's one I shouldn't care to undertake . . . Very well, then. In two hours from now."

"Operation successful," he reported. "The patient ought to be coming round in two hours' time, though it might be later. I wanted to plant two men there in case he came round earlier but they wouldn't have it."

Travers began sorting out the notes and scraps of manuscript, with, as he afterwards confessed, the wild hope that perhaps Pole had left a record of at least the outlines of that perfect crime of which he had once boasted. Wharton, having doubtless in mind what had been discovered from the counterfoil of a certain hotel cheque book, began opening the small inner drawers. Pole's current cheque book was soon found but there were no dramatic discoveries.

Then something struck him and he appealed to Travers.

"Take a look at these counterfoils, will you? See anything funny?"

Travers remarked that whereas all had dates and payee, one alone—the latest drawn—had neither. Scrawled on it was what looked like M.L.

"My God!" said Wharton. "M for Maud and L for Lettice!"

"You can't pay a dead woman money," Travers said. "Why shouldn't it be M for a thousand and L for pounds?"

Wharton stared, then once more went into action.

"There may be a chance. Ten minutes gone since the hospital rang up, so we've got plenty of time. It's the end of the quarter so that bank may be working late. Here, you take this and cut along. Knock the damn doors down if nobody comes."

Within five minutes he was being rung up for an identification of Travers and Travers himself was back from the bank inside the half hour.

"Plumb right, George," he said. "Pole cashed that cheque on the Wednesday morning, after you and I saw him here. It was for a thousand and he took it in pound notes, and as he hadn't that much in his accounts, he authorized the selling of securities the bank held for him."

"Blackmail," said Wharton, and licked his lips. "And who the devil should blackmail him? He wouldn't have minded owning up to that Lettice Smith affair?" And then all at once he was smiting his fist in his palm. "My God! suppose there's someone who knew he committed one or both of those murders—and made him pay through the nose."

"Then why did the blackmailer kill the goose that was laying such golden eggs?" Travers let the apt question settle, and then had another point to make.

"Do you know, George, when I came in here this minute ago, I noticed something strange about the room—"

Wharton was waving his hand for silence.

"I'll ring up that hospital and make sure. It scares me stiff to think he might come round and we shouldn't be there."

So he rang and patiently introduced himself. Travers gathered that he was making something of a nuisance of himself. Wharton confirmed the impression as he hung up.

"Well, they still insist that they're right. It's their funeral, not mine. Now what was that you were saying about the room being funny?"

"It's this," Travers said. "When I walked in here first I had eyes only for Pole. While I was here I thought in terms of Pole. When I came in again just now with a comparatively open mind I spotted at once that the room was different. Charlie's gone!"

"Charlie?"

"Yes. Charlie, the parrot, and his cage. You remember that marvellous parrot I told you about. Worth fifty pounds probably?"

"You mean the one who was here stole it?"

"Heaven knows. Fog or no fog, nobody could expect to walk about with a parrot in a huge affair of a cage and not be spotted. I know he might have had a car waiting outside. He shook his head. It might have been a joke on the part of one of Pole's intimates. He told me all his friends used to come up here to listen to it."

One of the print men had been pricking his ears. "You'll excuse me, sir, but there's a parrot cage in that room there."

The room was the study and the cage was in a corner behind some empty cases.

"Beginning to look fishy," Wharton said, and sent for Brown.

"Mr. Pole have any callers this morning?"

"Yes, sir. A man with a short stubby beard. Looked like some sort of workman. Carrying a little black bag, he was."

"Then why the devil didn't you say so when I was questioning you before?" glared Wharton. "What was his business?"

"I don't know, sir, and I didn't ask. He said, 'Party of the name of Pole?' and I told him where to go. That's all I know about it, sir."

"You didn't see him come down again?"

Brown shook his head. He thought he did, and then again he thought he didn't.

"Why the devil should he sell the bird and not the cage?" asked Wharton plaintively. "And if he sold the bird to this man, then it was to raise money; and what did he want money for when he could walk only half a street into the bank and get it?"

Then he nodded.

"I'm going to get the ins and outs of this."

He rang up the Yard. Two men were to get details from Brown of the man with the beard, and all local animal shops were to be questioned at once. He took no end of pains over that phoning and then warned Brown of what to expect.

"How's time now?" he asked Travers.

"Not too far off," Travers told him.

"You don't say so!" Two minutes later he was hurrying out to the dense fog of the street with Travers at his heels.

Pole was in a room by himself, with a nurse in a chair by the bedside. A doctor, strange to the Scotland Yard pair, was at hand.

"No sign of him coming round yet," the doctor whispered to Wharton. Then he made signs to the nurse and the three men drew back to the open annex. Travers could see the head of the injured man, with its swathes of bandages, and the face that was frighteningly pale in the dim light.

The doctor began talking about the operation and how straightforward it had been after all, and illustrating on Wharton's skull, and that was when Travers drew out of earshot, with all his old squeamishness at the thought of blood and brains. His own brains seemed all at once numb, with the over-tiredness that comes sometimes after a desperate concentration, and he had that queer depression again and felt the presence of ominous things. The smells of mortality were all about him and something of the silence of fate, and he fidgeted as he stood there and nervously wished for things to happen.

The doctor went to the bed again and stooped over the patient. Then he came back and whispered to Wharton and went away. Wharton sat stolidly on, with an expression that was almost morose. Half an hour went by, and Travers began a restless prowling about the small room. Then the nurse looked quickly in and indicated that the smallest noise was too much.

The doctor came back, smiled at Wharton and went through to the bed. Then there was more whispering when he came back.

"I don't care if it's only two words we get out of him, if they're the right ones," Wharton was saying. "I've done this sort of thing hundreds of times. You let me handle it and everything'll be all right. And soon as he tells us who it was that did it, then I've finished. The rest'll do when he gets round properly again."

The nerve-racking minutes went on. Then at long last the nurse was moving. The doctor flitted forward and was all at once at the bedside, and was making signs for Wharton to come. Two chairs were silently placed and Wharton and Travers took them. The nurse moved to the foot of the bed; the doctor stood by the pillow, eyes on the white, placid face.

Ten more slow minutes went by and then the crisis came. There was the faintest fluttering of eyelids, and before Travers was hardly aware, Pole was looking wide-eyed out. The eyes blinked and the doctor placed himself in their line of view. He smiled and stooped, his voice a gentle hush.

"You're feeling better now, aren't you? . . . You had an accident but you're all right now. . . . You were in your room and somebody struck you."

Wharton was all at once there. His voice was soft and somehow generous and pleading.

"Who did it, Mr. Pole? Just tell me who it was that struck you . . . Nothing else, Mr. Pole. Only just that."

Maybe Pole remembered then, for a quick stare of fright was in his eyes. Or perhaps it was a greater fear, for the eyes were on the motionless, watching figure at the foot of the bed, and he was realizing where indeed he was. His voice was a strangled whisper.

"Am I ill? . . . Am I going to die?"

"No, no, no." That was the doctor's soothing voice again. "Of course you're not going to die. You're going to be well in no time."

But he was making signs, and again Wharton drew abreast.

"Who did it, Mr. Pole? Just tell me who did it, and we won't trouble you a second longer."

Pole's eyes closed wearily. A frightening minute and they opened again. His voice was a halting whisper but its tenseness reached to where Travers now stood by the foot of the bed.

"The man with the squint . . . He dropped . . . his glasses . . . I saw . . ."

"My God!"

Wharton's startled voice cut in as Pole's last low whisper died. For Pole's head had fallen sideways and the doctor was waving them frantically from the room.

CHAPTER XII
A SHOCK FOR CHARLIE

THEY STEPPED THROUGH the doors to the pavement fog. Wharton stood there indecisively, coat collar hunched about his ears, and he was like a man whose world has suddenly been kicked endways. Then he whipped round on Travers.

"What do you make of it? Was he off his head? Or are you and I?"

"We may be, but he wasn't," Travers told him. "You could see he meant to get that something off his mind, if it was the last thing he ever said. Besides, a man's pretty sure of his words when he's been near the edge of eternity."

"How should he know that?" countered Wharton. "Didn't the doctor tell him he'd soon be all right?" He made a movement, halted again, and his hand went out. "I'm going back there. I'll let more daylight in on this if I have to stay all night. You go along to the flat. Someone'll be there by now if Norris isn't."

He was back through those doors at once. Travers groped his way along in the fog, and when each moment he heard those words that Pole had gasped out with what might after all have been his last communicable breath, he knew the world of theory and hard logic had collapsed and utterly gone. Now the urgent need of his own mind seemed to bare itself of every thought it had ever harboured. The slate must be wiped clean and a new writing be made. Previous values must be reassessed in the light of Pole's staggering disclosure.

As he stepped into the hall again he knew at least one clue that might await a search. Pole had known the attacker for the man with the squint because the glasses had come off. Perhaps they had broken, and the attacker had stopped before he fled, and picked up the larger fragments. But however small a fragment might be left, the experts could make a reconstruction and know the oculist's prescription.

As he came to the landing he saw with the constable at the door a sturdy-looking elderly man with a greyish beard. The door was open and Norris was just dismissing the print men. He came forward at once when he caught sight of Travers. He was of the patient, relentless kind, was Norris, and he heard with merely a shaking of the head all Travers had to tell.

"Well, we know where we are at last, sir, that's one good thing. And about the broken glasses, I'll see to it myself at once. Of course, we've got to contend with the fact that the glasses might have been ordinary plain ones, just coloured dark." Then he too saw the elderly man and remembered. There's a man there, sir, been waiting best part of an hour, to be questioned about a parrot.

Travers took his man to the privacy of the study. His name, he said, was Jonathan Porter, and he was head man and rough-and-ready vet to Padsley's of Long Acre. Travers offered him a cigarette and put him at ease.

"First I heard about it was this morning," he said, "when the guvnor said Mr. Pole was ringing up about a parrot what he'd bought from us. A rare nice bird and a clever one too, it was. Better take your little bag, he said, so I took my little black bag—"

"Like the doctors have?"

"That's right, sir." He gave a bit of a grin. "For all I knew, that parrot might have pupped. Well, I walked in here, sir, when the gent opened the door, and he reckoned the bird had got psitta-cosis"—he didn't pronounce it quite like that—"you know, sir, that there parrot disease. 'Lummy!' I says, 'what are you goin' to do about it, sir? Don't look to me as if there's anything wrong with it.' Then you ought to have heard him, sir. Was I there to carry out his orders or was I not?—and his orders was to destroy the bird there and then. But not while he was looking—oh, no! One o' them with a kind heart, he was, sir; so I told him when he was ready I was, so he went over to that desk there and I opened the cage and had Charlie by the neck and claws before he knew it and whipped him into my bag.

"'There you are, sir,' I says; 'broke his neck as clean as wink-ing'—making out I'd done the bird in, you see, sir? He didn't want to look in the bag—not him."

"You mean, the bird was all right shut up in that bag?"

"Course he was, sir—at least for a minute or two. So he gives me half a quid for myself and says I'm not to say anything except to my boss."

Travers was bringing out his note-case and examining its contents.

"Your boss will not be able to dispose of the live parrot, I take it—"

"This was between you and me, sir."

"No panic," smiled Travers. "It is between you and me. Let's cut preliminaries. I want that parrot, if it's healthy—"

"Not a thing wrong with it, sir. He must have got the wind up about it."

Travers selected a pound note and replaced the case.

"If it's a matter of strict confidence between the three of us, and I guarantee that everything will be satisfactory to Mr. Pole— if he recovers; he's been taken very ill, you know, but not from psittacosis—then there's a chance of my buying it?"

Porter gave a nod and something near a wink. Travers found a card and wrapped it in the note.

"Have it sent round to me—with the price. And see it's in a suitable cage. And you might give my man instructions how to look after it."

Porter whipped a rapid finger to the rim of his hat and was off at once. Travers came out to find Norris straightening his back after that search of the carpet.

"Not a thing here, sir, nor in that other room either. If he broke his glasses, it was a clean break."

The phone bell went then and Norris took the receiver. It was a longish business and Travers went back to the study and examined the parrot's cage, and rummaged about among the oddments. Norris found him there.

"That was Superintendent Wharton, sir, and he says there's no need for you to stay. He reckons Pole's in a bad way. His heart's unexpectedly gone dicky."

"What's keeping him then?" asked Travers, none too sorry to go.

"He had an idea, sir, that it might be possible to pretend you had a squint—just for the purpose of making out you were someone else. One doctor told him it wasn't possible and he's now seeing another." He smiled. "Rare one to cling hold when he's got his teeth into anything, sir?"

"Yes," said Travers, "but he'll have the job of his life trying to convince a doctor that a man can produce a convenient squint."

"You're right, sir," Norris said. "It doesn't seem a feasible thing to me." He screwed up his features into strange shapes in the personal attempt. "Beyond me, sir. But about that parrot business. What shall I say if he comes back?"

Travers smiled and begged the question. "I shouldn't worry. I don't reckon you'll find him in the mood to be interested in parrots."

He reached his flat no more than a minute before Charlie. The bird and cage were installed and the bill paid, and Palmer accepted the occurrence with the stolidity that might have accompanied the arrival of a tradesman's circular.

"Why did you tell Porter you knew all about parrots?" Travers asked.

"Your late mother kept a parrot, sir," Palmer reminded him.

"Lord! so she did," said Travers. "Pretty long time ago though. Still, you take him in with you. Got anything to put over his cage? Find something, if you haven't, because I don't want anyone to know he's here. Soon as anyone comes at any time, cover him up. Just a moment, though. Perhaps he'll give a small selection from his repertoire."

But the indignities of Porter's bag and the further strange surroundings of the last few hours had unsettled the bird, and no cajolements brought a word from him. Palmer bore him off, but remembered something as he opened the door.

"Before I forget it, sir, Mr. Cane rang up—the young gentleman who lunched with you the other day. He wouldn't leave any message, sir, except that it was nothing important, and he said he would ring you in the morning. About nine o'clock, I suggested, sir."

Next morning Cane rang up dead on time. He said that when he was in Mr. Travers's flat he had noticed some china in the cabinets. There were some pieces of his own that he had, and if they were of any value he would rather let Mr. Travers have them than sell them to a dealer.

Travers had the car out and was at Cane's place in under the twenty minutes he had stated. It was a depressing neighbourhood, though the fog had gone and a tentative sun was shining, and near enough though it was to the Tube Station, it seemed scarcely the best place to have chosen. Cane's first words were an apology and a recognition.

"Pretty grim sort of district, isn't it, sir. My mother liked it, though so I stayed on when she'd gone."

"There's many a worse," said Travers. "And how are you? Up to the eyes, I see."

A van stood outside the door and baize-aproned workmen were removing the furniture. There were four rooms and a kitchen in the flat and most were already cleared. Cane explained that he had sold everything to a dealer, as auctions were a cumbrous business and would bring in no more when expenses were all paid. Besides, he was sailing on the Monday.

"That's quick work," Travers said. "I hadn't an idea you were going quite so soon."

Cane said he had had a reply to his cable and had sent another to say he was sailing on the *Warakiki*.

"Half-past ten from Southampton she sails," Cane said, and grinned. "I feel like a kid going to a t-t-treat."

"I expect you do," Travers told him. "Even an old stager like myself can get a thrill out of the whistle of a liner. And have you shaken off the *Blazon* dust?"

"I wouldn't quite say that, sir." He shook his head. "They say absence makes the heart grow fonder, but honest, Mr. T-Travers, I had some good times there."

They had gone through the empty passage to the back room, which had been the living-room, and had a window overlooking a now dingy park, worn bare where lads and young men were kicking a football.

"Not a bad room this," Travers said. "Much better having a ground floor flat, don't you think? No stairs to climb, and all that."

"This is what I rang you up about," Cane said, collecting the three pieces of china from the bare corner where he had put them for safety.

"Ah!" said Travers, with all the collector's anticipation, and took the first from Cane's fingers. Then he grunted, and held both cup and saucer to the light. He grunted again.

"Chelsea undoubtedly. Typical decoration. See this little ladybird crawling towards the leaf?"

"There's two like that, sir," Cane said, producing the other. "And there's this plate. My mother always said that was very old. It belonged to my father's people. It's his sister's son I'm going out to in New Zealand."

"It is old," said Travers. "It's Swansea. Heavy bulbous roses. Unmarked, as I imagined. Pity it's got that slight chip." Then he chuckled. "You see how human nature gets the better of one? My dealer's instincts made me say that, to lower the price. However"—and he laid the pieces on the wide sill of the window—"just how much do you think I should give you for them?"

"I t-t-trust you, sir," Cane said. "Anything you know is fair. Would three pounds be too much?"

Travers thought for a moment or two.

"Ten pounds, I think. A dealer would ask six guineas for each cup and saucer and two guineas for the plate, but he's got a profit to make. Ten pounds I think would be fair."

Cane shook his head. "I don't want all that, sir."

But Travers overbore him. And then while he counted out the notes the collector's instinct again triumphed over the best of manners.

"That wasn't anything of value, was it?"

He was referring to what looked like a small picture standing in the same corner with its back to the wall.

"Not exactly, sir. Only something I was keeping."

There were two things there—a photograph and a small, framed oil of a man in military uniform of the Napoleonic period.

"My great-grandfather," Cane said. "We don't know who did it."

Travers had a good look at it.

"Not unlike the later Romney. I'd have this varnish off if I were you. It'd be worth spending a fiver on." He frowned. "Not Romney though—but quite well painted. And the other?"

But the other was merely an unframed photograph.

"My father, sir."

Travers nodded.

"A gunner, I see. . . . A father to be proud of. . . . Not unlike you either. . . . Killed early, was he?"

"At Loos, sir."

"A bad show that," said Travers, who had personal knowledge. He nodded sympathetically again as he gave the photograph back, then pulled himself up. "Well, I mustn't keep you any longer. But before I forget it. Which island are you bound for? North or South?"

"North Island, sir—Napier."

"Napier? Napier?" He frowned. "Didn't the Argills go to Napier? Or was it Auckland? I'll look it up. . . . Most delightful people, friends of mine," he explained. "Some time since I heard from them though. I'll look up Bill's last letter and let you know. You'd love them. If it is Napier, I'll give you a letter of introduction." He smiled away Cane's thanks. "No use thanking me for something that mayn't materialize."

Cane said he was staying at the *Maypole* in Danvers Street that night and traveling down to Southampton the next day, to avoid the Monday's early rising.

"Splendid," said Travers. "I'll know where to get hold of you then. Now I must bolt."

His hand went out and then he remembered something.

"You've heard about Pole?"

"Pole?" Cane smiled. "No. What's his latest?"

Travers thought for a moment. "Well, keep it to yourself, but he was attacked in his rooms early yesterday evening. Someone smashed his skull in and left him for dead. They rushed him to the hospital and operated. He came round all right but his heart's failing him."

"My God!" said Cane. "How dreadful!" Then his face lighted. "Couldn't they pull him round just long enough to make him speak?"

Travers shook his head. Then he smiled. "There spoke the old crime-reporter. But strictly between ourselves—" He broke off. "I can rely on you for secrecy?"

"Certainly, sir."

"Pole did speak. He said it was the man with the squint!"

Cane stared too and his mouth gaped.

"I know," said Travers. "You're itching to rush back to that desk of yours in Fleet Street."

Cane shook his head, and let out a breath.

"That's all done with, sir. But it's incredible. We all sort of t-t-took that as a joke."

"Well, there we are," Travers said. "It'll be public property by now, I expect—and it won't be a joke." Once more his hand went out. "You'll be hearing from me later. Great pity though, your sailing so soon. I had a great surprise for you."

"Had you, sir?"

"Only my young nephew," Travers said. "I was having him up in town next week-end and was asking you along. Thought you might like to compare Millborough and talk scandal."

"I'd have loved it, sir."

"He's not a bad fellow," Travers said. "Not like you though. He's all brawn and muscle, so to speak. Brains none too obvious. He's been doing pretty well at sport. You didn't have ambitions that way? Didn't even make the second fifteen? You ought to. You're the very spit of a good scrum half."

"I was in the second fifteen," Cane said, "but then I had to leave."

"I remember. Most thoughtless of me." His hand went to the wheel. "And now what's amusing you. The brick I dropped?"

"Oh, no, sir," said Cane. "I was just th-th-thinking about Tuke. You remember, sir. The news editor."

"Oh, yes. I remember Tuke."

Cane was still smiling. "I was thinking how relieved he'd be if that news got out. We used to call him the man with the squint—you know, sir, when the ramp started. Just a joke of course, but he got to know it. He was furious."

"I expect he was," said Travers, and nodded again and smiled as he moved the car off.

He drove the King's Cross way and through traffic incredibly busy, and while his eyes were on the road ahead or the back of a vehicle in front, in the slow-moving stream, his inner eyes were scanning the features of Tuke. Tuke, snappy and disgruntled; the man who wore heavy glasses; the man who had spied one day on Stowe and Pole.

So Travers cut through to Lapford Street and expectantly mounted the stairs. But Pole's flat was barred and sealed, as the porter came chasing to tell him. Thereupon Travers put the Rolls back and called up the Yard. Norris was out but Wharton had that minute come in.

"Just got an hour or two's sleep," he said. "Didn't turn in till daylight this morning."

"How's Pole?" asked Travers.

"In a bad way," Wharton said. "I wasn't very popular there when I went back. They reckoned it was me who knocked him out again."

"Did he come round again?"

"Not a hope," Wharton said. "Now he's clinging on by his eyebrows and developing pneumonia. That was the last news we had. If you can wait a minute I'll get the latest."

"It doesn't matter," Travers said. "Is it public property, by the way, who attacked him?"

"It'll be in this morning's editions," Wharton said. "You got any news yourself?"

"Only about the parrot," Travers said. "I've got it myself. There's a long story attached to it, which I'll tell you later. Pole got the wind up. Thought it had that parrot disease and wanted it destroyed. You know what a windy customer he was likely to be over anything like that."

"And so should I be," Wharton said with a grunt.

Travers, somewhat abashed, broke the news about Tuke. He could almost hear Wharton's brain at work while he took a minute to think it over.

"Perfectly ridiculous," he said. "Better get it cleared out of the way though. Could you slip along?"

"If you like," Travers told him. "But what was Tuke going to get out of it? There was a motive behind everything; that's one of the few things we've got to admit."

Wharton mumbled something about having heard that Tuke had been put on the back shelf.

"The fact that he wasn't made managing editor wouldn't be altered by committing three murders," Travers said. "All the same, I'll go along."

"I wish you would," Wharton said. And before he hung up, "And take my advice and be careful about that damn parrot."

Travers was smiling to himself as he made his way towards the Strand. Irony once more seemed the basis of emotion. What greater irony than that Pole should have been scared of a parrot and then have admitted surreptitiously to the flat the man who had murder in mind? Then the smile went and Travers began to wonder. Pole would never have parted with that parrot if he hadn't been sure. No man kills the thing he loves—Wilde or no Wilde—and when that thing is worth fifty pounds. As for parrot disease, it was no pleasant thing to die from. And the examination of the bird by Porter had most likely been a casual and avaricious one. Travers, in fact, was going hot and cold all over. Five minutes later he was well away from the Strand and in consultation with a vet of his acquaintance.

The vet said he would go along himself and make an examination and take the necessary precautions. Travers rang up to warn Palmer and left with his mind much easier. There was indeed only one uneasiness when he stepped out of the *Blazon* lift—precisely how Tuke should be tackled.

But while he stood there for a moment, thinking things out, Stowe came breezing up. Either he bore no malice or he had never connected Travers with that little fracas with Wharton; or then again he might have been seeing in Travers the man who knew the latest about Pole. In any case he hailed him with enthusiasm.

"Morning, Mr. Travers. Busy for a minute?"

"Not too busy," said Travers. "Why?"

"Tell you what," said Stowe, and whipped him round to the descending lift. "Let's go out and have a quick coffee. Little place next door."

Stowe was a fast worker in his own way, and an overwhelming one. Though he made no abrupt demand, "Well, what's the real dope on the Pole case?" he talked without ceasing till the coffee came and it amounted to much the same thing.

Travers countered with a sad shake of the head.

"I'd like to tell you, but you know how it is. Maybe if I get a chance later . . ."

"But about this man with the squint," went on Stowe. "What clues did you pick up? What did you—"

Travers smiled once more. "My dear Stowe, it's no use trying the exhaustive method. I'm far too wary a bird for that."

But he gave little unimportant snippets of information for which Stowe seemed grateful, and then changed the subject.

"You've lost young Cane then?"

"Not a bad kid," Stowe said. "Too highfalutin for this job though. You know, Mr. Travers, with all due respects to yourself, a man can write a damn sight too good English for a newspaper office."

"I'm sure of it," said Travers whole-heartedly. "How's Tuke, by the way?"

Then Stowe shot him a remarkably queer look. Travers bore it unflinchingly.

"Bit under the weather, old Tuke," Stowe said, and seemed to be assuming the indifference. "He isn't in today—wasn't yesterday neither. Coming Monday though."

"Murder on Mondays?" asked Travers, with a look of infinite craft.

Stowe shot another look, then grinned.

"Bit of a joke, don't you think, pulling his leg? You ought to have heard him when he overheard Ribbold alluding to him as the man with the squint. That's what you were thinking of, wasn't it?"

"Something of the sort," smiled Travers. "A bit awkward though, for Tuke, if he really has a squint?"

"Not he," said Stowe, and sneered. "That's one of the few things the old fool hasn't got. He can't stand the glare, that's why he wears those specs of his. He never wears them at home." Then he gulped down the last of the coffee and shot out a hand. "I'll be popping off now. See you later, Mr. Travers. Thanks for what you told me."

Before Travers could speak he had grabbed the ticket and was gone. Travers ordered a second coffee, and sat thinking things over. Then he went to the nearest call-box and rang Wharton.

"I told you there wasn't a thing in it," Wharton said. "But you don't happen to know his private address, do you?"

Travers smiled and remarked that finding it would be easy work for Wharton himself. Wharton gave a grunt and mentioned casually that he would be along at Pole's flat at two o'clock sharp. As a last after-thought he added that Pole had developed pneumonia in both lungs and was in a bad way.

As Travers stepped out of his own lift he remembered Charlie. But there was good news. The vet had left a note to the effect that the bird was in magnificent health. A bit droopy in the wing, but sound enough in constitution.

"I'm getting quite attached to the bird, sir," Palmer said. "A remarkable—er—animal, sir, if I may say so. Makes the most queer utterances, sir. I was actually forced to laugh once or twice this morning, sir."

"Good for your soul," Travers told him. "See lunch is on at one o'clock sharp, will you? If I get any spare time tonight, I'll have Charlie in and do some laughing for myself."

He was smiling as the door closed. The thought had come that possibly Palmer might prefer to call the parrot Charles.

CHAPTER XIII
FAREWELL TO ENGLAND

TRAVERS FOUND the door of Pole's flat open and Wharton inside. The greeting he received was unusual.

"Going down to Sussex this week-end?" It was Travers's habit to spend most week-ends at his sister's place.

"The squirrel's granary is full and the harvest done," quoted Travers. "In other words, the week-end's practically over. But why do you want to get rid of me, George?"

"We're going to eat humble pie," Wharton said. "We're having a try for the man with the squint. More men on the job and going down into the history of Luffham and Miss Delayne, to see if they ever knew such a man. Pole too."

"I still don't see it," Travers said.

"Give me time and you will," Wharton told him. "Pole's home town was Petersfield. That's where his people came from and where he was born. His father was a solicitor there, so we've discovered through his own lawyer. And Halstead's that way, isn't it?"

"Now I'm seeing things," Travers said. "With regard to the Luffham murder you're enquiring at Halstead about people who knew Luffham and also had a squint. The same at Petersfield, about Pole."

"That's the idea," Wharton said. "We want to go over the name of every pupil who's ever been at that school for the last fifty or so years. That's only one thing in the Luffham enquiry. What's happening is that Norris himself is going down to Petersfield tonight to open the Pole enquiry there. On the Monday he's going on to Halstead, and we hoped you might take him along and give him a suitable introduction—you know, smooth the way."

"Tell you what," said Travers. "When's Norris want to go, by the way? Any time to suit me? Then I'll get a call through to my sister and meet Norris outside the Yard at four o'clock sharp."

Travers used the hall phone while Wharton rang Norris at the Yard. Travers said the scheme would suit him admirably. He would leave Norris at Petersfield, slip back for two nights and a day with Helen and the Major, then pick up Norris on the Monday morning and so to Halstead.

Palmer had been rung to have things prepared, but it was yet short of half-past two and Travers lingered on.

"You know, we ought to have been certain from the first that this man with the squint was real," Wharton said. "He told a lot of lies to try and make us believe he was in the murder business long before last Monday week, and therefore he wasn't. Monday week was his maiden attempt. He was trying to confuse the issue and put himself in the limelight. That's why he owned up to that deformity. He was an exhibitionist, like poor Pole."

He gave a nod of satisfaction, then let his eyes run round the room.

"They say there's a lot in atmosphere. Doesn't seem to be doing me much good though. You got any ideas?"

"I wiped the old slate clean," Travers said. "All that's written on it now is the sequence—the sequence of related events that led up to Pole's murder. We might as well call it that."

"Yes, poor chap," said Wharton, who could weep like a crocodile. "And the sequence is?"

"This," said Travers. "I wrote it down during lunch."

1. Pole claims to be the victim of a plot.
2. Wharton tells him how to discover the Chief Conspirator.
3. Pole at once is bursting to go and do so. His look and manner showed it.
4. He left immediately to have things out with somebody, presumably that Chief Conspirator, who was therefore known to him.

5. But he got a shock that staggered him. Perhaps the C.C. brought it home to him that he was up to the neck in it himself.

6. Pole buys off the C.C. with a thousand pounds.

7. Gets the C.C. surreptitiously into the flat to do so.

8. But the C.C. insists on a further appointment. He forces Pole to admit him again, and then, because Pole knows too much, murders him—or thinks he has done so.

"A bit muddled in tenses," said Wharton irritatingly. "But it's a sensible document. A most sensible one. Do you mind if I keep it?"

"Do," said Travers. "Tenses and all."

Wharton ignored the mild riposte.

"There was something I was trying to think out myself, while I was having my humble snack and half-pint. Talking of conspirators and being in the swim, and this paper you've just given me, your idea is that the man with the squint and Pole started off on a scheme?"

"That was part of the sequence."

"Well, let's take the first two murders and see what we can't get away from—say in the connecting link line. Pole and Stowe were mixed up in both. Pole was a likely suspect and Stowe was absent from the first and wouldn't own up where he was."

"What about motive?"

"I was coming to that," Wharton said. "Motive's the main clue in any murder, and I've proved it all my life long. Pole got tremendous and profitable publicity out of the first murder, and so did Stowe. Stowe took jolly good care not to miss it. The second murder gave them a bit more."

Travers gave a wry smile.

"That virtually makes either Pole or Stowe to be the man with the squint! After all, he committed the third murder."

"I'm not going to go so far as that," Wharton said. "I say the man with the squint was in partnership with Pole, and perhaps Stowe. But Pole couldn't have been the man with the squint for the simple reason that he didn't murder himself. Stowe couldn't have disguised himself as the man with the squint, because his hulking great form doesn't lend itself to disguise, and Pole must have recognized his voice. Therefore the man with the squint was a third, distinct person."

"Very well then," said Travers. "Accepting the logic of that as I do, I merely ask what the man with the squint expected to get out of the partnership?"

"He got a thousand quid, didn't he?"

"Oh, my hat!" said Travers. "I want to know what he got out of scheming to murder Luffham and Laura Delayne."

"All in good time," said Wharton. "It's got me beat, and I'll own as much. But you'd better be pushing on, hadn't you? It's getting on for three."

"What are you doing yourself?" Travers asked him.

"Don't know yet," Wharton said. "But it's Saturday night and I'm not going home." And to Travers's polite look of enquiry, "B.B.C. brand of humour on tonight, by the *Radio Times*. They've been bally-hooing this week about a new fresh-to-the-minute song by Giggling Gilbert."

Travers had known Norris before his Chief-Inspector days and had always liked him. And though Travers had never an ounce of snobbery in his make-up, he was glad Norris was going to handle the Halstead end of the enquiry, for Norris was a man for whom there would never be blushes. He had small Latin, and the only Greek he knew might he the name of a street, but Norris was versed in tongues of which Halstead had never heard, and carried about with him that honest simplicity which some consider the perquisite of gentility.

Norris said he would be quite at home cooperating with the local police over an enquiry into the Pole history, but owned up to a nervousness at the thought of entering the portals of an old historic school like Halstead.

"History's nothing to do with it," Travers told him. "Besides, bishops read detective novels, don't they? Smuggle them under their aprons if everything's true in the publishers' adverts. But I've got in mind a man after your own heart. Tattler, they used to call him. Tatheman, his name is. Well over sixty, and was a master there in my own time. Was a boy there too. He'll know every lad of the village who even looked like having a squint. Excellent fellow in himself too. Most unorthodox."

"Here, at nine o'clock on Monday morning then, sir," said Norris, when they parted at the Petersfield fork a quarter of a mile from the town.

"That's right. Meeting on Mondays."

Norris grinned and swung off with his attaché case. Travers pushed the Rolls on and reached Pulvery at that annoying hour which is far too late for tea and hungrily remote from dinner.

That night he and the Major sat yarning till the small hours. Next morning they played golf, with Travers parting with half-a-crown, not being able to make up on the roundabouts of cunning approaches what he lost on the full swings. But there was always something in the air of Pulvery that induced sleep, and dinner was midday on a Sunday, and Travers hungry. So when the Major disappeared for his usual half-hour's nap, Travers drew his own chair in to the drawing-room fire. It seemed only a minute later that he was rousing himself, but an hour and more had gone by the clock.

"You talk in your sleep," Helen said. "You rolled disgracefully in the chair and then you said something. You've always denied it, but now I know."

"I deny it still," said Travers. "What was it I was supposed to say?"

"Something that sounded like—*thenks*. Like a little cockney typist—"

"Good Lord!" said Travers, and pulled a wry face. "I don't know that you aren't right. The fact is I was dreaming about a man called Stowe—a newspaperman. You wouldn't know him."

He was smiling to himself then at the preposterousness of the dream, and how he still seemed to hear Stowe's words of thanks. Travers had been telling him that he was going to be murdered on the Monday and had warned him to get out of the *Blazon* building, and Stowe had grasped him by the hand, with, "Thenks, Mr. Travers."

"Very funny," said Travers aloud. Then his face fell. "My hat! there's something I've forgotten to do. Helen, what part of New Zealand did the Argills go to? Napier, wasn't it?"

"Not Napier," Helen said. "I'm sure it wasn't Napier. Some name like—like Gettysburg—"

"Hardly be that," said Travers urbanely.

"Will you let me think, Ludo—please." She frowned. "I tell you it was Gettys something. Now where're you going?"

Travers came back with an atlas, and they spotted it at once.

"Gisborne," she said. "Didn't I tell you so!"

"We'll say you did," Travers told her. "And it's not so far from Napier. You haven't got the address, presuming you're quite sure it is Gisborne?"

"Ludo!" she said. "What on earth should I do with their address. They were your friends, not mine."

"That tears it then," said Travers. "I promised their address to a man who's sailing tomorrow morning. A nice boy. Went to Millborough. I had the vaguest idea that if he hadn't been sailing so soon, he and Peter might have met at my place in town." He got to his feet, still somewhat perturbed. "How is Peter, by the way?"

"Knocked out, poor darling," Helen said.

"Rugger?"

"How very awkward you are sometimes, Ludo. You know they play Rugger only in the winter term and hockey in the spring. It was a hockey ball that hit him on the knee. Very painful for the poor darling, but he's almost got over it."

"Sorry," Travers was saying, "but I'm afraid I must go back to town after all."

The Major came down from the bathroom in time to hear.

"What's this about going back to town?"

Travers was polishing his glasses and blinking away at space.

"Something I've forgotten. I'll be back in time for supper. And will you warn Palmer that I'll be there at about five. I may bring him back with me, by the way."

"Five?" said the Major. "That'll be pretty good going, won't it?"

But Travers had already gone.

It was an unperturbed Palmer who was bringing in tea within a couple of minutes of Travers's arrival.

"Sorry about all this bother," Travers said, but I had to keep my word to Mr. Cane about that letter of introduction. You remember Colonel Argill?

"Certainly I do, sir," Palmer said. "How is he getting on out there, sir?"

"Haven't heard recently," Travers told him. "Mr. Cane's going out near him however. Sailing in the morning."

"If you're writing to the Colonel, perhaps you'd permit me to send my best respects, sir."

"Why, of course," said Travers. "He'll be delighted to hear about you."

Helen had been right about the district though it was as well that Travers had not trusted to the name of the township as sole address.

"I'd rather like you to come back with me," Travers said when Palmer came in for the tray. "The only thing that worries me is the parrot."

"He will be perfectly all right, sir," Palmer said, and smiled.

"Been amusing you, has he?"

At that very moment there was a squawk, followed by a flow of words. Travers cocked an ear, and Palmer stood approvingly by as if he were the eccentric deity who had endowed the bird with speech.

"Is that you? Is that you? Hallo! Hallo! Are you there? Are you there? Breakfast for one. Breakfast for one."

"Stop him for the love of Heaven," said Travers, thinking all at once of Pole, and finding something distressingly raucous in the mimicry. Then while with a wince he saw Pole's white face again and heard his urgent, frightened words, Charlie was speaking, and with it there was a laugh—a queer, uncanny laugh—that Travers had never heard.

Travers was getting to his feet. The fingers that had reached fumblingly up stayed rigid by his glasses. Then he called:

"Palmer! Bring him in here. Bring him in at once!"

There was something so unnatural and peremptory in the tone that Palmer shot him a puzzled look as he came back with the cage.

"See if he'll talk," Travers said, eyes on the bird as if it might suddenly be transformed to some new miraculous shape.

But Charlie refused to talk. Palmer uttered words and sounds of cajolement, but the bird was tantalizingly obstinate.

"All right," said Travers. "You can take him back. And I won't write the letter here. I'll write it in the car, and you must drive. As soon as you're ready, we'll go."

It was well after dusk when the car came down the drive again. The Major was standing on the porch as if on the look-out.

"Back again all right, then?" he said. "A telephone message came for you about an hour ago. I took it myself. To say that someone was dead and you were to know. Someone of the name of Pole."

It was slightly before time the next morning when the car drew up at the Petersfield fork, but Norris was waiting. Travers made him sit in front so that they could talk.

"What luck at Petersfield?" he asked.

"Not a thing," said Norris. "But I don't know that we expected it, sir—not yet. What we wanted to do was to put the local police on the right track. You heard, by the way, that Pole is dead, sir?"

"Yes," said Travers. "And it wasn't Murder on Mondays. Anything strike you about that?"

"Only that you can't always wait for a Monday," Norris suggested.

"That's what struck me," Travers told him. "There may have been murders that fitted very conveniently into a publicity scheme, but this was a murder in tremendous earnest. No trimmings, Norris. Just damn serious, bloody murder—and with intent."

"Pardon me, sir," Norris was suddenly saying, "but are we going some different way? I thought Halstead was a bit north-west?"

"Sorry," said Travers. "I forgot to tell you. I've got to see a man off at Southampton. Half-past ten will be early enough at Halstead?"

He explained the situation. Then they went on talking about Cane and so to emigration and liners and colonies. Norris said he never heard about a liner without thinking of Crippen who had thought himself safe and had then been unluckily bowled over by the new application of wireless. That brought them back to murder again, and Luffham's murder in particular, and they were still hard at it when the docks were in sight.

"You might as well come," Travers told Norris. "Palmer will be staying with the car. We're very bright and early so Cane mayn't be aboard. If so I'll stay long enough to leave a written message and then we'll push on to Halstead."

At the gangway head Travers made enquiries. Mr. Cane was on board and a steward was sent to find him, and Travers took the precaution of sending a preliminary message. So Cane's face, when he came up, was all smiles and gratitude.

"It's very good of you, sir," he said, "but you shouldn't have given yourself all that bother—just for me."

"Not bother," Travers told him. "It was my own forgetful fault or I'd have given you the letter in town." He had noticed Cane's look of polite enquiry. "Oh, this is a friend of mine—Chief-Inspector Norris. We're just off to Halstead. Some enquiries into the Luffham case."

Cane shook hands and said he believed he had run across the Inspector somewhere before.

"I've been down here before many a time," Norris said. "I've had more than one who thought himself snug aboard."

Travers laughed. "Steady on, Norris. Mr. Cane's looking quite perturbed." He explained jokingly to Cane. "The worst of all policemen is that they see everything in terms of crime. When I told him about calling up here to see you off, all he could think of was Crippen. What sort of a cabin have they given you, by the way?"

"Would you like to come and see it, sir?"

"Lord, no!" said Travers. "We can't spare more than a minute for one thing, and looking through port-holes always makes me giddy. You have port-holes, I hope?"

"Port-holes?" said Cane blankly, then smiled. "Oh, yes, there's one port-hole, if not two."

"I was thinking about the Red Sea," Travers said. "You'll find them fine things to open when you get there. I've had experience and I know." The thought made him shiver in his heavy ulster. Cane was looking a different person in that fine new overcoat and the smart grey hat, though he had the collar turned up against the cold.

"Do come downstairs, won't you?" Cane said. "It's a bit chilly up here."

"No," said Travers abruptly. "We've got to be going. And at once." He smiled. "Well, I'll say good-by. If you ever do see Colonel Argill, tell him how you left me. Now I'll get away in a hurry. I don't want you to read all the unblushing things I've told him about you."

Norris put out his hand. "Good-by, sir—and good luck to you."

Travers all at once gaped.

"Good Lord! Coming all this way and then going after all without giving you the letter!" He put it in Cane's hand. "There we are then. Good-by. I hope to have news of you soon."

He almost bolted then to avoid Cane's thanks. He and Norris stopped at the Customs shed corner and looked back, but Cane had already gone.

They made such good time that they looked like being no more than a few minutes late. Travers slowed the car down as they came to the ridge of the Downs, with Halstead no more than a mile away, and he looked back to the far distance where Southampton lay, and beyond it the open sea. Norris had a look at his watch and smiled.

"Well, another one left the old country, sir?"

"Yes," said Travers, and moved the car on again. "Another one gone, as you say."

"A long journey too, sir."

"Yes," said Travers again. "About as long a journey as there is. He was one of Wharton's suspects, you know."

"I know," Norris said. "He casts a pretty wide net, the General does." He heaved a sigh. "Well, Pole's gone, and he was one of them. This young gentleman's gone—though he never was one, not really. All that's left is somebody you and me know."

"Stowe, you mean."

"Yes," said Norris. "There's that Tuke the General's got his eye on, but I don't know. I can't see where he fits."

The car was passing the first houses of the village and Travers slowed down to almost a crawl.

"It's Monday, Norris," he said. "What's the betting there isn't another murder?"

Norris pulled a face. "Well, I'm not much of a betting man, sir, but I'll lay you ten to one there ain't."

Travers gave a queer smile as he shook his head.

"Sorry, but I can't take you. It wouldn't be fair. You can't bet on a certainty."

Norris looked at him, as if he had suddenly gone mad.

"Murder on Mondays," said Travers, and shook his head again. "There'll be a murder, and it'll be the last. It must be the last."

"My God, sir, how you talk!" Norris was licking his lips. "You mean to say you know there's going to be another murder?"

"I know it for an excellent reason," Travers told him.

"Reason, sir?"

"Yes," said Travers. "For the very excellent reason that I'm going to commit it myself."

CHAPTER XIV
ONE WAY OUT

NORRIS WAS SHAKING his head. Travers, he knew of old, was a queer character, but while he pondered some new retort, the car was stopping at the village post-office: Travers found an envelope back and began to write, and Palmer was asked to stand by.

"One thing I've got to be sure of," Travers said. "Everything depends on what reply I get to this."

He handed Norris the request, which was for a statement of Stowe's whereabouts at the vital times of Pole's murder; reply to be sent if possible within an hour. Palmer was to ring the Yard from the call-box.

"I still don't see what you're getting at, sir," Norris began. But the car was passing through the ancient gateway and turning right by the chapel quadrangle. Travers drew it in at Morgan's Plat, by the mulberry tree.

"Sacred to the staff only," he said to Norris. "Now grab your documents and we'll get things going."

The Yard had sent a covering letter and Travers had phoned from Pulvery, so the Head was prepared. He was a well-meaning, earnest soul—next year to join the bishops' bench—but there was little mention of his scandalous predecessor. It was indeed with considerable and dexterous haste that he handed the two over to Tatheman, who took them along to what he called his registrar's office.

Tatheman went warily for a bit, thinking it necessary, no doubt, to put on a soberness in the presence of a Chief-Inspector who was so obviously awed by the antiquity and air of overwhelming erudition of his surroundings. But Tatheman could never keep up that pose for long, and something Norris said started him off.

"You've got a fine place here, sir?"

"In parts," said Tatheman, and gave Travers a wink.

"You mean, some parts are older than others?" He shook his head. "A bit different to the school I went to myself."

"I don't know," said Tatheman. "I expect you think as much of yours as Travers here does of this."

"Mine, sir?" Norris shook his head and smiled mournfully. "The first one I went to wasn't so bad. It taught me everything I ever picked up. Then they sent me to a grammar-school, and that did it. I was what they call expelled."

"Good man," said Tatheman admiringly. Travers laughed. Norris imagined a brick had been dropped.

"Not for anything serious, it wasn't. I used to play truant a bit and the headmaster said it was bad example." He gave an apologetic look. "I don't reckon you have anything like that happen in a place like this, sir."

"Don't we, by Jove!" He gave Travers another wink, as much as to say that Norris was a man after his own heart. "You remember the Lamb episode, don't you, Travers?"

"Lord, yes," said Travers. "You mean when Tom Lamb started a bookmaker's business, with his brother as clerk, during Lewes races."

"That's it," Tatheman said. "But by the way, won't Inspector Norris have some beer? If he's going to work in this room, he'll find it uncommonly dry."

"Make it two," Travers said. "I hope to do some research work myself."

While the tankards were coming, Tatheman showed this and that in the room. It was his own idea, with every conceivable record for the last fifty years, and everything card-indexed. Then the beer appeared and the room relaxed again.

"Mind you," Tatheman said, taking up the talk where pushing the bell had left it, "the funniest case we ever had here was not so very long after the war. Now there was a stout lad who always had my sympathy. He was what I'd call a genius in lying. Forget what his name was at the moment, but he came to us from a well-known prep-school. Clever young devil too. And the quiet sort of cove you'd never suspect of doing a thing. But what do you think he did? He used to make out at home that he was being roped in for all kinds of expensive extras that had to be paid for on the nail. His fond parents swallowed that—hook, line and sinker—and our young friend amassed quite a deal of wealth. He planned it well ahead till he had enough saved up and then he proceeded to spend it. Informed his people that he was staying on here for a week on some special course, and then went up to town, and stayed at some slap-up hotel, and made out he was a Persian prince. Had his face coloured, and a man to look after him and everything. It took the management nearly the week before they got suspicious. The great T.P.L. was furious. Personally I thought it damn funny."

Norris was shaking his head sadly at the errors of youth.

"But we mustn't keep the Inspector from work," Tatheman said. "Would you like to see the new reredos, Travers? Or have you seen it already?"

"What I'd like to see—in very strict confidence—is the full record of the Persian prince," Travers told him. "Perhaps you might start Norris off on that squint business first."

"The *lusus naturae* in question may be found here," Tatheman said, indicating the health rolls and the gym-sergeant's reports. "I think you're on the wrong trail. I'd have remembered anybody here who had a squint."

No sooner had Travers been shown the confidential details of the Persian prince than he was being called to the phone. When he came back it was to give Tatheman a shock.

"Sorry to be so explosive, and all that, but Inspector Norris and I have to go back to town at once. Really desperately important. Not a minute to lose, in fact. Thank the Head, and make our apologies, will you? Unpardonable of us to have given you all this trouble. . ."

The Rolls was headed for town. Norris asked no questions and apparently was taking things as related. But after a mile he was wondering about Stowe.

"Got something on him, have they, sir?"

"All we've got on him is this," said Travers. "From half-past three last Friday till four o'clock, he was making his own enquiries into the case of Laura Delayne, and he has a witness to prove he was at the hotel."

Norris frowned. "That isn't having anything on him, sir. That sounds to me like a damn good alibi."

"Yes," said Travers. "That's certainly what it looks like." He smiled. "Wharton threw in a bit of extra information. He hasn't anything on Tuke either. All he's been able to pick up is that Tuke was genuinely indisposed that time, and the neighbours say he quarrels like hell with his wife."

"Sounds like a cross-word puzzle to me," said Norris.

"Yes," said Travers, and amused himself by adding one last mystery. "Tuke and Stowe—working in the same building. Even more simple than Wharton thinks."

It was well on the way to noon and he pushed the car on. Just over Kew Bridge he drew in at a pub.

"If a man's committed murder, what precautions ought he to take?"

Norris fell in with the joke.

"Take damn good care the police don't get him."

"Exactly," said Travers. "And just one other thing. Aren't there certain snakes that infallibly track down the one who kills their mate? I'm sure I've read something of the kind, but you see what I'm getting at? The murderer has to dodge the police and protect himself at the same time."

"Lie doggo, in fact, sir," grinned Norris.

"Exactly," said Travers again, and called Palmer across.

"I want you to take the car home," he said. "Garage it and then carry on normally. But mark this most carefully. You'd better write it down, in fact. If anyone rings up, asking for me, but won't give a name or gives a name that you don't know and speaks in a voice you can't identify, say this: 'Mr. Travers is in the country but he's sent word that he'll be back at seven-thirty sharp this evening. But he'll only be in the flat a short time as he has to dress and go to a dinner at eight o'clock.' "

Palmer got it word-perfect.

"I'll keep in touch with you by phone," Travers went on. "Further instructions will depend on what happens."

"And what now, sir?" asked Norris, when the car had disappeared round the bend.

"A quick lunch," Travers said. "I don't know about you but I breakfasted early. And if I'm going into hiding, I shall want a square meal inside me."

"Then you've committed that murder of yours already?" grinned Norris.

"Oh, dear, no!" Travers said. "I very much doubt if it'll be committed for quite a good time yet. Sandwiches, I think, and plenty of them, don't you? And of course beer. Pretty thin after the Halstead brew, but murderers can't be choosers."

"Nor cops either," added Norris.

They had a corner to themselves in the private bar. The plate of sandwiches was almost cleared when Travers dropped the general conversation and reverted to crime again. His voice had a tremendous seriousness.

"I want you to do something for me, Norris."

"Certainly, sir. What is it?"

"I'll accept full responsibility," Travers said, "but there's just the chance—if things miscarry—that Wharton may rear up very high on his hind legs. That doesn't worry me. All I want to know is if you, on your own responsibility, can do something for me."

"Depends what it is, sir."

"Precisely. It's this, and I'm speaking in dead earnest. No jokes, Norris, and no blether. I consider that tonight I may be in danger of my life—"

"You really are murdering someone, sir?"

"Yes," said Travers, "but there's also a no. But what I want you to do is to be at St. Martin's Chambers at seven o'clock tonight." He scribbled something on the back of a card. "Give this to the hall-porter. It tells him to follow your instructions. But you must on no account be seen, either entering or when you're actually in. Use the service door in Marryon Street. Use it also for two good men of your own. They can be posted in a linen room at the end of the corridor which runs past my door. If at any time after half-past seven anybody approaches my door and rings or knocks, one of your men must emerge from the linen room—which will make him appear an ordinary resident—and go by my door as if he was making for the lift. But he'll grab the man who was at my door, and if he wants help the other one in the linen room will know it."

"And suppose it's a person on lawful business?"

"I'll take the responsibility as owner," Travers said. "Mistakes can always be smoothed over. But somehow I don't think there will be one."

"I can manage that all right for you, sir," Norris said. "You're afraid for your life and you've approached me. That's good enough. The only snag is that I may have to lie doggo the rest of today in case I get sent anywhere."

"Wharton thinks you still at Halstead," Travers said. "I gave him that impression, so you're all right that far." He got to his feet. "Everything understood?"

Norris nodded. "Yes, sir. I've got you. Where do I go now?"

"I suggest to the pictures," Travers said. "I'm drifting off back to town in penny numbers, like they published the classics, and phoning at intervals. I'm also making an appointment with Wharton at the Yard at six-thirty or so. In case anything happens in the meanwhile, you ring up Palmer at the same time and he'll pass any message on."

Two o'clock found Travers at Shepherd's Bush, and ringing up Palmer. Then he took a bus to Notting Hill Gate and spent an hour looking into the windows of the antique shops, after which he rang up Palmer again. Then he took a bus to Euston Road, and from there rang up the Yard and fixed an urgent appointment for Wharton at half-past six. Then he left Tottenham Court Road for side streets but came out at it again at a cinema. He nipped into that like a man afraid of being seen, and it was six o'clock when he came out again.

Now he crossed the road warily and waited in a side street for a cruising taxi. Next came a quick tea near Westminster Bridge, at a high-brow tea-shop with an upstairs room. He was five minutes late for the interview with Wharton, and the General commented on the fact.

"What did you and Norris get?" he said. "Anything good?"

"Afraid not," Travers said. "As far as we've been able to ascertain, there was never anybody born into this moral world with a squint."

Wharton grunted, then shot a look over his spectacle tops.

"Well, aren't you going to take off your coat and sit down?"

"Afraid not," said Travers again. "The fact is I want you to come at once to my place. There's something most urgent I want to show you."

"Then why didn't you bring it along?"

"Bit too big to carry," Travers said.

Wharton grunted again, then went over to his coat and hat.

"Well, what is it? It isn't too big to tell me about, is it?"

"I don't know that it is," Travers said. "But I'd rather wait. You might get wrong impressions."

They took a bus and traffic was awkward so that it was nearly seven when they circled round by St. Martin's steps. Wharton took the familiar way, but Travers drew him gently aside.

"This way, George. We're being a bit wary."

The word seemed scarcely apt. Mysterious and annoyingly secretive, Wharton thought it, for Travers gave a knock at the service door and Palmer had it open at once. Travers dodged in quickly, Wharton having already been propelled inside.

"Everything all right, Palmer?"

"Everything, sir."

"No more enquiries?"

"Yes, sir. The same enquirer, sir, but I repeated the instructions."

Travers nodded and up they went by way of the main service lift. Travers peeped cautiously out along the short corridor, then nipped across into Palmer's door.

"Everything all right in the study?"

"Everything, sir."

Travers nodded back to Wharton and led the way. He closed the study door behind him and locked it. The windows, Wharton noticed, were curtained.

"What'll you drink, George? Sherry? Whisky? Or what?"

"A whisky. A long one," Wharton said. "And what is all this? Some game or other?"

"Sh!" went Travers. "Damn serious, George. In fact I've got on to something. Tonight we ought to-know all we've been looking for."

He poured Wharton's drink and one for himself.

"Let's talk quietly, George. The last thing anyone must suspect is that I'm where I am now. And believe me, there didn't seem any other way of doing it but this way. I may have seemed a trifle flamboyant, but you're going to understand."

Wharton's fingers were tight around the glass, but the glass was unraised.

"You know?"

"I think so," Travers said. "I know there'll be no more murders. You see—well, the fact is I was seeing off young Cane. He left England for New Zealand this morning. On the *Warakiki,* from Southampton He'll be a good many miles out on the open sea by now."

"Cane?" said Wharton, and was still staring. "But you were the very one who proved that he couldn't have had a thing to do with the murders! Especially the Delayne murder. He was at the *Blazon* at the time it was done and he was here with you when Stowe was being rung up to go to the hotel!"

"I know," said Travers quietly.

"And he didn't do Pole's job. He hasn't a squint—and never did have."

"I know all that."

Wharton took his first swig, set down the glass and scowled.

"Then what in God's name are you getting at? Cane's on the high seas, isn't he?"

"I hope so," said Travers. "But I wish you wouldn't talk quite so loudly, George. I tell you it's imperative no one should know I'm here."

"I get you," said Wharton. "Young Cane was in it, and now he's out of it. You're expecting a call from someone else who was in it too."

"You're right—partly right," Travers said, and gave a quick look at the clock. "But may I tell you my suspicions against Cane? What I've discovered, in fact?"

Wharton took another swig.

"Go on," he said. "I'm listening."

Travers took a long pull at the drink as if to steady himself.

"I'm going to keep to facts," he began. "I'm saying nothing that isn't so utterly true that it's beyond questioning. I told you some time ago that I thought Cane just a little too good to be true, when he withdrew so gracefully at Stowe's unexpected return. He was handling the Murder on Mondays business very well indeed himself, and it didn't seem human nature to draw so gracefully aside. But I told you also at the time that Cane *tried to give the impression* that he was drawing gracefully aside, and that's very different. As a matter of fact, he was losing badly, and in spite of his attempts to appear chivalrous and even quixotic, he was unable to conceal his real vexation. But the main point is that even when he'd had a nasty set-back, he took refuge in trying to pose. So much for preliminaries."

A listen at the door, a quick glance at the clock, and he resumed.

"My mind has always therefore been prepared to receive suspicions, and it speaks well for Cane that he gave me none, and he even eradicated that one uneasy impression. So to the first fact. I was with Cane on Saturday morning and the talk got round to Millborough, which was Cane's school, and to my young nephew who also happens to be there. Cane told me he was in the second fifteen at Millborough—a fact which I should never have suspected, but which gave me a certain pleasure. But on the Sunday, at Pulvery, there was certain talk about Millborough, and all at once something startling dawned on me. Millborough, until five years ago, was a soccer school. Therefore when Cane was supposed to be there, there was no such thing as a fifteen. Therefore he was never there, and he was a liar and a poseur. But when I remembered the first day I met him and how Maylove was under the impression that Cane and myself had been at the same school, then I suddenly knew that Cane had really been at Halstead, *and under Luffham* therefore. That gave me a line on the first murder."

"Yes?" said Wharton. "Go on."

Travers gave a shrug of the shoulders. "That's all, George. I said I'd stick to facts."

Wharton stared. "You mean to say that that's the sole evidence you've got against Cane?"

"It is," said Travers. "But it was a foundation on which I could build a whole series of superb hypotheses. Which in fact I did. I came back to London yesterday afternoon to get the address of a man in New Zealand to whom I'd promised Cane a letter of introduction. I never wrote that letter of introduction. I wrote for an hour, while Palmer drove, and I wrote down the whole of the case against Cane, as built on one fact. This morning just before Cane sailed I handed him that supposed letter of introduction, and then I bolted in case he should find out before I left. What I'd determined to do, you see, to commit murder."

Wharton shot him a look, grunted, and waited.

"What I did was this," went on Travers. "I took the law into my own hands. When Norris and I were talking to Cane just before he sailed, I'd tried to make him uneasy by several cryptic allusions. I'd reminded him, for instance, of the fact that a modern liner was a death trap for a wanted man. But to get back to that long letter which he must have read soon after Norris and I had gone."

He broke off then, for the clock showed the half-hour. He whispered, and his manner was quiet and assured, and somehow sad, like that of a doctor at a hopeless bedside.

"We'll get in the other room now. I'll carry on there. Pay no attention to anything I may do."

Back in the main room he first tried the outer corridor door, but it was securely locked. Then he began talking aloud to an imaginary Palmer. A moment's silence and he was whispering to Wharton again.

"At the end of the letter I incited him to suicide, which means murder. I assured him that I had his spiritual welfare at heart and I'd never told my suspicions to a single soul—Sh! . . . Did you hear anything?"

They listened, breath held and eyes straining. Wharton shook his head.

"I told him Scotland Yard suspected nothing. The only way for him was to drop over the ship's side. If he had not done so by midnight tonight, then I should put Scotland Yard in possession of the facts, the liner would be hove to, and he'd be arrested and brought home."

He listened again, ears intent.

"I don't think so, Palmer," he said aloud, as if the man were there. "No, I shan't want you again for a bit."

Another long listen and he resumed his whispering.

"If he does commit suicide, then we'll know facts which we'd otherwise never have been able to prove—"

He broke off, eyes alert and mouth gaping. His hand tightened on Wharton's arm. Wharton was rigid too, for the rap on the door had been like thunder in the silence, and the quiet room was suddenly filled with the threatening of unseen things.

CHAPTER XV
THE OTHER WAY OUT

A MOMENT, and there was a questioning voice, as of a passer-by in the outer corridor. The words came clearly to the silence of the room.

"Anyone you were wanting?"

"It's all right, th-th-thank you."

"Cane!" That was Wharton's hiss, and Travers's hand closed on his arm again. Then there was a noise—a lumping noise and a grunting; a kind of shriek and the running of feet. There was a man's deep growl, a heavy smashing against the door—and then a shot!

Quick as Wharton was, Travers beat him to the door, and had the bolt back and the door open. Something lay on the floor and three men were looking down. Wharton thrust them aside.

"What's all this? What're you doing here, Norris?"

Norris gave him a look but it was to Travers he spoke.

"Looks as if we've made a mess of it, sir"

"Dead, is he?" Wharton was stooping and feeling his heart. Then he sprang up. "He's still alive. Why didn't you send for someone?"

"Palmer's in there now, sir," Norris told him quietly. "He's ringing up the hospital."

Travers looked down at the crumpled body of Cane. Then he shook his head and turned away.

"His own gun, was it, Norris?"

"His own, sir. What he was reckoning to do you in with. Sort of half disguised himself too, with a false moustache thing. Who let the gun off, Edwards?"

"Don't know, sir," the man said. "It looked to me as if he knew the game was up and when we was struggling for it, he sort of dipped his head and let himself have it. That was just as Frank tripped him up."

Palmer came to say the hand ambulance and a doctor were coming.

"Let's hope they'll have better luck with him than they did with Pole," Wharton began. Then his look changed queerly, and he stooped. Norris leaned over, and was shaking his head at Travers, and frowning.

"No need for that ambulance," Wharton said, and sneered. Then he drew himself up and looked round the small group. "There'll be trouble about this, and I wouldn't like to be in the shoes of them that's responsible."

For the first time in his life Travers and Wharton were chin to chin.

"There'll be no question of responsibility," Travers said.

"Oh?" said Wharton grimly. "I'll see about that."

"No, you won't," Travers told him. "I'm entitled to police protection if my life's threatened. I had it. Nobody can be blamed for the rest."

"A man was allowed to slip through our fingers when he was wanted for murder."

"Murder?" asked Travers. "Cane wanted for murder? Who says so?"

"What's the idea?" asked Wharton. "You said he was, sir. You were going to give me the whole case against him."

Travers looked amazed. "Sorry, but there must be some mistake. I know nothing."

But he turned back at the door.

"Look round his waist, Norris, will you? See if he's wearing a money belt."

"My God! sir, he is," Norris said. "And it's crammed full of notes . . . Pound notes!"

Travers nodded, and turned once more. Palmer had long since gone and the door closed behind him. But he listened for a moment to the whine of the lift, then gave a slow shake of the head again, and made his way back to the study.

A quarter of an hour later, Wharton tapped on the door and walked in.

"Ah! thought I should find you here," he said. "You and I were losing our sense of proportion just now."

"Were we?"

"Come now." Wharton gave a chuckle. "You don't want to be on your dignity. Maybe there wasn't any other way than the one you chose. Maybe we'll once more have to say the cases were cleared up to the satisfaction of the police."

"And no one's for the high jump?"

Wharton waved his hands. "I don't see why we can't give a satisfactory explanation. I mean to say, I would like to hear anything that—well, any ideas you might have had—"

Travers smiled. "Sit down, George, and pour yourself another drink. I'm having one, as you see. Shook me up a bit—what was outside there. Him, I mean, not what might have happened to myself."

"I expect it did," said Wharton, and showed his humility by pouring out the merest tot. "But tell me now, will you, just what it was that you put in the letter? You must have hit a good many nails on the head?"

"I tried to force out the truth," Travers said. "I knew there was too much ever to prove. All I knew for certain was enough to make him either slip over the side of that ship or else come here and do in the only one who knew."

"Very shrewd," said Wharton. "Very shrewd. And what was in the letter?"

"A lot of truth, a lot of hints, and some puzzling blether," Travers said. "I'll re-edit for your benefit, and make it what I now believe to be all truth. And I'll start at Little Tarfold when—I say it bluntly, but not, I trust, vulgarly—Francis Powell put Maud Smith in the family way, left her and bolted abroad, came back to think himself safe, but for even more safety changed his name to Ferdinand Pole."

Wharton grunted. "So that was the way of it, was it? They were carrying on so blatantly that the village noticed it, so that Mrs. Crow said."

"Maud had money of her own," Travers went on. "You may trust Lettice to have been at least just. Where Maud went we do not know but she must have made herself out a widow, and she kept her name of Smith, which is quite a good name for anonymity. Her son was born, and christened Theodore. He went to a prep school, was clever, and got a scholarship to Halstead. Which brings me to the tale I heard this morning—the tale of the Persian prince."

"My God!" said Wharton, when he had heard it. "He was an exhibitionist all right. No need to ask who his father was."

"You yourself noticed Cane's auburn hair and somewhat high voice," Travers said. "But to get on. I should say the Smiths moved when he was expelled from Halstead, and I'd say he induced his mother to change their name to Cane; he changing his own to Tristram, instead of Theodore. Or she—romantically minded—might have suggested it. I'd also say that Cane was a constant handful to his mother, and cost her a good bit, because they'd come down to living in a poorish neighbourhood. And as he boasted to me how close to each other they were, I take it as proof that he made her life hell. I'll also say he was a fly-by-night. Haroun-al-Raschid sort of stuff, you know, looking for romance; Soho restaurants, and so on. That's how he came to spot Luffham. I'd say too that it might be worth while to enquire how many different jobs he had in Fleet Street and why he left them.

"Then about six weeks ago, the mother died, and when she knew she was dying, she told him things: who his father was, and how she had discovered her sister and approached her for help years ago and had been turned down. How she had found out Pole I don't know, except that publicity and press photographs cut several ways. But you see the effect of the revelations on a mind like Cane's?

"He planned a spectacular and profitable revenge, even if it did run away with him in the end. Did you read either of his detective novels, by the way? They're in the first person, which gives his hero the chance to be his diffident and secret self, and they're amazingly clever. He'd already planned that Murder on Mondays letter to put himself well in with the *Blazon,* but he went to Pole and offered the idea to him. He made it a most secretive visit, and that was the first occasion when Pole got the hall porter out of the way. Pole fell for the scheme at once, and he and Cane pretended ever after to be total strangers. Early that Monday morning, Cane murdered Luffham. Pole accepted the murder as a miracle and hailed the publicity.

"Now how Cane came to meet Luffham we never shall know. We know how he recognized him, because he told us as much in a man with the squint letter. I'd say that when he recognized Luffham he threatened to expose him. He used moral blackmail, in fact, and, if Luffham recognized him, he told him that he was going under the name of Pole. Luffham knew no Pole. What was the Napoleon of Crime to him? Murder Leagues were not in the vocabulary of a man like Luffham.

"You see, Cane guarded against any writing that Luffham left, and its possible mention of names. He also dropped Pole's card in the waste-paper basket. And now a shrewd point. I'd say Cane had mapped out a series of man with the squint letters, and intended to send one admitting the crime and asking if the elastic was found. For if Cane was to get all the publicity of the *Blazon,* and maybe Stowe's job, then it had to be proved that Luffham was murdered. But Cane didn't have to write a man with the squint letter. I was the mutt sent by Providence to find the elastic and do the proving."

"That's good," said Wharton, and gave a nod or two. "You can bet your life that's what happened."

"Now to the next step," Travers went on. "Stowe came back and cooked Cane's publicity goose. Stowe became someone who might embarrass him, and therefore must be removed. Cane had hoped that we should have arrested Pole, so in the next murder he tried a double. He sent Stowe to discover Laura Delayne's murder and he rang him up unmistakably in Pole's voice.

"As to Laura Delayne. Think of Cane's feeling when he heard about her and his mother. There would be furious anger that she should have turned his mother away in her need. He would think of what would have meant to himself to have an aunt who was well off and famous. Then he would sneer to himself and say that though she had drawn her skirts away from his mother, he himself—bastard as he was—would make her sing a different tune. So Cane was the ghost she saw when one day he introduced himself. He demanded money, and she gave it to him. Then he rang her up and asked for a further interview, which she gave. That wasn't a bloody murder. Probably he told her in a quick sentence or two the hell of hate he had for her, and then there was simply a whipping of a knife into her back and a quick getaway, even before the blood seeped through. I'd say he killed her before midday, then he rang me up from the call-boxes outside and made out he was speaking from the *Blazon*. We took all that for granted because he was never a real suspect. Just before one o'clock he was ringing the *Blazon* from the call-box under this very window, and imitating Pole's voice to Stowe. Then he came up here. While Palmer came to the study here, he slipped the clock hands back, and remarked to me that he was early. When he was in here he made an excuse to fetch his handkerchief or something, and slipped the hands forward again. Palmer never noticed a thing, I admit, but it's perfectly feasible. That brings us back to Pole."

"Yes," said Wharton. "That sequence you wrote down. I can see it now."

"I know," said Travers. "It might have been easy then, if Pole hadn't had to lie. When you advised him how to discover who was the Chief Conspirator, he guessed young Cane at once. He called on Cane or asked Cane to see him. That gave Cane his chance. He told him all there was to tell. He asked a thousand pounds and promised to go abroad. He threatened Pole with exposure about himself and he threatened to tell about how he and Pole had agreed about the writing of the Murder on Mondays letter, and I shouldn't be surprised if he threatened to swear that he'd seen Pole coming out of Luffham's flat the night of the murder. All we know is that he had Pole badly scared. Pole paid up and Cane announced that he was going to New Zealand, after having broached the topic to me first. Then Cane worked the final gag again. He demanded a last interview with Pole, and Pole managed it. Cane had to have that interview and he had to kill Pole, because Pole might lose his nerve after all and blab. What was said and what excuse Cane made for coming I have no idea, but Pole rang down to the porter to clear the coast again. Say that Pole did the speaking down—not Cane. Cane wouldn't have had the nerve to imitate Pole's voice just after he had struck Pole down. But as Pole moved away from the tube, Cane hit him murderously three or four times and bolted, after he thought him dead.

"Next morning Cane rang me up. Nothing had got out to the press and he made the selling of some china an excuse to try to find out from me what had happened. He had a bad minute or two when he knew Pole was still alive but a tremendous relief when he knew Pole had said the attacker was the man with the squint.

"You can see Pole's mind working when he said that, by the way? He daren't tell the truth—not if he was going to live. Can you hear him, George? Asking so plaintively if he was going to get better? Certainly, said the doctor. Then Pole relaxed. His mind suggested the only safe answer—the man with the squint.

The rest he could think out during convalescence. Meanwhile—the man with the squint. The answer of a Murder League mind."

"And that's the lot?"

"Yes, except for oddments. Cane did some exhibition stuff with me that same Saturday morning. Showed me a picture of an ancestor, and a photograph of his father, supposed to be a gunner officer killed in the war. Which reminds me of a clue that I missed altogether, in the early stages. Remember the clue of the worn sole? That's something we might have caught Cane out by, if he hadn't died and we'd been holding him for carrying a gun without a license. You see, Cane was with me on the landing when I told him how I'd found footprints showing a worn sole. He stared, then he bolted. I thought he was bolting to get back to the *Blazon*. When I saw him a short time later, he'd done a most artistic thing. He hadn't changed merely his shoes, which would have been a drawing of attention. He'd had a complete change from collar to shoes, which left the shoes unnoticed."

"You're right," said Wharton. "We'll find the shoemaker who did his repairs—just to clear things up." He poured himself out another and more ample tot, and took a hearty swig. "And all that just because Cane hadn't taken the trouble to read up the school he was supposed to have been at."

"That's it," said Travers. "A little too much posing, and a slip of the tongue. When he first went to the *Blazon* he'd blow a bit about Halstead, knowing nothing of that escapade of his would ever come out. Later on, when he knew things, he had to pretend Halstead was a mistake. He was too busy after that to look up Millborough."

Wharton finished the drink and wiped mouth and moustache with wide sweeps of his voluminous handkerchief.

"Well, I'll see you tomorrow and clear up the rest. Norris and I are going to be busy with the Commissioner. You ought to get a pat on the back too."

"God forbid," said Travers hastily, and drew back for Wharton to pass through. "At least, not in public. Pole may have gone but the Murder League, I fear, goes on for ever. There may be more invitations and correspondence."

"Murder League!" Wharton snorted, then suddenly thought of something. "One thing puzzles me, by the way. That chap Stowe. What'd he lie for about that holiday? Pole hadn't let him into the secret, had he?"

"Stowe," said Travers, and gave a queer shake of the head. "The man who used to call in on the Tukes. Who called Mrs. Tuke by her Christian name of Rhoda. The Tukes quarrelling. Old Tuke hating Stowe and spying round. Mrs. Tuke in the Cornish cottage and Stowe on leave in—shall we say?—Switzerland. Now do you guess why Stowe wouldn't own up where he really was?"

"Yes," said Wharton, and frowned. "I guess all right." Then he heaved a sigh. "Well, everything's clear so far—What the devil's that!"

Palmer had come in belatedly with the evening papers. Charlie had greeted his departure with a series of whoops.

"Pole's famous parrot," Travers said. "And there might have been another clue. Do you know why Pole wanted him put out of the way? Charlie knew too much."

"Pulling my leg?"

"Heaven forbid!" said Travers again. "I'm in earnest, George; never more so."

He pushed the bell for Palmer and the bird was brought in. Maybe in Wharton's face he saw a contemptuous humour, or in the vast overhanging moustache there were dim ancestral memories of primeval forests and home; but whatever it was, Charlie refused obstinately to talk.

"Never mind," Wharton said. "Some other time."

"But I want you to hear him," Travers said. "There's something he's added to his repertoire that you've got to hear. The something that frightened Pole and made him want to have the bird destroyed."

So they tried again but Charlie proved exasperatingly taciturn. Wharton gave a nod and then moved off to the door.

"Don't you trouble to see me down. I know all the tricks of that lift. Besides—"

He broke off, for Charlie was all at once talking.

"Hallo! Hallo! Is that you? Good morning. Good morning. Breakfast for one. Breakfast for one."

Wharton grinned, and took a step or two back towards table and cage.

"Is that you? Is that you? T-t-take it or leave it. T-t-take it or leave it."

"You hear that?" Travers's hand was grasping Wharton's arm. "Cane's stutter, when he was nervous or excited. And there's a queer sort of laugh. An uncanny laugh."

Wharton nodded. The two stood motionless, eyes on the cage, but once more the bird was struck with an utter dumbness.

"I've heard enough to get the hang of things," Wharton said at last and turned to the door again. Then as his fingers closed round the knob there was a kind of squawk and once more Charlie was in full gabble.

"Hallo! Hallo! Breakfast for one. Breakfast for one. Good Lord! Good Lord!"

"Good Lord!" said Travers himself, and stared.

Wharton fairly roared.

"Well, if that don't beat cock-fighting! Got you to the life, and only a day or two to do it in."

Travers was smiling quietly and shaking his head.

"See you some time in the morning, George. Up here, shall we say? I think I'd rather you came here. I might have a surprise."

Wharton stared.

"Nothing to do with murder," Travers said. "I've had enough of murder to last me for quite a time. Relief's what I want. Maybe I'll spend the rest of tonight teaching that bird to imitate you."

Wharton shot him a look, then glared.

"Teach that damn bird to say Murder on Mondays, and I'll wring his neck."

Travers took his arm and pushed him gently inside the lift.

"Suspicions wholly unjustified. If I taught him anything, it'd be to grunt, and damn the *Blazon*."

Wharton beamed.

"That'd be something like—if you left out the grunt." Out went his hand. "Well, good night, and thanks. But for you I don't know where we'd have been."

Travers shook his head. The lift moved and he stood there smiling till the last whine had gone, then slowly moved back towards his own door. His hand went out to the knob, and as his eyes fell, the smile had suddenly gone. His long arm reached out again and opened the door, and his long leg took a stride so that it was as if he stepped over some obstacle, and into the room.

But before he closed the door behind him, he stood for a long minute looking down at the thing over which he had stepped. A smear still darkened the carpet where the body of Cane had fallen, and for a moment that body had still seemed there. Cane—and the things he might have done and been. Youth, and its infinite possibilities—and all that was sure was a smear of reddish-brown on a corridor carpet. And as Travers knew that and his one hand closed the door, his eyes were blinking and his other hand was rising to his glasses.

THE END